Praise for Susan Meissner's novels pours in from readers and reviewers everywhere...

Why the Sky Is Blue

Tracy Farnsworth, at www.roundtablereviews.com, says: "Bring out the Kleenex; you are certain to need them. Susan Meissner's debut novel is... impressive and leaves me hungry for more."

A book group leader reports: "*Why the Sky Is Blue* was one of [our] favorites out of all the ones we have read...We discussed the characters in depth and how you made them so real. One woman said you have a gift for allowing the reader to identify with each one, rather than with just one or two. A few shared how they had cried as certain parts of your story touched their hearts in various personal ways...We are a diverse group of readers with quite a range in ages and in tastes. Only a few books have been as well received by this bunch as was *Why the Sky Is Blue*."

Roxanne Henke, author of *After Anne, Becoming Olivia,* **and** *Always, Jan,* says: "*Why the Sky Is Blue* was so real it broke my heart, then, somehow, mended it. I loved this book!"

A Minnesotan says: "Wow! What a brutally honest, beautifully expressed, compelling book! I simply could not put it down. I will definitely recommend it to many, since I work in my local public library. This book is so personal. I thought I was reading a diary or personal letter..."

A Window to the World

A high school teacher in Minnesota says: "I just finished *A Window to the World*—it was amazing! I could hardly put it down and snuck it to school to finish the last couple chapters because I just couldn't wait...There is so much in this novel! You really made each character come to life and filled the events with meaning at every turn...Thank you for writing one of the most entertaining and thought-provoking books I have ever read."

A teenager in cyberspace says: "I am only 14 years old, but I bought your book and couldn't put it down...I just wanted to tell you that your book doesn't only have an impact on grown-ups, but also on teens. It really made me understand how bad things that happen to us are also a way that God is shaping us, even though we may not realize it till later."

Sara Mills, at www.christianfictionreviewer.com, says: "POWERFUL... When I finished the last page, all I could think was, WOW...I highly recommend this book and applaud Susan Meissner for writing so eloquently what is almost impossible to put into words."

The Remedy for Regret

Kelli Standish, at www.focusonfiction.net, says: "This timeless story, and Susan Meissner's lilting, lyrical prose, entranced me from the first page…and climaxes with a…scene that is so powerful and laden with such an unmistakable sense of the Divine that it had me in tears. And the message of the story is so poignant and gentle, you feel as though you've been hugged. Bottom line? Meissner's incredible gift with words has never shone truer than in *The Remedy for Regret,* and this book is a must for any discerning reader's library."

Marilyn in Iowa says: "You did it again! I have read all three of your books—just finished *The Remedy for Regret* and love it!!! Can't wait for number four!!!!"

In All Deep Places

Kelly Klepfer at firstnoveljourney.blogspot.com says: "Ms. Meissner writes Christian Fiction the way it should be written, with threads and hints and God webs interwoven into not very rosy pictures of broken lives. *In All Deep Places* contains tinges of hope, an aroma of life, a slight glow of light, and a lingering trace of poignancy. And that is the stuff of life, the moments when we are forced to think, to face our smallness and the immensity of God."

Jamie in Minnesota says: "Once again you created a cast of chracters that make me feel!…FEEL."

Andrea Sisco at Armchair Interviews says: "*In All Deep Places,* Susan Meissner has once again skillfully examined the basic truth of what it is to be alive in the world, with all the good and all the bad that is there. But she doesn't leave it at that. She gently reminds us that it is God's grace and love that will see us through the night…Meissner's books are must-reads. Their beautiful messages are yours there for the taking. What a gift to her readers!"

Novelist Mary DeMuth, author of *Watching the Tree Limbs,* says: "Lyrically written, sensitively wrought, Susan Meissner's *In All Deep Places* captivated me from page one. Meissner's strength is displaying the inner emotional landscape of her characters, this time putting the reader in the head of a male protagonist. Woven in such a way that beckons instead of dictates, Meissner's message of redemption and heaven will stay with the reader long after she puts the book down."

A
Seahorse
in the
Thames

Susan Meissner

HARVEST HOUSE PUBLISHERS

EUGENE, OREGON

Cover photos © Neo Vision / Photonica / Getty Images; Michael Mahovlich / Masterfile

Cover by Left Coast Design, Portland, Oregon

A SEAHORSE IN THE THAMES
Copyright © 2006 by Susan Meissner
Published by Harvest House Publishers
Eugene, Oregon 97402
www.harvesthousepublishers.com

Library of Congress Cataloging-in-Publication Data
Meissner, Susan, 1961-
    A seahorse in the Thames / Susan Meissner.
       p. cm.
    ISBN-13: 978-0-7369-1760-5 (pbk.)
    ISBN-10: 0-7369-1760-8
    Product # 6917608
    1. Sisters—Fiction. I. Title.
    PS3613.E435S43 2006
    813'.6—dc22   2006001330

Printed in the United States of America

06 07 08 09 10 11 12 13 14 / LB-MS / 10 9 8 7 6 5 4 3 2 1

For Chelsey

Your courage and perseverance
have taught me to see grace and beauty
where I least expected to find it.

Acknowledgments

Nick Harrison, Kim Moore, and Kimberly Shumate, editors
    extraordinaire,
      Your combined skills and insights have made me a better
      writer and allowed the tiny seahorse to truly shine.

Judy Horning, my mom and willing proofreader,
      Thanks for finding every lost apostrophe, every doubled
      period, every missing preposition.

Siri Mitchell, friend and fellow author,
      Thanks for your expert French translation skills. *Merci,
      mon ami!*

Don Pape, friend and agent,
      Your confidence in my ability to tell a story enables me to
      tell it.

God, the One and Only,
      Thanks for showing me that lovely things are often
      hidden from plain sight.

"Brian Baker was thinking about returning to port on the morning tide, yet as he hauled up his nets from the shallow waters of the Thames Estuary, once the outlet for the dirtiest waterway in Britain, he was about to get a surprise. He spotted among the seaweed a scrap of aquatic life not seen in these waters for more than a generation. The short-snouted seahorse, *Hippocampus hippocampus*, that he caught measured no more than 15cm in length, but it is a source of great local pride. On display at the Southend Sealife Adventure Centre, it is being hailed as an important sign that the Thames Estuary is returning to ecological health. It is also being seen by some as an indication that the waters are steadily warming…"

Jonathan Brown,
The London Independent,
June 16, 2004

Stephen's wounded body lies just inches from me. His eyes are closed, but I cannot tell if he is awake or sleeping. Luminescent red numbers on a tiny black screen blink at me, silently registering every beat of his heart; the Demerol the emergency room nurse gave him has slowed it some, but the drug seems to have taken the edge off his pain. A broken arm and ankle are thankfully the worst of the injuries Stephen sustained when he fell off my roof. Bandages here and there cover the places where his skin tore away from his body, but he will need surgery to repair the broken bones. I look at him lying there, an injured man I barely know, and all I can think is, *So this is what it's like to fall in love.*

I must be crazy.

I have known Stephen for only four days.

And knowing someone for four days doesn't mean you really *know* that person.

I don't know what it means. I just know I cannot pull myself away from his hospital bed, even though he is surely no longer in any danger. The fall did not kill him. I am grateful for the Indian hawthorn bushes outside my kitchen window that broke his fall. The branches poked him, puncturing skin all over his arms, face, and legs, but they held him up from the unforgiving ground. I cannot bear to think what would have happened if he had fallen off the east side of my roof to the concrete driveway below it.

My next-door neighbor, Serafina, saw Stephen fall. It was just after eleven this morning, a little more than an hour ago. She came running to my front door, pounding on the screen and yelling in her melodic Spanish accent, "Alexa! That repairman has fallen from your roof!"

"What?" I had said, coming to the door from my bedroom, certain I hadn't heard her correctly.

Serafina's long braid of gray hair, usually wound up on her head, was hanging loose, making her look like Pocahontas at age sixty-five.

"That man has fallen from your roof!"

That man. Stephen.

"I was out by the curb!" Serafina had continued, words flying out of her mouth. "I saw him standing there at the top and then he fell! Over the back!"

"Call 911!" I yelled to her and then I had dashed out my back door. Fear was pulsing through my veins, making the four-inch-long incision under my arm beat with pain. I had a simple lumpectomy six days ago. Simple in that the walnut-sized tumor was benign. It still hurt like the dickens. But it was why I was home and not at work while repairs were being made to the triplex where I live. It was why I knew Stephen's name at all. If I had been at work, I never would have met him. And I wouldn't have been home when he fell.

I had winced as I threw open the door with my "good" arm. It still hurt the "bad" one. The moment I stepped out onto the patio I saw Stephen's crumpled body half on and half off a line of hawthorn in bloom along the south wall. I could see that his left arm lay at an odd, sickening angle. I wanted with all my heart to ease his broken body off the protruding hawthorn branches, but I knew I couldn't and shouldn't. I knew I could never maneuver his 6' 2", at-least-190-pound body to the ground—even if I didn't have stitches under my arm. I also knew it is never a good idea to move an injured person unless what they lie on is on fire or about to collapse. I just stood there, bending over him, speaking his name, and waiting for the ambulance. Stephen wasn't moaning or moving. That's what had scared me the most.

Stephen stirs now and my breath pauses. He makes a tiny sound in his throat.

Does that mean he is awake?

I am suddenly anxious that he will open his eyes and be shocked to find me standing here in his hospital room at San Diego's Sharp Memorial Hospital. Won't he wonder why I'm here? I'm not his wife or fiancée or girlfriend. Perhaps I'm not even his friend. Can I say I'm his friend? I've known him for only four days.

But this is what I told the paramedics when they arrived. I told them the injured man was a friend of mine, not a handyman hired by Rose Marvelle, my landlady.

"What's his name?" one of the paramedics had asked, after they had gently pulled Stephen's body off the bushes and placed him on a stretcher. The one who spoke to me eased a cervical collar on Stephen's neck. The other one was speaking into a radio transmitter pinned to his collar.

"Stephen Moran," I said. Stephen Moran the Handyman.

"How old is he? Is he allergic to anything?" the paramedic continued, while the other paramedic started saying Stephen's name, asking him if he could hear him. Apparently Stephen could not. He made no sound.

"He's not coming around," the other paramedic said.

"He's thirty-two. I don't know if he's allergic to anything," I replied, my stomach in knots. There are just a few things I do know about Stephen, but the paramedics didn't ask me where Stephen grew up. Santa Cruz. They didn't ask me if he enjoys surfing. He does. They didn't ask me if he is kind to strangers and little kids. He is.

They asked me if he has any family.

"His mother lives in Riverside," I had said, remembering all the short conversations we've had over the last few days, when he took breaks or drank my lemonade or when he asked for some Tylenol for a headache or when he helped me back inside my house on Tuesday when my post-op pain medication caused me to faint on my lawn while reaching for the morning paper. Stephen had told me on Monday, the day I met him, that his mother is his only family. He had been married once, but he only spoke of this in one sad moment of reflection while I watched him tear out rotting floorboards on the front porch. The marriage had ended badly. He doesn't even know where his ex-wife is.

"I wasn't the man then that I am now," he had said. And I had wanted to ask what kind of man is he now. But I didn't. Anyway, I think I already know. I was already feeling the attraction to him. I was already falling for him. And that was just the first day.

"Do you know how to reach her?" The paramedic had roused me from this remembered snippet of conversation. He was removing the tool belt from Stephen's waist, but he was looking up at me.

"Why?" It suddenly and horribly occurred to me that maybe Stephen was dead and the paramedics needed to notify the next of kin.

"If he doesn't regain consciousness by the time we get to the hospital, we'll need someone to sign the medical release."

"Oh."

"Do you know how to reach her?"

"What? Um, I...maybe," I stuttered. Stephen's mother doesn't even know who I am. At least I don't think she does. Did Stephen call her earlier this week? Did he mention in passing that he is working on a repair project on a triplex in Mission Beach? Did he tell her he met one of the tenants? Did he tell her the tenant fainted on the grass and he carried her inside her house? Did he say he twice stayed after quitting time to talk to the tenant on her patio, that she gave him lemonade, that he made her consider—for the first time since she was twelve—what it means to have a relationship with God?

No, I was certain he had not. Why would he?

Did I call *my* mother?

I had nearly laughed at this thought. My mother has no phone. She hates phones. She hasn't had a phone in her house for seventeen years. It's e-mail, snail mail, or doorbell with her. But thinking of this had given me an idea.

"Let me get his cell phone," I said, but I didn't wait for permission. I knelt down and quickly slipped my hand into the cell phone holder on Stephen's belt. On impulse I also gently removed his wallet from his back pocket. I blushed when I did that. Despite the flush of my cheeks, I quickly scanned the contents of the wallet to see if there was anything else the paramedics should know about him. Driver's license. Not a bad picture. Hair the color of toast. Perpetual tan from working day after day in the legendary San Diego sunshine. I saw his address. A street in Encinitas. A Visa card. Triple A. His contractor's license. A medical insurance card.

"Here." I extended the card to the paramedics.

"Aren't you going to follow along in your own vehicle?" the paramedic asked. It was more like he requested I follow. I felt a rush of importance. I felt invited. They assumed I am Stephen's close friend.

"Oh. Yes, of course."

The paramedic turned away from my outstretched hand and back to Stephen lying motionless on a stretcher.

"Just bring it with you," the paramedic said, motioning with his head to the card. "We're taking him to Sharp Hospital. They have a trauma center—just in case. Do you know where that is?"

"Yes."

"Use the emergency room entrance."

The paramedics whisked Stephen away into their vehicle. As I watched them place Stephen inside, I noticed for the first time that Serafina was standing beside me and probably had been there the whole time.

She crossed herself as the siren began to wail and the vehicle pulled away. And then she uttered a prayer for the handyman as I hurried inside to get my purse and car keys.

The emergency room was not especially busy when I arrived, and for this I was grateful. I had not thought much about where I was headed until I was in my own car, making my way to

Sharp Hospital. I avoid emergency rooms the way some people avoid spiders or commitments. I have to work extra hard to avoid them because I actually work in a hospital as an occupational therapist. But it can be done. You can work for five years at a hospital and never set foot in the emergency room. I am living proof.

I have been like this ever since my sister Rebecca's car accident. It's not so surprising, I guess. Trauma can do that to you— produce in you an aversion to something because it reminds you of the ordeal.

Even though Rebecca survived that accident, I still lost her in a sense. Rebecca emerged from her many injuries a different person; forgetful and dependent, but also chatty and childlike. Her head injury swept away her brilliance and assertiveness, but it also erased her obstinacy and tendency to be selfish. She became what I was. An amiable twelve-year-old. And that's where she has stayed. Seventeen years later, and at the age of thirty-six, she still has the mind of an adolescent.

I still think of that night from time to time. I know how pivotal it was for all of us. We were still a family before that night. My parents were still married to each other. We still lived in Mount Helix. My twin sister, Priscilla, hadn't stopped talking to my father. My mother still had a phone in the house. But in the quiet darkness of that one night we all crossed a line. And we quickly found there was no going back to the other side of it, the familiar side.

It happened on a late June evening. Rebecca had gone out with her best friend and college roommate, Leanne. She didn't say where they were going, but I remember Rebecca seemed anxious and distracted. I figured it was because she wasn't thrilled with being home that summer after having tasted freedom at the University of California, Santa Barbara, where she spent her freshman year. Rebecca, Leanne, and a third roommate named Mindy Fortner were planning to head back to UCSB at the end of the summer. Rebecca left the house in a grumpy fuss—typical for her—when Leanne came for her. Leanne didn't even come to the door. She just honked. Mindy was not with them that night.

Dad was on a business trip in Tokyo, but Mom, Priscilla, and I were at home watching TV when the phone rang two hours later. Mom answered it. There had been an accident. Leanne was dead. Rebecca was alive, but she had been rushed to Grossmont Hospital in critical condition. No other cars were involved. Leanne had struck a mighty sycamore head-on at full speed. It was unclear what caused her to run off the road.

Priscilla and I kind of pieced this together from the scattering of words that came out of our mother's mouth between the time she picked up the phone and said "Hello?" and the moment she dropped the receiver to the floor.

I had barely processed the news when my mother rushed out of the house into the velvet shadows of the evening. She said nothing to Priscilla or me as she grabbed her car keys. She just dropped the phone, sailed out of the house, and ran to our car. Priscilla ran after her. I followed Priscilla. We climbed into the back of the car, barely getting the door shut before Mom peeled out of the driveway. She drove like a mad woman to the hospital, screeching to stops, running red lights, and jumping over curbs. I reached over to Priscilla and grabbed for her hand as we drove. She let me have it.

The emergency room that night was hellish. There had been an accidental shooting, and family members from both sides were warring over whose fault it was that a six-year-old now had a bullet in his chest. Someone else had nearly severed a finger slicing a bagel. Someone else held a toddler in her arms sweating with fever. Someone else had a foot with shards of glass sticking out of it. I saw all of this as we were led to the room where Rebecca was lying, awaiting a surgeon's arrival and a parent's signature. It was like being inside someone's nightmare.

My mother's face turned ashen when she saw Rebecca, her firstborn, lying battered and bruised on the gurney. Ruptured spleen, fractured pelvis, punctured lung, multiple contusions. I heard the doctor say all these words, but I wasn't entirely sure what any of them truly meant. When you are twelve, the word "contusion" means nothing to you.

Then the doctor said something about a head injury, bleeding on the brain, and "we must relieve the pressure," and I somehow knew that my life would be different after that night. That even if Rebecca survived, which she did, my life would be different.

That was the night I learned to hate emergency rooms.

That was the night my mother learned to hate telephones.

Stephen was nowhere to be found when I had walked into the emergency room at Sharp. He had no doubt been there for many minutes already. Unlike the ambulance, I had to drive at the posted speed limit and then hunt down a free parking place.

I had made my way to the reception desk, passing only two other people in the waiting area: a man with an arm in a home-made sling and a whimpering little boy on his mother's lap with an ice pack over one side of his face.

The nurse at the desk looked up at me and smiled. "Can I help you?"

"I'm Alexa Poole and a...my friend Stephen Moran was brought here by ambulance. He fell off my roof while replacing shingles. I think he has a broken arm. I mean, I am not sure... I didn't actually see him fall..." I was babbling. I sounded as though I were trying to assure an angry judge that I hadn't pushed Stephen off the roof myself. I stopped mid-sentence and just stared at her.

"It's okay," the nurse had said gently. "The ER is kind of a scary place, but your friend is in good hands, all right?"

I nodded like a three-year-old.

"Do you know how we can reach Mr. Moran's family? Someone who can give us some information so we can better care for him? Getting his signature on the release form was about all he could manage."

"So he's awake?" I had said, feeling strangely giddy.

"Kind of in and out," the nurse said. "Do you know anyone in Mr. Moran's family?"

I had completely forgotten about trying to reach his mother. I had been so engrossed with nasty emergency room memories, I hadn't even tried to see if her phone number was stored on his cell phone.

"Oh! I...I will try and call his mother," I stammered, fumbling in my purse for Stephen's cell phone. My hands brushed across his wallet. I lifted it out, slipped the insurance card into my free hand, and handed it to her.

"Thanks." She handed me a clipboard with an admittance form attached. "Do you think you could fill any of this out for us?"

"Maybe just his address and his age," I said.

"Well, that's a start."

I took the clipboard and walked over to a row of chairs by a window. I withdrew Stephen's cell phone and fumbled through the menu, looking for his stored numbers. I found "Mom" under the "M's."

I pressed the button for "Mom" and waited as somewhere in Riverside a phone rang. A woman answered it on the fourth ring.

"Mrs. Moran?"

"Yes?"

"Um, my name is Alexa Poole, and your son Stephen is working at my apartment building doing some repair work."

I paused for just a second.

He hadn't called her. She had said nothing when she heard my name.

"And, well, while he was on the roof today, he fell. I'm with him at Sharp Hospital in San Diego."

"He is okay? Is he hurt?" I could hear tension and panic in her voice. I recognized it. I had heard it before, seventeen years before, actually, when my own mother received a call somewhat like this one.

"I think he broke his arm, and maybe his leg or ankle. He has some scratches. He fell onto a hedge outside my kitchen window, but he wasn't exactly conscious when the ambulance came and took him, so I don't know what else may be wrong."

"Dear Jesus!" Mrs. Moran had said.

"Mrs. Moran, I am at the emergency room with him, and they need some information from you."

"Oh, of course. I can talk to them."

I had walked back over to the front desk and handed Stephen's cell phone to the smiling nurse. She motioned for me to hand her the clipboard as well. The nurse began to ask Mrs. Moran questions, and I stood there, unashamedly watching her fill in the blanks. Blood type B positive. Tonsils out when he was eight. Father deceased. Doesn't smoke. No childhood illnesses. No prior broken bones. Has mentioned headaches the last few weeks. Exercises regularly. No known allergies.

Is kind to strangers and little kids, I wanted to add. The nurse looked up at me as though she had read my thoughts. I suddenly felt very awkward standing there, eavesdropping. It didn't feel right. I stepped away from the desk.

When she was finished, the nurse smiled and extended the phone toward me. I walked back over to her and took it.

"Your friend's mother is on her way. She should be here in an hour or so."

I slipped the phone back into my purse.

"Thanks," I said, not knowing what else to say. I had no idea what to do next.

"Would you like me to ask when you can see him?" she said.

Her question took me a little by surprise. She said it as though she assumed I would want to.

In the seconds before I answered her, I thought of the way Stephen had carried me into my house two days ago, how he gently laid me on my couch and brushed away my hair from my face as I came out of a fog of semi-consciousness. How he looked away when I tried to sit up and my robe fell partly open. How he got me a glass of water. How he stayed with me, listening as I spontaneously told him what I had told no one else. That for several long weeks I didn't know if my tumor was benign. That I couldn't tell my mother I even had a tumor under my arm. Not her. I told him about Rebecca, my thirty-six-year-old sister who still plays Candy Land. I told him about her accident. I told him my parents had once lost another child, this one for real. There had been a son, my brother, Julian, who died within hours of his birth of a congenital heart defect four years before Priscilla and I were born. I told him Priscilla hasn't been home in four years, that she moved to London seven years ago and has only made one trip home since. That my dad has a new wife, a new home, a new son, a new life.

"There was no one I could tell how scared I was," I had said. A little weepy, I might add.

I think somehow he knew it wasn't that I don't have friends I could have told my fears to. I do have friends. I have friends at work and the joggers I share my favorite beach with and Serafina. I have some kind acquaintances at her church where I sometimes attend. I think he somehow knew this was just one of those private, personal things I had wanted to share only with someone who truly loves me, someone who would have worried with me, been scared for me that I might have had cancer, who would have fought with me if I did, and who would have wept for me if it killed me.

He sat there and listened to it all.

"You are very brave," he said, when I was finished.

"No, I'm not…" I started to say.

"Yes, you are. Look at how you have suffered to spare your mother pain. She's the reason you said nothing to anyone about your fears, isn't it? Because of what happened to your sister? And your baby brother? You didn't want her to think for a moment that she might lose you too. You are very brave. And unselfish."

I could think of nothing to say.

Stephen rose from where he had been sitting—on the couch

next to me. He handed me the newspaper I had gone outside for in the first place.

"I'd better get back to work," he had said, "if you're sure you'll be okay?"

I had nodded and then watched him walk out onto the porch where new planks of wood waited to be nailed into place.

The nurse is waiting for my answer.

"Yes, please. I'd like to see him."

I have been in Stephen's room now for twenty minutes. He has been moved to a regular room while we wait for Ivy Moran to arrive from Riverside. The operating room has been prepared. Stephen will need two pins in his arm to hold his broken elbow in place while it heals and a steel plate in his shattered ankle. Doctors are guessing that when Stephen fell from the ridge-line of my roof, he landed on his elbow upon his first contact with the roof and his ankle on the second. One of the doctors is concerned about why Stephen fell. He keeps talking about the headaches Stephen seems to have been having. He has asked me twice if I saw Stephen fall. I have told him twice that I did not.

Stephen stirs again and licks his lips. I see his eyes flutter open.

He sees me.

"Alexa?" he whispers.

I move toward him. Instinctively, I reach for the hand that is not wounded.

"Yes, it's me."

"*What* was in that lemonade?" he says, a faint smile breaking across his face.

"You fell, silly," I reply. "Onto my hawthorn bushes."

"Am I still in one piece?"

"Broken arm, broken ankle, lots of cuts and scratches. But I think you will still be able to play the violin."

He grins, but it turns quickly into a grimace. He is in pain.

"I should call my mother," he whispers.

"She's already on her way," I reply, squeezing his hand. "I filched your cell phone and found her number. She'll be here soon. Then you will go in for surgery for your arm and ankle."

He nodded.

"What hit me in the head?" Stephen mumbles a moment later.

"What?" I ask.

"What hit me in the head?"

"I don't know, Stephen." I don't know what to say to this. Serafina never mentioned anything about seeing something hit Stephen in the head. A second of silence passes between us.

Then I ask what I feel I must. Better to know right away if his heart is spoken for.

"Stephen, is there anyone else you want me to call?"

I wonder if he knows what I mean. I don't mean should I call my landlady, Rose, and tell her she will need to find someone else to finish the repairs. I don't mean does he have a pet and do I need to call a neighbor to ask them to take care of it. I mean is there *someone* else.

He opens one eye, and I feel his hand move.

"No," he says, and his pinky touches mine.

He drifts off again.

I am falling.

I do not let go of his hand.

2

Ivy Moran arrives in a flowing caftan that billows past her as she makes her way down the corridor to Stephen's room. I hear her footsteps first, flip-flops slapping the shiny floor, and I poke my head out of Stephen's door. I see her moving toward me, her long, mostly gray hair moves across her shoulders like wheat in wind. I know this woman coming toward me is Stephen's mother; I can see his features in her tanned face. Ivy is wearing a collection of Native American jewelry. She looks as though she spends a lot of time in the sun.

"You must be Alexa!" she says to me when she reaches Stephen's door. She embraces me as though I am a long-lost relative. "How can I ever thank you for everything you've done today?"

She says this as she pulls me back into Stephen's room. I know she is anxious to see him.

"I was happy to do it," I say.

But now she has eyes only for her son.

"Stephen, I'm here," she says, and she is at his side in an instant, stroking the hand that I had been holding.

Stephen opens his eyes and smiles as best he can. "But it's Thursday afternoon. You will miss Bunco."

"It's okay. I never win anyway."

"Guess I really did it this time."

"You will mend," she says, but her smile disappears a little.

"I can barely keep my eyes open. They gave me something…" Stephen does not finish his sentence. His pre-op sedative is starting to take effect.

At that moment, a bed on wheels arrives, pushed by two nurses in pastel scrubs.

"Okay, who would like to go for a little ride?" one of the nurses asks cheerfully. She pushes the bed inside, parallel to Stephen's bed.

Getting Stephen, groggy and with broken limbs wrapped in splints, onto the bed is going to be tricky. And he is wearing nothing but a pale blue hospital gown. I step out into the hall while the nurses and his mother help him make the transition.

A moment later Ivy joins me and the bed appears at the doorway. One of the nurses eases it through and begins to turn it for the push down the hall. Stephen holds up his good arm.

"Just a sec," he mumbles.

The nurse stops.

"Alexa," he says.

"I'm here."

"Tell Rafael I'll show him the curve ball another time. Told him I'd see him today…"

Rafael. Serafina's and Jorge's eight-year-old grandson.

"I'll tell him."

He says nothing else, but he waves his hand in my direction. I resist the urge to take it, raise it to my lips, and kiss it.

Kiss it. What in the world am I thinking?

The nurse finishes her turn, and the rolling stretcher starts to move down the hall. Ivy turns to me before following it.

"God bless you, Alexa, for everything you've done for me and Stephen. I'm in your debt!"

I want to ask her if she needs a place to stay the night or if she wants me to wait with her while Stephen is in surgery, but my mouth refuses to produce these questions. I simply nod and she dashes off, the caftan flowing like a sail on a slim boat.

I stand there watching them until the stretcher disappears into an elevator.

My incision is starting to ache.

I don't know what to do. Should I stay? Maybe I should go. Is Ivy the kind of person who can handle something like this on her own? She seems calm and self-assured. Maybe that's just how she appears on the outside. Maybe she needs me to stay.

Who am I kidding?

This is not about staying for Ivy.

This is about wanting to be where Stephen is.

This is nuts.

I'll come see him tomorrow.

I head for the elevator. Not to go to the OR, I tell myself when I step inside. "L" for lobby, that's where I am going. I don't even know which floor the OR is on. Which is fine. I don't need to know. I am going home. "L" for lobby. I press it. The doors close. I feel myself descending.

Oh, how I feel myself descending.

Stephen is not the first man I've ever fallen for. There have been a few other men in my life who have left me breathless, scatterbrained, and captivated by their touch. Okay, two. One in high school. One in college. But this honestly feels different. I'm not sure how to describe it. Everything that comes to mind sounds like the goo and syrup that oozes from a poorly written greeting card. This attraction I feel for Stephen begins somewhere deeper within my being than the fascination I've felt for other men in the past. I don't feel the visceral pull of physical attraction, though I'm sure it must be there. There is a stronger draw than just the mere appeal of a handsome member of the opposite sex. This deeper attraction is all I can sense, making me wonder if this is what people really mean when they say "love at first sight." I am not drawn to Stephen just by what I see in him. It's as though I'm drawn by what I see in me and other people when I am with him.

I didn't feel this way with Greg Oldenburg in high school. And I seriously doubt Greg felt this way about me. Ours was an association of convenience. I think Greg and I both got what we wanted out of our relationship. We both wanted to be paired with someone for our senior year. We both wanted to have someone to go on dates with on Friday nights, someone to hold hands with in the hallways, someone to be seen with, someone to make us feel we were both worthy of being dated, someone to go to prom with, someone with whom to experiment the art of kissing. Someone to show us how to begin to understand the emotional and mental differences between men and women.

I also wanted to be like Priscilla, who had a dozen high school guys chasing after her. Despite being identical twins, Priscilla was the one the boys at our high school were attracted to, not me. It didn't matter that we looked alike, sounded alike, and shared each other's clothes. She was the one who turned heads. I think she liked that, though. And to be honest, I would not have wanted that much attention. Priscilla liked the thrill of having multiple young men longing for her company, and I was happy just to experience the joy of capturing one boy's complete attention. It was just one of the many ways we were different from each other. And probably still are.

I honestly don't know where Priscilla drew the line with her dating relationships. We drifted apart along with the rest of the family after Rebecca's accident. As for me, I know Greg wanted more from me than I was willing to give him, but I couldn't bring myself to let him have every inch of my body and soul, even though his physical touch was electrifying. I had enough sporadic exposure from our family's infrequent attendance at church to know that God frowned on premarital sex. I knew it somehow cheapened the relationship as well as the very act itself. I knew my parents wouldn't approve. But it wasn't just because I felt it morally wrong that I refused Greg's advances. I was primarily scared to have sex with him. Scared of being naked with him. Scared that it would hurt. Scared that he would find me repulsive. Scared that I would find *him* repulsive. Scared I would never be able to fully love another man. Scared I would get pregnant. Scared that I wouldn't find anything pleasurable or good in giving my body away to a man-boy I knew I would not marry.

I let Greg kiss me, passionately, I guess you could say, and on more than one occasion he wove his way through my resistance by touching me in ways that threatened to lead us to the very thing I wanted to avoid. So I broke up with him the week after we graduated. I think he was relieved. Like I said, we had both gotten what we wanted. High school was over. We were headed to different colleges where no one knew us, and where no one would particularly notice if either one of us had a date or not on Friday nights. And I figured at college he could probably find someone who would give him what he wanted.

I wish I could say I was as smart about my next relationship. I got through my freshman year at San Jose State without any romantic entanglements. I was too thrilled to be on my own—out of my mother's lonely house where there was no dad and no telephone. And since Priscilla had opted to go to Berkeley, there was no one to compare me to. I was just *me*.

But I met Rick Fortrell my sophomore year. And I fell for him as quick and as hard as Stephen fell off my roof. And I ended up with injuries just as Stephen did, albeit emotional ones. Rick was handsome, intelligent, motivated, and a smooth-talker. Greg had no idea how to talk me out of my fears about being intimate with a man, but Rick had already mastered this form of communication, though I didn't know this at first. I ended up giving myself, every part of myself—including my soul, it seemed—to Rick because I thought he was going to ask me to marry him. He didn't, of course. In fact, after six months of living in as complete a relationship as I have ever known, Rick became bored.

While he was deciding we were through, I was imagining what my wedding dress would look like. I still shudder at how his departure from my life surprised me. It was what I least expected would happen.

Wounded, angry, and feeling very foolish, I crept into the biggest downtown church I could find on the day he left me; one where I could just melt into an empty pew and stay anonymous. Easy to do on a Thursday. The sanctuary of the Presbyterian church I happened upon was open and empty. I went in because I didn't know where else to go. I didn't know whom to turn to but God.

I appealed to the heavens.

I let Rick have everything! Every part of me, God! My very soul!

I don't know if I whispered this or cried it aloud or screamed it within my head. But I did hear something back. It's the only time I can ever recall feeling as though God had specifically spoken to me. Perhaps that is because it was one of the few times I had specifically spoken to *him.*

Not every part, the holy voice said. *Not your very soul. That is still yours to give to whom you will.*

Stunned into silence, I said nothing else. And neither did the Voice.

But I left the church that day feeling as though I had been given something back. It got me through the rest of the school year.

I didn't date for a long time after that. When I graduated a couple years later, I was still unattached, and I felt strangely unnecessary. The same month I graduated, Priscilla abruptly moved to London without so much as a phone call to let me know. Then my father's second wife had a baby. To top off the month, my mother took her inheritance from her parents, sold my childhood home, bought a condo on Coronado Island, and started raising pugs.

And there I was with a college degree but no job. And no significant other. I desperately needed to feel useful.

The only person who I knew who really needed me was Rebecca. She was living in a group home—and still does, actually—near Balboa Park. Her material and physical needs were being met, and she had been given a job of sorts to help her feel that she has a purpose for her life, but I knew my mother's visits to her were usually stress filled—for both of them. When I graduated from college, it had been ten years since Rebecca's accident, but I honestly think my mother still expected her to "get better." Mom was in the mode of impatient expectation. Rebecca had relearned how to walk, how to write, how to do math, how to understand a joke; it seemed reasonable to think she would re-become the person she had been before the accident changed her: a promising scholar, a driven perfectionist, an independent thinker. But that's not what happened. My sister's injuries left her with low to average intelligence, frequent bouts of short-term memory loss, and a childlike wonder that I confess I found enchanting. Mom was visiting Rebecca once or twice a month back then. It is even less now. My father didn't visit Rebecca much back then, either, even though after the divorce he moved only an hour and a half away. I'm sure he thought—and still thinks—"Well, how often do parents need to visit their adult children?" After all, when I graduated from college at twenty-two, Rebecca was twenty-nine. She had been living at the group home for nine years. She had a life of her own, right? And Priscilla? Priscilla only came back to San Diego once after she left for Berkeley. Once. After she was handed her college degree, she boarded a plane to London, landed, and then just stayed there. She has a flat, as she calls it, overlooking the Thames, and she works as a translator for an import company. That's her life. It doesn't really include the remnants of her family. Rebecca has seen her once in the past seven years.

Rebecca and I, on the other hand, get along great. I've never told anyone this, but I like who she became after her accident. I would never have wished it on her, but it wasn't the worst possible thing that could have happened to her. The worst possible thing would have been to end up like Leanne.

So I was pretty sure Rebecca would be thrilled if I could spend more time with her, see her regularly, take her places for lunch. And being needed by Rebecca, my brain-damaged sister, was better than being needed by no one.

I applied to all the San Diego hospitals, hoping to get a job close to Rebecca's group home. I moved back to San Diego, found the triplex after a chance meeting with Rose, the owner and landlady, in a parking lot, and hoped the right job offer would come my way. It finally came at just about the time my meager reserve funds were about to run out. I got a job at Mercy Hospital, just a few minutes away from Rebecca's group home.

So the job worked out, I found a wonderful place to live near the beach, and I was and still am able to see Rebecca every week.

But it's been seven years, and here I am still waiting for my life to move on to the next phase. Nothing ever seems to change for the better. I don't want to win the lottery or move to France or sail around the world. I just want what millions of other women have and probably find unremarkable: a husband, children, and a home to love them in.

I just don't seem to run across many suitable men to date. I long ago decided not to get mixed up with another Rick. Trouble is, I didn't know what Rick was like until I had been with him for many months.

Rose's son, Patrick, who lives in the last third of the triplex—on the other side of Serafina and Jorge—made an attempt to woo me early on, but it was clear from the beginning that he only wanted my company if it included sex. It was obvious to me then, and still is, that Patrick dates beautiful women for show, average women for sex, and rich women for—what else?—money. This is why Patrick is still chasing women at a frenzied pace; eventually, they all figure him out. This is also why I refuse to even go with him to a movie. I barely tolerate him as a neighbor.

There are some nice single men at the hospital where I work, but no one who has ever taken my breath away. Not the way Rick did. Not the way Stephen does.

The thing is, there is something about Stephen that is unlike Rick in every way. I've seen it in everything he has done in the short time I've known him. It's a quality I find hard to define. I've seen it in his every conversation with me, with little Rafael, even. He seems so...genuine.

Yesterday he came to my back door and grudgingly asked for some Tylenol because he had a headache; grudgingly because he said he usually keeps a bottle in his truck, but it was empty. I didn't mind, of course. I gave it to him and told him he should rest a few minutes before continuing in the hot sun. He agreed, and I invited him into my kitchen and gave him a glass of lemonade.

We started to chat about little, trivial things, and then for some reason I can't recall—even though it happened just yesterday—we got on the subject of church. He asked if I went to one, and I said sometimes I go with Serafina and Jorge. He asked why just sometimes. I shrugged and said I just go when I feel that I've missed it.

"Alexa, can I ask you something? What's your relationship with God like? Do you have one?" His question unnerved me a little, but I answered him.

"Doesn't everybody have a relationship with God?" I said. I didn't mean to sound glib. I just don't see who *doesn't* have a relationship with God.

I felt the need to explain. "I mean, that's like asking me if I have a relationship with air," I said. "Of course I do. Even the atheist has a relationship with God. He denies God exists. That's his relationship. One of denial."

"Okay, fair enough," he had said. He was grinning.

"Why do you ask?"

His answer moved me. "Because you seem as though you have been carrying around a lot of pain, a lot of bad memories, a lot of grief," he said, never taking his eyes off me. "I can see that you miss your family, the one you lost when your sister had her accident. I can see that you're still hurting over what you lost. But I can also see that you still have hope. You're not bitter. That's usually the evidence of the grace of God in someone's life."

I could only look at him in speechless confusion.

He downed the rest of the lemonade and then rose from the table. "I didn't mean to pry. Sorry," he said. "Thanks for the drink and the Tylenol. I'm feeling better already."

He went out the back door and I watched him go, utterly silent, in my chair.

Thinking of it again now makes me tremble.

This, then, is that quality in Stephen that beckons me, this quality he has that no other man I've known has had.

Stephen cares for my very soul.

The one thing I have not given away.

3

I awaken on Friday morning to the sound of the morning commute and the cry of seagulls looking for breakfast. There is no pounding of a hammer or screech of a saw this morning. Stephen is not outside beginning his fifth day of repair work to the triplex. I rise from my bed and stretch carefully, mindful of my incision. My doctor wants to check it this morning since it's been a full week since the tumor was removed. This will technically be my last day of sick leave. I'm scheduled to return to work on Monday, and I'm suddenly wishing I had asked for two weeks off instead of one.

I bathe, wary of getting the bandage under my arm wet, and I wash my hair in the crazy way I concocted on Sunday, the day after I got home from what was supposed to have been same-day surgery. The anesthesia made me so nauseous I had to stay overnight. I tip my head back, off to the left, and dump a mega-Slurpee cup full of water over my head. Half the water seems to pool in my right ear. Washing the suds out of my hair with one hand also has its limitations, but I get through it.

I dry off, run a comb through my hair, and slip on a cotton sundress with a button-up front, figuring I won't have to completely undress if I can slip out of the bodice when my doctor checks the incision. My stroll outside to get the paper seems uneventful. For the past four mornings, Stephen had been there to greet me.

Four days ago, when my incision was just three-days old, I tentatively made the same short trek outside in just my robe. I had forgotten Rose had hired someone to fix the sagging porch on my side of the triplex as well as replace the roof along the entire length. I was dizzy with pain, and I am sure I made quite a few ugly faces as I tottered out to fetch the *San Diego Union Tribune*.

That's how I looked when Stephen first saw me.

"Need some help?" a voice said.

The voice startled me. I flinched, and a throbbing jet of pain coursed through my upper body. I made a noise. The kind of noise someone makes when they have been stung by a couple of angry wasps.

Stephen was at my side in an instant.

And that's how I first saw him.

Tall, muscular, and tanned, and he smelled nice. When he ran to me, his tool belt made all kinds of deep, manly noises.

"Are you okay?" he asked, genuinely concerned.

I had stopped midstride, intent on not screaming out a word unfit to be heard on a sun-drenched residential street. I looked down at my feet.

"Y-yes," I muttered, wanting to look up at him, but knowing

I must look like a hag. I hadn't even run a brush through my hair.

He started to reach for my right arm—to support me, I guess—and I turned away, releasing another arrow of pain through my torso. I bit my lip and swallowed the yelp that begged to jump out of my mouth.

"I had some minor surgery on Friday," I mumbled. "Under my arm. Haven't taken my pain medication this morning." Which was true, I hadn't. The following morning I *did* take it before going out to get the paper, and then I promptly fainted. "Just want to get my paper."

That was when I looked up. I couldn't believe what I had just told Mr. Handsome Tool Belt. I didn't even know his name yet.

"Oh," he said, letting his arm fall back. He reached down for the paper that was lying a few inches off my front path and handed it to me. "Here you go."

I reached for it with the arm that wasn't in spasms of pain. "Thanks," I said, looking at the paper, not at him.

"I'm afraid I'm going to be making lots of noise today. I apologize."

Surprise made me look up into his face. "What?"

"Your landlady hired me to make a lot of noise today. I'm really sorry. You probably were hoping to get some rest."

I remembered then. I remembered Rose calling me and Serafina and Jorge last week to tell us this would be happening. Patrick was supposed to tell us, but he had not.

"It's okay," I said. "It's not your fault."

"Can I help you get inside?"

It had been a long time since I had been in the company of a man as chivalrous as Stephen was. I realized I see way too much of Patrick, even though I try not to pay any attention to him.

"No, thanks," I said, and I think my voice and eyes betrayed how touched I was by his thoughtfulness.

He smiled at me. "I'm Stephen Moran. Stephen Moran the Handyman." And he laughed.

"Alexa. Alexa Poole," I replied.

"Nice to meet you, Alexa," he said. He started to turn away and then turned back. "You sure you'll be okay?"

I nodded. "Nothing that a little orange juice and codeine can't fix." I said it to be casual and funny, but it sounded as though I were condoning substance abuse.

He smiled, but I know he watched me make my way slowly back up to my apartment. When I got inside I threw the unopened paper on the couch, filled a glass with orange juice, and popped two pain pills into my mouth. I lay back down and slept away the rest of the morning, despite the loud noises outside.

I never did open that paper to read it.

Later that afternoon I felt well enough to sit outside on my porch. I took a book with me and a glass of iced chai. I had just sat down on my wicker chair when Stephen came around the corner with a crowbar and some other wicked-looking tool.

"Alexa. Hello." He seemed startled to see me. He stopped at the railing to the porch.

"Hello."

He looked at my book and my glass of chai.

"Feeling okay?"

"Yes. Thanks."

He paused.

"Going to read for a while?"

Well, it seemed kind of obvious to me that I was planning on reading. "Yeah, thought I would."

"Oh."

He didn't move away from the railing.

"Is something the matter?" I asked.

"I just…I just told Mrs. Marvelle I would start on the porch this afternoon."

Of course. The porch. I felt very stupid.

"I'm sorry. I'm in your way." I started to get up, wincing a little as I rose.

"No, please, don't get up!" He took a step toward me. "It can wait."

"Don't be silly. This is why you're here."

"You're not in my way, actually. Not yet, anyway," he said, stepping onto the porch itself. "It's these boards between your place and the place next door that need to be replaced. You don't have to move, but it might be distracting if you're trying to read."

He looked at me in a kind way, so ready to accommodate me. It was already starting to grow on me, this way he had of dealing with people. Of dealing with me.

I stayed.

I didn't read.

Instead Stephen asked me about my job, where I'm from, if I had family here. That first day I told him the short version: I told him where I worked, that I had been born right here in San Diego, that my parents were divorced, and that I had two sisters; one of them being my twin. Then I asked him about his family, his life. And that's when he told me he was born in Santa Cruz, that he is thirty-two, that he loves to surf, that his mother lives in Riverside now, and that he's an only child.

I asked him if he is married, and he paused and said, "I used to be."

I waited to see if he would say anything else. He didn't say a lot about his marriage; just that it had been a long time ago. And that the way it ended was not something he was proud of.

And that he had been a different kind of man back then.

I went back inside a few minutes later, as my pain medication had worn off. I took two more pills, laid down, and when I awoke it was late afternoon. I heard voices outside my bedroom window. I sat up slowly and stood, pulling away the curtain from the window by my dresser. Stephen was measuring boards on a sawhorse, and little Rafael was standing nearby, asking Stephen a million questions. Stephen was attentive to his work, but he was smiling at Rafael and answering every one of them.

The day stretches before me with a full agenda of things I want to do. My appointment with my doctor is at nine thirty, and then I had made plans to have an early lunch with Mom. I also told Rebecca I would be able to see her later this afternoon in addition to our usual Sunday afternoon get-together because I had the week off from work. I didn't tell Rebecca in advance why I was off. I'm not entirely sure she would have fully comprehended what having a tumor, even a benign one, means, nor what my surgery would entail. Besides, it was probable she would have forgotten anyway. It's better just to tell Rebecca something at the moment she needs to know it. If it isn't important to her, she tends to forget.

Then, of course, I want to see Stephen.

While I eat my breakfast and ponder my reasons for wanting to see him, I mentally somersault back and forth between how to make my visit seem natural.

If I go, will he be glad I came? Surprised? Concerned? Will

he think I'm just a compassionate person concerned for the handyman who fell from her roof? Or will he be able to see right through me? Will he be able to pick up on my growing attraction to him? Perhaps he has already! Perhaps he is flattered by it. Perhaps he is bothered. Humored? Annoyed.

I feel like a timid, unpopular high school girl with a crush on the star quarterback on the football team.

I want to have a bona fide motive for seeing Stephen that he won't be able spend time guessing about. The motive comes to me as I scrape my cereal bowl in the sink.

I still have his cell phone and wallet in my purse.

My doctor's appointment is routine. Dr. Chou is happy with the way the incision is healing and certain I won't need even a small amount of reconstructive surgery. The tumor, though walnut sized, was removed with a fair amount of surrounding fatty tissue. If I walk around the rest of my life with my right arm raised, people will see a divot and a scar, but since I'm not a nude model or a trapeze artist, this does not concern Dr. Chou or me. He tells me to make an appointment to have the stitches removed on Wednesday.

With a fresh and smaller bandage snuggled under my arm, I head out into the late June sunshine and to my mother's world on Coronado. I actually love the drive to my mother's island home. I love making the heady, short journey across the Coronado Bridge, whose arc over the sparkling bay is like a white-and-blue rainbow. I love her little house too, even though it's less than twelve hundred square feet and yet cost her nearly a million dollars. I'm learning to like her dogs, Humphrey and Margot, though this has taken considerable time and effort on my part. Her pugs are cute little things, but the way she fawns over them is rather nauseating. Humphrey and Margot have produced three litters so far, tiny suede bundles of canine cuteness which Mom has been able to sell for substantial amounts of money, considering that they are, after all, just little dogs. Everything now revolves around them, especially when there are puppies expected or puppies in the house. I'm fortunate that Humphrey and Margot are "between jobs" today, or I doubt my mother would leave the house to have lunch with me.

She is watering baskets of lobelia on her porch when I arrive. My mother—Mom to me and Eileen to her dogs and friends— is quite attractive, I think. She wears her graying hair short and stylish and usually sports long, dangling earrings. Mom exercises to a video tape every morning, drinks water all day long, and never eats anything fried, unless it's tempura. She loves the opera, the color lavender, and falling rain. She has her flaws, though, just like all of us do. My mom can't move past what happened to her first two children. She can't forgive Dad for being in Tokyo when Rebecca was nearly killed, though it certainly wasn't his fault. She can't find a way to reconcile her relationship with Priscilla, which I think is sad. Mom has the money and the time to go to London and force Priscilla to visit with her, but she doesn't do it. Can't leave the dogs, you know. She can't think a nice thought about my dad, even though my parents have been divorced since my sophomore year in high school, twelve years ago. And I think her worst weakness is her inability to love the Rebecca that I love. The one God left us with, if I may be so bold as to say that. I get the feeling Mom thinks Rebecca is terribly unhappy with her second life, but I just don't see it that way.

She waves as I drive up and sets the little metal watering can on the porch floor. She puts her hands on her hips as she watches me get out of my car and walk up the little curving path to her front door.

We step inside and I am greeted with the familiar and the foreign. Half of the furnishings in her nicely arranged living room are from my childhood home, half have no meaning for me. The framed photographs sitting on the glass-and-wrought-iron table by the entrance to her dining room are the most unusual pairings of old and new. The table is new; the photographs are not.

There are four of them; one for each child my mother has borne. Rebecca's is at the far left, at the beginning of the sentence, if you will. It's one of her high school senior photos, taken the year before her first life ended. Her cocked head, easy smile, and Audrey Hepburn eyes exude tenacity and potential. It must pain my mother to keep that picture up, yet she does. Julian's photo should be next, but it isn't. Priscilla's and my senior pictures follow. Being six minutes older, Priscilla precedes me. She's wearing a blue turtleneck; I'm wearing yellow. She looks clever and perceptive and I look naive and hopeful, yet people said they couldn't tell us apart.

Then there is Julian. I have never had the courage to ask my mother why he is last and not second in the line of photographs. I long ago convinced myself that it doesn't really matter. I love this picture, but I don't like to look at it. The photo was taken when he was minutes from death. He lived a total of seven hours, twenty-six minutes. Julian fought for survival the way all human beings do, regardless of their age, but there was no way to win against such a grotesquely malformed heart. My parents refused to speak of it, but my paternal grandmother told me a long time ago that Julian died as peaceful a death as one could wish on an infant doomed to die. He simply drifted away, leaving the hospital and my mother's arms like a feather on the wind. Julian doesn't look as though he is dying in the picture; he looks like an adorable, sleeping baby. But I know he was dead minutes after the shutter opened and his likeness was etched on film.

I look away from these pictures as we step into my mother's kitchen.

I wait for a second to see if she will ask how my appointment went. I didn't really think she would ask, so when she doesn't, it's not a surprise. After our greetings to each other and as she ushers me inside, I simply tell her what she wants to hear. That everything is fine.

"The incision is healing fine. Just the way it's supposed to," I say as Margot and Humphrey run to smell my ankles and beg for attention.

"Good, good," she says, but in a distracted way. And I honestly don't mind changing the subject for her benefit. Last Friday was hard for her. Even though I waited until I knew the tumor was benign before I told her I was having surgery, she still didn't like hearing it. She didn't like taking me to the hospital for the surgery, didn't like waiting while I had it, and thoroughly didn't like my violent reaction to the anesthesia after I awoke. She nearly hugged me in relief when I told her in between retching that she should just go home and come back in the morning to take me home. So I move on. I ask her if she would like to come with me to see Rebecca this afternoon.

Mom is at her back door, locking it as we prepare to leave the house for lunch.

"But I just saw her last Tuesday," she says.

And that's that.

We get in my car and it's on the tip of my tongue to tell her I have met someone. She is usually interested in hearing about new developments in my love life. Well, at least she asks about it now and again. Most of the time there's nothing new to tell. But I decide not to. I am only on Day 5. Besides, my someone is lying in a hospital bed with broken bones and a body full of punctures. She will not want to hear about that.

I ask her about the dogs.

And that's what we talk about.

It is a little after two when I pull up to Rebecca's group home. She's waiting for me on the verandah—pacing, actually.

When I get out of my car, she comes running—in her slightly leaning way—to greet me.

"Alexa!"

"Hey, Becca," I reply. She seems quite happy this afternoon. Her eyes are alight with joy and something else. Anticipation, maybe? Something good must have happened today. Or will happen. I wonder if she plans on telling me what it is.

I follow her into the large lobby of the Falkman Residential Center. It's a nice place, really, with beautifully landscaped grounds. Thirty people live here, eighteen women and twelve men. The men's dorms are on the second floor and the women's are on the first. Rebecca shares her room with a twenty-eight-year-old woman with Down syndrome named Marietta. She is the friendliest person I know and the perfect roommate: quiet, serene, and able to listen with interest to anything Rebecca says. Most of the residents are like Rebecca; they are functioning adults but need assistance living independent lives. Many of

Rebecca's housemates were born with their disabilities, but several became disabled, as Rebecca did, when they were just out living normal lives. The residents all work in a little building behind the center where they make colorful rugs on giant looms. The rugs are actually quite beautiful. When the rugs are sold, each resident earns a "paycheck." It's a great arrangement, which is why there is a waiting list for the Falkman Center with more than a hundred names on it. The facility is heavily endowed by the Falkman Foundation; so heavily, in fact, that Rebecca's state disability check plus the four hundred dollars my parents split and chip in every month pays her room and board. It feels like a real home because it is. The Center is a private institution; any resident is free to leave at any time.

Rebecca lived at our home in Mount Helix for the first year after her accident. Actually, she lived in the hospital for three months during her recovery and then nine months at home while waiting for an opening at the Falkman Center. With her short-term memory problems, finishing college seemed out of the question. And even though Rebecca couldn't live a completely independent life, she didn't want to live at home for the rest of her life, either. But those nine months she was home, still recuperating, was a very strange time. My parents were still kind of shell-shocked when Rebecca was finally discharged, and I can see now that they hadn't a clue how to acquaint themselves with her new personality. My parents quarreled often, even before Rebecca's accident, but it got ten times worse afterward, beginning the moment Dad came home from Tokyo. The more they fought, the more Priscilla retreated into a sort of self-imposed solitary confinement. Before Rebecca came home, there were days when I felt as though I were an only child.

While Rebecca was still in the hospital, there was an army of visitors and well-wishers, especially in the beginning. But as the weeks wore on, there were fewer and fewer visitors, so that by the time Rebecca came home, there was really no one for whom my mom had to put on a happy face. The only people who came to visit Rebecca with any kind of regularity were Leanne's very wealthy father, Gavin McNeil, and his son—Leanne's older brother, Kevin. I remember thinking back then that they probably felt terribly guilty about what happened because Leanne was the one who had been driving, or that they wanted answers and hoped Rebecca could give them, which she couldn't. Gavin and Kevin came, anyway—one or the other or both—three or four times to the hospital and another three or four times to the house after Rebecca's discharge. But I don't think Rebecca ever regained her memory of that night. Leanne's mother, so I heard, was inconsolable after Leanne's death. I imagined Gavin and Kevin hoped they could relieve Mrs. McNeil's agony by giving her an explanation for the car accident that claimed her daughter's life, but none of us ever learned the reason why Leanne went off the road that night. After a while Gavin and Kevin stopped coming.

Rebecca now tugs on my arm, pulling me toward her room to get her Scrabble board. We usually play a game on the patio when I come. Her brown hair is pulled back with a red plastic headband, one of two headbands—the other one being a blue one—which she insists on alternately wearing every day. Her left arm is slightly bent at the elbow and she walks with a tiny hitch in her step—two lasting visual reminders of her long-ago accident. That she walks at all is amazing. When she first emerged from her coma, there was doubt her wounded brain would allow her the use of her legs. But while her head

injury made her less oppositional, it didn't make her less motivated. She worked hard in therapy to learn to walk again. It
was while watching her day after day exert herself to exhaus-
tion that I decided to become an occupational therapist. I was
the only one of us that cheered her on in the therapy room.
My parents and Priscilla had a hard time watching those ses-
sions, watching Rebecca sometimes collapse in frustration, but
I didn't mind being there. There were just as many triumphal
moments.

Rebecca and I enter her room and Marietta is there, brushing
the hair of a baby doll while she sits on her bed.

"Hi, Marietta," I say. Marietta smiles at me but doesn't say
anything back, which is not unusual for her. Marietta doesn't
say much, but she is forever in a good mood. I don't think I
have ever seen her grumpy or agitated. I hear drawers being
opened and shut behind me, and I turn to see that Rebecca is
going through her dresser as if looking for something. She turns
toward her closet and then turns back to the dresser, looking
flustered. She opens her underwear drawer and rifles through it
with a perplexed look on her face. Rebecca is clearly not looking
for the Scrabble board.

"What are you looking for, Rebecca?" I ask.

"I thought I knew where it was," she says softly, as if to no
one.

"Where what was?"

She turns to face me and the look on her face is a mix of hesitation and panic. As though she suddenly wishes she hadn't
given away that she was looking for something. As though
maybe her timing had been off. As though she had forgotten
Marietta and I were in the room with her.

"Rebecca?"

"Do you want to see my fish?" she asks, but as soon as she says this, her brows instantly wrinkle, as though she has just decided this, too, is not a good subject to talk about. Rebecca has had the blue-and-silver betta for three months. I was with her when she bought it, and I can sense that she remembers this. She is trying to change the subject.

"Cosmo," Marietta says and Rebecca whips her head around to look at Marietta, making it seem that she is annoyed Marietta would know the name of the fish. Well, of course she does. She shares a room with Rebecca and the fish she named Cosmo.

"I don't want to talk about my fish," Rebecca says gravely, speaking to me but looking at Marietta.

"We don't have to," I assure her. I sit down on Rebecca's bed and purposely look away from her fish.

As Marietta begins to hum "I've Been Working on the Railroad," Rebecca suddenly launches into a monologue about what she had for lunch, what she did on break, and what she watched on television last night. I can see that she is going to make this one of those visits where she just chatters away about everything and nothing. Scrabble is forgotten.

I don't mean to, but I start to tune her out. I'm thinking about Stephen and how I feel about him. I'm thinking about my mom and how I wish she were the kind of mom who asked how my doctor's appointment went. I'm thinking of how I miss Priscilla, different though she is, and that even though we e-mail each other frequently, it's not the same as being with her. I'm thinking how every once in a while Priscilla hints that she might consider coming home for a visit, but that she never follows through. And that she never invites me to come visit her.

Marietta continues to serenade us as I only half listen to Rebecca's rambling. I have too much tumbling about in my head, and I can see that this visit is pointless. I'm not mentally prepared to visit Rebecca today. It's not her fault; it's mine. When she pauses, I tell her I need to get going, that I need to visit a friend in the hospital. Which is true.

She seems both annoyed and relieved that I'm cutting our visit short. I stand and hug her goodbye and try not to cry out when she enthusiastically hugs me back. She rubs on my incision, but I elect to tell her another time about my surgery, if at all.

"See you Sunday, Becca." She looks back at me wide-eyed, as though she has forgotten we having a standing date on Sundays.

I leave her and Marietta to their childlike world and head back out to the lobby. I have my hand on the front door when Frances, the day manager, calls out from behind me.

"I'm glad I caught you, Alexa," she says, coming up to me. "I wanted to ask you something. I was just wondering if you've noticed anything unusual about Rebecca lately?"

Her question startles me. Not that she asked me a question about Rebecca. I mean, with my mother having no phone, I'm the main contact person for Rebecca when the Center needs to get ahold of the family. And my visits to Rebecca are regular, unlike my mother's. It's just the question itself that startles me.

"No. I mean, I don't think so. She was kind of chatty and distracted today," I reply, "but that's not unusual for her."

Frances thinks for a moment. "It's probably nothing. She just seems to be a little secretive around me. That's a new behavior for her. I was just wondering if you had noticed anything... new."

I shake my head. I just want to go see Stephen.

"No, not really."

She smiles. "Like I said, it's probably nothing. Thanks, Alexa. Have a nice rest of the day."

"Thanks. You too."

I slip into my hot car, roll down the windows, and head to Sharp Hospital.

4

I'm nervous as I make my way into the hospital lobby and ask a receptionist for Stephen's room number. As I inquire it suddenly occurs to me that perhaps Stephen was discharged this morning. A broken elbow and ankle aren't injuries to keep one hospitalized for very long. I really don't have a plan if they tell me he has gone home.

"He's in Room 304," the lady says, and then she tells me where to find the elevators.

So he's still here.

I try to calm my nerves as I head to the elevators and press the up arrow.

This is not a big deal. You are just returning his cell phone and wallet. You are not in love with him. You have known him less than a week. He is not in love with you.

This is what I tell myself as the elevator trudges up its cables, but I don't feel any different when the doors pull apart and I step out onto the third floor. I'm still as nervous as a schoolgirl.

I follow the signs to his room, smiling at the nurses and orderlies I pass as though I'm at ease with the state of the entire world.

Stephen's door is partly open. I knock.

"Come in."

Stephen's voice.

I see Ivy first. Her smile is wide and genuine. She is sitting in a chair with a tall back, wearing different clothes, so I assume she drove home last night and came back today. She stands when I walk in.

"Alexa. How wonderful to see you." And she says it as though she really means it.

"Hello, Ivy," I say, stepping farther in. My eyes are drawn to Stephen sitting up in bed. His wounded leg is elevated on a pillow. So is his elbow. His face and neck are streaked and spotted with scrapes and cuts from the hawthorn bushes. But he smiles when he sees me too. I cannot tell if he's delighted or amused by my visit, but I can safely file away "bothered" and "annoyed." He does not appear to be either of these.

"Hey," he says.

"Hi, Stephen." I step as close as I can to him without touching his bed.

"Must be kind of quiet around your place today. Or did my friend show up?"

"Friend?"

"I called a colleague of mine and asked him to finish up the job for me. He didn't come?"

"Oh. I've been gone most of the day, actually. He could be there now, I suppose."

"You've been out? You must be feeling pretty good. That's great."

I don't know how we so easily got onto the topic of how I'm faring, but I want to ask him how he is.

"You didn't go to work today, did you?" he continues.

"Uh, no. No, I had a checkup and then lunch with my mom, and then I stopped to see Rebecca."

"Rebecca's her sister," he says to his mom. "The one who was in the car accident."

I am bewildered, I must admit. He has told his mother about Rebecca. Which means he must have talked to her about me. What else did he tell her?

"Oh, of course," Ivy says. "Well, I'm sure she must have liked that. Alexa, would you like to sit down?"

I turn to Ivy to tell her I'm fine with standing, and I notice that she looks a little tired. No, not tired. Sad, maybe?

"It's okay. I don't mind standing," I tell her. "I won't stay long." She takes the chair instead of me.

I turn my head back to Stephen, and he seems to be searching my face for a reason for my visit. I hesitate and then insert my hand into my purse and close it around his cell phone and wallet.

"I forgot to give these back to you yesterday," I say, placing them atop the wheeled tray next to him where a water bottle sits and the remote for the television.

"Oh. Thanks," he says, and I'm certain there is disappointment in his voice. Is it my imagination, or is he disappointed that returning his cell phone and wallet is the only apparent reason I came?

I don't like the look of disappointment on his face.

I take the plunge. "So, are you okay? Are you in much pain?"

His features soften.

"The bones will mend. And the pain is nothing that a little orange juice and codeine can't fix."

I smile at this, at his attempt to make light of his injuries. "So you'll be going home soon?"

He doesn't stop smiling, but he looks over to Ivy and I follow his gaze. She smiles too. But it's a weary smile.

"In a couple of days, maybe," he replies as he turns his head back to me.

A tremor of foreboding slices through me. "Couple of days?"

Stephen clears his throat. "The doctors want to check something out, that's all."

"Check what out?"

He doesn't answer right away, and the moments of silence give me plenty of time to realize I have no business asking such a question.

"I'm sorry...I had no right to ask that..." I say, practically tripping over my words.

"No, it's okay—" he starts to say.

"No, it's not."

"Alexa, don't beat yourself up about it. I don't mind telling you if you really want to know."

I hear Ivy shift her weight in her chair.

"Is something else wrong?" I ask, and now I hear the apprehension in my voice.

Stephen holds my gaze, and it feels as though he's holding me with his arms. He is being the strong one.

"Well, the thing is, when I was thirteen I had a brain tumor," he says easily, as if he were telling me that when he was thirteen he had a dog named Rex. "I had surgery and radiation and we licked it. But the doctors are concerned about the headaches

I've been having and why I blacked out when I was standing on your roof. They just want to make sure the tumor hasn't returned. So I'm going to stay a couple days, get an MRI, and then we'll know."

He says all of this as though he's not a part of it, as though he's a spectator or a journalist or even one of the doctors.

I look over at Ivy, and she's smiling that same weary smile, but her eyes have grown misty. She's looking at Stephen, her only child, and not at me, but the look of a hurting mother is something I cannot bear. I feel my own eyes glaze over with moisture, and I look away from her. When I raise my eyes to meet Stephen's, I see that he's deeply moved by my response.

"It could be nothing," he says, and I'm sure he's speaking to both Ivy and me, but he's looking at me. And I sense in his eyes that he already suspects it is *something*. He has been down this road before. And so has Ivy.

"Sounds kind of scary," I manage to say.

He leans back a little on his pillow, as though he's comfortable with being honest with me. "Yeah. It's kind of scary."

"So…so when will you have the MRI?" My voice sounds shaky in my ears.

"Tomorrow morning."

Tomorrow. I already know how life can change in the span of twenty-four hours. I have seen it happen. I've felt it happen. And now I feel weighted by the prospect of *tomorrow*, and at how everything that defines you can change within its confines. Added to this weight is a crazy notion I feel welling up within me that Stephen's dilemma is somehow pulling me closer toward him, whether I want it to or not, and that I'm about to cross a line with him. One of those inevitable points of no return. The line of personal involvement. He probably doesn't even know I stand at this line. That I'm standing at a place where I will choose.

"Would you mind if I came by tomorrow afternoon, afterward?" I ask, slightly amazed at how easily this question falls off my lips. It's clear that the outcome matters to me.

"No," he says, and I stiffen for a second. But he continues. "No, I wouldn't mind at all."

I'm wrong about him not knowing I stand at the line.

He knows.

When I arrive back at the triplex, a quartet of men is finishing up the roof. One of them is descending a ladder as I pull into my driveway. I get out of my car and stare up at the finished project.

"There's no rain in the forecast, but if there was, you'd be all set," the man on the ladder says as he jumps off at the third rung.

"Wow. That was fast," I reply. "Stephen said he'd called someone. I figured that meant just one person."

The man gestures with his hands to the other workers. "Well, I knew these guys would have just frittered away the afternoon watching soap operas, so, you know…"

One of the other men on the roof throws an old shingle down, intending to hit the man from the ladder, but he ducks. All four men laugh. I can see these guys being friends with Stephen. I can see him being the man on the ladder. I can see him being the man who jokingly threw the shingle. And I can see him abruptly changing his Friday afternoon plans to help a friend.

I walk into my house and decide to get a pitcher of iced tea ready to offer Stephen's friends. But the men outside are pulling away in a red truck when I get to the front door ten minutes later. One of them is driving Stephen's vehicle, which had been left at the curb last night. I wave to them. And they honk a farewell.

I take the tea and glasses back to the kitchen, feeling perplexed. I open the fridge and look at my options for dinner. Nothing looks appetizing and yet I'm hungry. I grab an apple and take it outside. I haven't been able to run on the beach since my surgery, one of my favorite pastimes, but I feel well enough to walk on the wet sand. And I feel the need to.

The shoreline of Mission Beach is only three blocks away, so within minutes I'm standing at the threshold of the blue expanse of the Pacific Ocean. I stand at the water's edge, eating my apple and watching after-work surfers head into the waves. I immediately think of Stephen. This is something he told me he loves to do. I picture him as one of the figures far out in the waves, glistening in black as his wet suit catches the sun's rays. I have never attempted to surf. I'm too afraid of the bigger waves' power. But I can imagine I see Stephen bending at the knees, arms held out like the wings on an airplane, riding on the fury of water as if to tame it.

And yet I know some things cannot be tamed. Stephen didn't say the word "cancer" today, but didn't I feel as though he had? Wasn't the echo of it swirling about us?

I could see in Stephen's eyes that he pretty much knows what the MRI will reveal. Perhaps he had already started to suspect something was wrong. Perhaps he was figuring it out two days ago when he realized he had consumed all the Tylenol that he keeps in his glove box. Perhaps today it all made sense to him when he fully realized nothing hit him in the head as he stood on the ridgeline of my roof.

The surfer I have been watching has taken the wave to where it ends. He's standing in knee-deep water and bending over his board. He grabs it and runs back into the froth. Jumping over the little waves that want to break upon him, he heads out to where the true swells gather momentum.

I have never had the courage to try surfing.

I wonder if somewhere within me that courage nevertheless lives, untapped.

Saturday morning arrives warm and without the usual thick, coastal cloud cover. I rise and step into the kitchen to make coffee. I notice that my incision feels itchy today, not sore, as I go outside to retrieve the paper.

I walk back inside and toss the paper onto the living room table. I'm restless. Stephen will have the MRI this morning. Maybe he's having it now. Maybe the radiologist is at this very moment looking at the tissues in Stephen's brain. Maybe at this very moment he sees something that isn't supposed to be there...

I will myself to stop letting my imagination run wild. I go back into the kitchen, yank a mug out of my dishwasher with my good arm, and fill it with coffee. I go back to my bedroom, intending to switch on my computer to see if Priscilla has e-mailed me, as is her custom on Saturdays, but the phone rings. I pick up the cordless phone on my bedside table and answer it.

"Alexa, it's Pauline." Pauline is the new weekend manager at the Falkman Residential Center. She sounds agitated.

"Hello, Pauline."

"Alexa, is Rebecca with you? Did you take her out last night? Did you forget to sign her out?"

A cold rivulet of fear spreads over me. "No!"

"Does your mother have her?"

Oh, dear God. "No! Mom doesn't have her!"

"She's gone, Alexa!"

"What do you mean, she's *gone?*" I yell.

"I mean she's not here. Her little overnight suitcase is gone. She left a note for someone to feed her fish. If you don't have her, I don't know where she is."

My mind instantly swirls to come up with explanations of where Rebecca could be. I can think of nothing. She has never done anything like this before.

I blurt out a question that makes sense to only those of us who know her.

"Did she take her headbands?"

"Yes." Pauline answers, and I can hear her begin to break down in tears. She has only been a Center employee for a few weeks, and I'm sure she doesn't know what it's like to "lose" a resident. It happens sometimes. One of the residents will wander off, but within hours a helpful policeman, a kind neighbor, or the frantic Center employee who went looking for them brings them back.

But usually when a resident wanders off, they do not pack. They don't take their headbands. They don't leave a note to please feed their fish.

Rebecca didn't just wander off.

She left.

"Did she leave any other kind of note? Anything at all?" I ask. "How long has she been gone?"

"I don't know. The night manager says Rebecca was in her bed last night at eleven, but when I got here this morning, her bed was empty. She had made it. And there's nothing but the note for the fish."

My mind is reeling as I pace. "Did you call the police?" I ask.

"The police?"

"Yes, the police!"

Pauline hesitates. "But..." she finally says.

"But what?"

"She's not...she's technically free to leave here whenever she wants. All the residents are."

"I'm not suggesting she was kidnapped, Pauline. I'm just saying the police should know. What if she's wandering around on the Interstate? She's a vulnerable adult!" Even as I say this, I know Rebecca is certainly not strolling down the median on I-5. She has the mind of an adolescent, not a toddler.

"Oh! I think I need to call Frances first," Pauline replies, and again she's close to tears.

"I'll call the police myself!" I say. "Look, I will be there as soon as I can. Ask Marietta if she knows where Rebecca went."

"I already did. Marietta wasn't able to tell me anything. I'm not sure she even knows what I was asking her."

"You call Frances. I'll be there as soon as I can get there."

"Okay."

With shaking fingers, I press the "off" button.

My incision has stopped itching and is now starting to burn.

What am I supposed to do? How am I supposed to handle this? And what can the police do? Rebecca is disabled but not incapacitated. I don't have power of attorney over her and neither does my mother. Despite Rebecca's mental condition, she is a consenting adult. She still has the IQ of a functioning member of society.

But she is alone in a world that is often hostile. Especially to the innocent.

At least I think she is alone.

What if she is not?

With an anxious heart I pick up the phone to call the police anyway, wishing with all my heart I could call my mother instead and let her be the one who has to worry.

5

The Falkman Center looks as tranquil and undisturbed as it did yesterday; the manicured lawns and swaying palms seem to mock my unease as I park my car. I do not feel any better for having called the police. The policeman I spoke with was kind and sympathetic, but when I hung up the phone after talking with him I was simply more convinced of what deep down I already knew: Rebecca is a disabled American citizen, with all the rights U.S. citizens have, including life, liberty, and the pursuit of happiness. As the facts appear, my sister packed a bag, left a note for her fish, took her headbands, and is presumably now out pursuing happiness. The police can keep a lookout for her, and they can alert other law enforcement agencies, but Rebecca is technically not a missing person. Not yet. The policeman did say that if it appeared in any way that Rebecca was forced or coerced into leaving the Falkman Center that he wanted to hear back from me.

Before I got into my car to leave for the Center, I had taped a note to my front door. It's remotely possible that Rebecca might hail a taxi and come to my place. The note is addressed to her, and in it I tell her the location of my spare key and that she should go inside and wait for me.

I get out of my car now and walk up the cement pathway to the lobby doors, wondering for the umpteenth time if I should have gone to Mom's first. Or maybe I should have called Mom's next-door neighbor, Mrs. Devore, and told her to relay the news of Rebecca's running away to my mother. But I only consider this once. If Rebecca has indeed run away—can a thirty-six-year-old run away?—Mrs. Devore should not be the one to tell her. It should be me.

Pauline is waiting for me at the door, and behind her I can see Frances in the administration offices just inside. Frances is talking on the telephone and wearing sweats. I have never seen Frances wear anything but tailored slacks. She must have decided to come in when Pauline called her at home and told her one of the residents had left in the middle of the night.

"Alexa, I'm so glad you are here," Pauline says, pulling the door closed behind me and ushering me into the office, where Frances stands in her weekend clothes.

Frances hangs up the phone.

"Well, I guess you and I probably got the same information from the police," Frances says, calmly but with heaviness. "It doesn't look like there was any foul play, Alexa. I've looked in her room. The windows are still locked from the inside. There's no sign of a struggle in her room or at the front door, where we must assume she left the Center. The back door triggers a fire alarm at night, and it didn't go off. "

"I see," I mumble. It's a thing to say. I don't really see. Rebecca has thoroughly amazed me. I honestly cannot come up with a reason why she would do this. She loves living at the Falkman Center. She loves Marietta. This is her home. It has been for more than a dozen years.

"Can I see her room?"

"Of course," Frances says, and I can tell she, too, is worried for my sister.

The carpeted halls are quiet this morning. Many of the residents are on home visits or already involved with one of the Saturday activities the Center plans each week. Rebecca's half of the room looks the way it did yesterday. Neat, though not overly so. Her bed is indeed made. I walk over to her desk and pick up the note that is resting against the side of her fishbowl.

Don't worry about me. I am fine. Please feed Cosmo.

There is no mistake that it is Rebecca's handwriting and there is no frantic slant or agitation to the round letters of her script. She did not write it under duress. I walk over to her closet and open the door. Her pink suitcase is gone, as are half her clothes. Her three church dresses are gone, along with her dress shoes. The empty hangers in a neat line make me think she took time packing. Or she was being quiet so as not to wake Marietta. Or anyone else.

A few of the old shoe boxes on the top shelf of her closet are in mild disarray, suggesting she needed or wanted something from one of them and had stood on tiptoes to look through them. A bound stack of invitations from the weddings of her high school friends rests on its side rather than on top of the boxes, where it usually sits. Inside those boxes are treasures from her past: swimming medals from high school, postcards from friends, photographs of the people she loves, and other things, such as candy wrappers, movie ticket stubs, and napkins from restaurants. I reach for the one that sits at the oddest angle; perhaps the one she looked in last. It's a shoe box, a large one, and I know it holds most of her dearest belongings. I lift the lid and notice immediately that the photo of Julian that is usually right on top is gone. So is the photo of the three of us—me, Priscilla, and Rebecca—taken the spring of her eighteenth birthday at Anza Borrego when the desert was in bloom. The absence of the photos suggests a painful truth to me: Rebecca planned her escape.

I turn to face her dresser, knowing the headbands are gone, but needing to see the empty space where they would be if Rebecca were here. The dresser top is nearly empty. The headbands aren't the only things not there. Her rosewood jewelry box and her hairbrush are gone, and so is a little statue of a fairy kneeling down to rub noses with a butterfly. I open the top drawer where she keeps her underwear but also things she doesn't want to lose or misplace, like her address book, the take-out menu of her favorite Chinese restaurant, and her pass to the community swimming pool. Most of her under garments are gone, as is her address book. In their place, however, is a folded-over piece of paper with my name written on the top flap. I snatch it up.

"What is that?" Frances says.

"She left me a note," I say. I open it and begin to read what Rebecca has written, hoping she has told me where she has gone.

Alexa:
I have looked everywhere, but I cannot find it. Please, please, if

you find it, throw it away. I don't want it anymore. And remember, it's a secret.

Love always, Rebecca

PS. I will write.

I have absolutely no idea what she is talking about. None. It's not unlike Rebecca to forget to tell me something, but it is a little unlike her to think she *has* told me something when she hasn't. Although I can't say it has never happened. It has just never really mattered before.

"What does she say?" Frances says.

"She just wants me to uh…throw something away for her," I mumble. "She doesn't say where she's gone. She does say she'll write to me."

"Write?" Frances says. We both know what this means. It means Rebecca intends to be gone a while.

"I can't believe she did this," I mutter, stuffing the strange note in the back pocket of my denim skirt.

Frances touches my arm, communicating with her touch that she empathizes. "Alexa, do you remember yesterday when I asked you if you had noticed anything different about Rebecca?" she asks. "That I got the feeling she was being secretive around me? I think maybe she has been planning this for a while."

I sigh. "I never saw it coming."

But then I immediately think of how Rebecca was acting yesterday. How distracted she was. How she seemed to forget I was even in the room when she began looking for whatever it was she was unable to find. How she first mentioned her fish and then abruptly changed the subject. How flustered she seemed.

And then I think of how I was acting yesterday. How I had

Stephen, my mother, and Priscilla on my mind, and I had tuned Rebecca out.

A second groan escapes from me.

"I'm so sorry, Alexa," Frances says. "I wish I had been more insistent in my comments to you."

"It's not your fault, Frances. I should have guessed Rebecca had something on her mind yesterday. She wasn't acting like herself. This is my fault, not yours."

"Don't blame yourself. Rebecca has her limitations, but she makes her own choices. She's an adult, you know."

"That doesn't mean she knows how to behave like one," I counter, shaking my head. "What will she do for money? How will she get around? What if she gets lost?"

Frances smiles at me. "We can hope that she *does* get lost, that she does indeed run out of money. I think she'll call us then. All kids call home when they need money. Hopefully she'll be in a safe place when that happens. I think she'll be mindful of danger, Alexa. I really do. Rebecca has immature ideas, but she's not ignorant of danger. She still looks both ways when she crosses the street."

I let myself sit heavily on Rebecca's bed. "We can't just let her run off and do nothing but wait for her limited funds to run out. We have to do something."

"I'll ask our residents today and on Monday when they are all back if they know anything. And I've already called the train station and the bus station downtown. Pauline has called the homeless shelters, and tomorrow I'll go to the church that the Center takes part in and see if she shows up there."

Again, I sigh. "Thanks, Frances."

But this isn't enough. I can't just sit by while Rebecca doles out whatever money she's been able to save. What if she wanders into the wrong neighborhood? What if she's approached by a madman? What if she accepts help from a would-be rapist?

I have to look for her.

And I can't do it alone. This city is huge. The world is huge.

I have to look for her.

But first I need to go to Coronado.

And I am dreading it.

I'm sitting in my mother's living room with Humphrey and Margot vying for my lap when I tell my mother Rebecca decided to leave the Center without telling anyone where she was going. I carefully avoid saying Rebecca has run away.

"What do you mean she didn't tell anyone?" Mom asks, wrinkling her brow.

"I mean, she left sometime last night with her suitcase. She wrote a note asking that her fish be fed, but she didn't tell anyone where she was going." I say nothing of the other note. Rebecca obviously wants that kept between her and me. Whatever *that* is.

"Are you telling me no one knows where Rebecca is?"

Her eyes do not betray what she is thinking. It could be anything. Mom could be on the brink of hysterical crying or an angry tantrum or just in wordless shock. I hesitate before telling her it's true. That no one knows where Rebecca is.

Mom closes her eyes and shakes her head slightly, as though she just had a tiny, silent conversation in her mind and part of her asked a question and the other part said, "No, we're not going there."

She says nothing audibly.

"Mom?" I search her face for clues as to what she's thinking.

"Rebecca packed a suitcase?"

"Yes."

"Did she take everything?"

"No. Not everything."

Mom sits back in her chair a little. Margot gets off the couch where I am and hops onto my mother's lap. "Then she will be back," Mom says, patting her dog, but her hand is shaking.

Of all the responses I was picturing my mother having, this was not one of them. She has completely detached herself from the very real possibility that Rebecca could be in danger.

"Mom," I reply, "she just took what she could fit in her suitcase. She took the photograph of Julian!"

Mom seems to flinch a little when I say Julian's name. It's a name not mentioned often in her presence. I didn't mean to so easily say it just now, but I think by taking Julian's picture Rebecca was offering us a glimpse into her plans. She took what was most precious to her because she doesn't know when she is coming back. Or maybe she took it because she has no plans to come back at all.

"I cannot deal with this, Alexa," my mother whispers. "I really cannot."

"Mom, we can't pretend there's nothing wrong here!" How can she so easily decide she will not deal with this?

"She's an adult..." Mom says feigning ease.

"She's a disabled adult!"

My mother winces. She hates that word. Disabled.

"Mom."

My mother raises her eyes from the dog on her lap to look at me. "What are we supposed to do, Alexa?" she asks and the tone of her voice is tense and laced with sadness. "If Rebecca wants go somewhere, who are we to stop her? She's a grown woman."

"Mom, she's a vulnerable adult!"

"As are we all," Mom says, looking back at Margot.

"So you're not going to do anything about this?" I ask, my words are evenly spaced with tiny flecks of anger in each one.

Mom doesn't answer right away. She continues to stroke the dog. "The police will find her."

"The police aren't looking for her, Mom."

She looks up at me and says nothing. It's as though she already knows the police are not combing the streets looking for my sister. I'm speechless for several seconds.

"She's my sister. I love her," I finally whisper.

At the word "love" I see the faintest of tremors run through my mother's body. I know she loves Rebecca, but I don't understand the way Mom loves. I haven't for a long time.

"If Rebecca had wanted you to know where she was going, she would have *told* you," Mom says.

For a second or two I'm silent as I ponder this.

"I can't just let her go and not do anything."

"Then do something." My mother's words, though whispered, sound strangely urgent. Her eyes, when she raises them, are ablaze with emotion she refuses to give in to.

It's after noon, and since I haven't had breakfast, I'm ravenous, but I decline Mom's offer to make me a sandwich. I want to get home to see if Rebecca has shown up on my doorstep. I decide to call my father on my way back to Mission Beach. We don't talk often, but I call him anyway. Perhaps he will be able to make some decisions about what to do about Rebecca since my mother refuses to.

Dad, who is on the golf course when my call comes through, has the same reaction as my mother to Rebecca's disappearance, although his is delayed. At first he's genuinely concerned, but then the more he hears—that Rebecca made her bed before leaving, that she packed a suitcase, that she took Julian's picture, that she left a note about the fish—the more he begins to temper his concern.

"So you've called the authorities, then?"

"Yes," I answer, and I tell him what I was told.

"Alexa, I don't know what else we can do except wait and see."

"That just doesn't seem like enough, Dad."

"Well, what else can we do? We can't walk the streets of San Diego putting up fliers on telephone poles. She's a grown woman."

I'm getting really tired of hearing that.

"What about a private investigator?" I venture.

Dad thinks for moment. "Maybe," he replies. "But I think it's a little soon to take such a drastic measure."

"I don't think it's *drastic* to want to find her." I'm driving with one hand, holding my cell phone with my "bad" arm and becoming increasingly agitated.

"You know that's not what I mean."

"Well, what do you mean?"

He pauses. I hear the wind whistling around the mouthpiece of his cell phone.

"Let me ask around and see if there's a private investigator we can ask to look into this."

"How long will that take?"

"I haven't the foggiest, Alexa. I've never had to call one before."

He's getting ticked. He doesn't want the responsibility of having all the answers.

"What should I do until then?"

"I guess that's up to you. If you really think you can make headway by combing the streets of San Diego, then I'm not going to tell you not to."

I say nothing in return. I don't know what to say. Truth is, he's right. Combing the streets will probably not reveal where Rebecca has gone.

"Look. Call me tomorrow, okay? Maybe you, your mother, and I can get together and decide what, if anything, we can do."

This is actually a gracious offer on his part. Mom makes no attempt to hide her contempt for my father's new life when family matters bring us together. My parents' marriage, which faltered when Julian died and which they somehow resurrected the year Priscilla and I were conceived, disintegrated when Rebecca nearly died. Within two years of her accident my parents were divorced and Dad quickly remarried. Seven years later, Dad's second wife gave birth to a son who lived.

"I'll call you in the morning," I say.

"Don't think the worst, Alexa. She could be just in need of a little break from the routine. You know?"

"Yeah. Maybe."

"Okay, then, for now?"

"I guess."

I wait for a second to see if he will ask about my surgery, how it went, but then I remember I didn't tell him I was having it. I guess I want to believe that I can get along just fine with his minimal intrusions in my life, that I'm like Priscilla in at least this one way: I don't need more than the little he is willing to give. I don't know if this is exactly why Priscilla reacted so strongly to my parents' divorce—actually, to my dad leaving my mother, but I do know Priscilla has no desire to patch things up. And the fact that Dad apparently has no desire either just fuels her resolve to leave things as they are.

"Okay. Talk to you later," my father says.

I toss the phone on the seat next to me and take my exit off the Interstate.

Somehow I know when I get to my apartment that there will be no sign of Rebecca having been there. The note is where I left it. The secret place where the key is hidden is undisturbed. I go inside and head straight for the phone, fully intending to call Priscilla and unload on her. But I don't do it. She has always been the rational, calm, intuitive one. I hate appearing so terribly desperate and needy in front of my mirror image. I decide to eat something first.

It isn't until I finish eating leftover macaroni and cheese that I remember Stephen had his MRI this morning. As I place my bowl in the sink, I'm torn with wanting to go see him and wanting to call Priscilla before it gets too late.

I decide to make the call. It's Saturday night in London. In all likelihood Priscilla will be out and I will miss her anyway. We e-mail each other once a week, but I usually only call her twice a year, on Christmas and on our birthday. She will be surprised to hear my voice. She will also be surprised to hear that Rebecca has run off. But she won't be worried like me or detached like our mother. She will be realistic, like our dad. That's the ironic thing about my father and Priscilla, those two who refuse to speak to each other. They are so much alike.

When the call goes through and Priscilla's voice picks up on the other side, I'm almost expecting to hear the rest of an answering machine message. But it's Priscilla on the other end, not a machine. She's at home in her flat overlooking the Thames.

"Good Lord, Alexa, what's up?" she says, and I can hear that seven years in London is finally rubbing off on her. She sounds slightly British. It was bound to happen. Priscilla is a master at languages. She speaks fluent French, Spanish, and Italian, and she recently learned to read and write some Mandarin. It's why she is paid so well at the import company where she works as a translator.

"I know it's kind of late, Pris, but I need to talk to you," I say, and I tell her everything—all of it—including Rebecca's mysterious note, which is quite possibly not what Rebecca would have wanted. I even manage to get in the news of my benign tumor and the injured man I have unbelievably fallen in love with, an injured man who probably has cancer.

"Anything else?" she asks, half in jest and half not.

I offer a tired laugh. "No, that's about it."

"Well, first off, Lex, why don't you subtract your tumor off your list since it was benign and you're healing well, yes?"

"Yes."

"And the prognosis is favorable?"

"Yes."

"Then let it go, love. And as far as Rebecca goes, I hate to say it, Lexie, you know I do, but you can't find someone who wants to be absent, especially if that person is of reasonable intelligence."

"But she is gullible and naive," I counter.

"So are most high school graduates, and yet we hug them,

wish them luck, and send them on their way with a lot less than a suitcase and headbands."

"Aren't you the least bit worried about her?" I'm a bit miffed.

"Of course I'm concerned. But face it, Lex. She wasn't abducted. She *left*. With a suitcase. She may not want to be found."

"I feel like there's got to be something more to do than just wait."

"Like what?"

"Well, like go through her room. Go through her trash, her pockets, and her closet. Maybe there's something hidden away that will tell us where she went. Maybe this 'thing' she wants me to find and throw away is a clue as to where she went."

"I guess it can't hurt. If it's what you want to do and if you think it's best, you should do it."

Her voice, so like mine and yet so not, is soothing to me, despite her flair for being shamelessly candid. I so wish she were here. The wish falls from my lips before I can catch it and analyze it. "I wish you were here, Priscilla."

"Do you really?"

Her response surprises me. I expected her to say how we all need to find the place where we bloom best and how she's found it.

"Yes, of course I do. I always do. But especially now."

"It's interesting you should say that because I've been thinking of coming over for a short visit. I've been thinking about it for quite a while. This may actually be a good time. There's...there's something I need to tell you."

I don't know which statement to address first. Coming over for a visit? She hasn't been home in four years. This may a good time? A *good* time? Has she been looking for a reason? And what is this something she needs to tell me? What kind of something? Is it bad news? Is she sick? Maybe she is engaged. My head is reeling.

"Alexa, are you there?"

"Yes!" I finally say. "Are you serious? Priscilla, are you really thinking of coming?"

"Is that all right?"

"Oh, Priscilla, that would mean the world to me. And Mom too. I know it would mean a lot to Mom." I don't mention Dad's name. "Especially with what's happened with Rebecca."

"I honestly can't stay longer than a week, Lex, no matter what happens with Rebecca. You understand that, don't you?"

"Of course. If you can't, you can't." It's on the tip of my tongue to say, "If you won't, you won't," but I don't want to say anything to break the spell. "Can you tell me what it is you want to tell me? I'm not sure I can wait."

"I think it's best you find out when I get there."

"Priscilla, is it..." but I don't finish.

"It's nothing that will rock your world, Lex. Don't fuss over it, all right?"

"Okay."

"I have some vacation time coming to me that I need to take or I'll lose it. I'll see if I can get a flight out tomorrow evening. I have loads of frequent flier miles. That would get me in Monday sometime. Would that work? If you can't get to the airport, I can rent a car."

"Of course it will work!" I exclaim. "I'll take another week of sick leave. I'll come for you, don't worry about that."

"And, Lexie, I want to stay in a hotel this time. I don't want to stay with Mom."

I don't want to consider what aversion Priscilla has to staying with Mom. I can think about that later. But I don't want Priscilla staying in a hotel, either.

"Please stay with me," I reply. "Please, Pris?"

"Lex, you have a one-bedroom apartment. Don't be silly."

"But I have a queen-size bed. And I have a sofa bed in the living room. I can sleep in the living room and you can have the bedroom. Please, Priscilla! Please? Please stay with me."

She hesitates for a moment as though she is making a huge decision. I don't see what the big deal is.

"All right."

"Great. It will be better than staying in a hotel, you'll see."

"I'll e-mail you tomorrow when I know the flight number, but right now it's late and I want to go to bed."

"Okay!"

"And, Lexie, don't worry yourself to death about Rebecca. Worry won't bring her back."

"I'll try not to."

"And don't fret over falling in love with this man who might have cancer. If you really have fallen in love with him, and I mean *really* fallen in love with him, well, there's probably not a whole lot you can do about it. You know, you wouldn't be the first."

"The first?"

"Lex, every man who has cancer has some woman in his life who loves him, even if it's just his mother. So you would be no different than a million other women. There are worse things than loving a sick man."

"Oh, really? Like what?" I ask, challenging her.

"Well, like loving an unfaithful man. Or an abusive man. Or a dishonest man. Or a heartless man."

Priscilla the Sensible. "Okay. I see your point. I'll try not to worry about either one."

"Right, then. See you soon, yes?"

"Yes. Goodbye, Priscilla."

We click off, and I feel joy for the first time today.

The feeling empowers me to run a brush through my hair and freshen my makeup in preparation to see Stephen.

The sick man I am in love with.

6

As I retrace my steps to Stephen's hospital room, I find myself mentally wrestling with Priscilla's words: *There are worse things than loving a sick man.*

I really do know that she's right.

I know it's worse to love a man who beats you or who lies to you or who ignores you.

And I suppose it is also worse to have no one to love at all. I already know what that is like. I have been living *that* life for years.

But the prospect of falling for a man who has a brain tumor scares me witless. And yet, according to Priscilla, if I have indeed fallen for Stephen, then there's little I can do to reverse it. You can't fall back up. You can only fall down. You can climb out of something, but I'm not sure I would know where to start, where to look for the first foothold. My life has become increasingly complicated. I don't even know which direction is *up*.

I decide to brace myself for bad news. I pretend as I walk that

I already know the outcome of Stephen's MRI. If it has revealed nothing, then I will be in for a nice surprise. It's better to imagine the worst than to be upended by it.

The door to his room is half open, like yesterday. I knock softly and his voice reaches me.

"Come in."

The first thing I notice is that Ivy's chair is empty. Then I see Stephen sitting up in his bed. Above and across from him, the TV is turned to ESPN with the sound off. Pillows again elevate his leg and arm and lying open across his chest, pages down, is a Bible.

"Hey," he says, and he offers me a smile.

"Hi." I come to his side. My eyes are drawn to the Bible on his chest.

"You okay, Alexa?"

I don't know how he knows I have had a difficult day, but my demeanor must give it all away.

"I had a crazy morning, but I'm sure you don't want to hear about it," I answer, dismissing his concern. "Besides, I came to see how you are."

"Is everything all right? What happened?" he asks, ignoring my reason for coming in the nicest way possible.

"We don't have to talk about me, Stephen."

"Is it about the roof? Did my friend not show up?"

"No, no, he came. And he brought friends. The roof is done, Stephen. And they took your truck. I suppose they drove it home for you."

"Oh, good." Stephen nods his head. "Sit down, Alexa. Please."

I take the chair that Ivy was sitting in yesterday. It's pulled close to his bed. I leave it there as I fold my body into it. "Your mom isn't here?"

"I sent her down to the cafeteria to get something to eat."

"Oh. Okay."

"What happened this morning?" he asks. He delays talking about himself. Perhaps it is best.

So I tell him. I tell him everything that is making my world sway. That Rebecca has disappeared. That my mother is in denial. That my dad may or may not hire a private investigator to look for her. That Priscilla has decided to come home for a visit after a four-year absence and that she has something to tell me.

I don't tell him about Rebecca's second note, nor do I tell him that I've fallen in love with a man who may have a brain tumor.

"It sounds like you want to try finding Rebecca yourself." He says this as though it's not the most ridiculous idea he's ever heard. I don't feel foolish answering him.

"Well, I'm just thinking that maybe she left clues as to what she was planning in her room. A note, a scrap of paper. Something."

"It's a good idea," he says. "Worth a try, anyway."

I'm about to murmur my thanks for his not making light of my plan when he continues. "You must be pretty excited that Priscilla is coming."

"Yes. Yes, I am. I miss being with her. I've learned to ignore how much by concentrating on my job and caring for Rebecca, but I do miss her. She's like the half of me that makes sense of things. She's always been the wise one."

"Well, I hope you have a wonderful visit. And I hope

whatever news she has to tell you is happy news," he says, and immediately his countenance seems to fall a bit.

He has news to share too.

I think he senses that I know already it's not happy news.

"So you had the MRI," I say.

"Yes."

"And?"

"The tumor is back."

I let the words penetrate my mind, my heart.

"What does that mean?" Despite my resolve to be brave, my voice quavers a bit.

He notices the tiny shift in my voice. I can see in his eyes that he notices.

"Well, the last time doctors were able to remove most of it. Radiation took care of what they couldn't," Stephen says, saying every word carefully and methodically. "This time surgery isn't an option. The tumor has attached itself to a place where surgery isn't safe. So it will mean heavy doses of radiation to shrink the tumor, and chemotherapy to kill it, if the radiation can't do it alone."

"So...so it's bad," I murmur. Dumb thing to say. An inoperable brain tumor is never good.

"Well, brain tumors usually are, because they have no room to grow," Stephen says. "The bones of the skull box them in, but they grow anyway. That's the bad part. But you work in a hospital. You probably already know that."

I look down at the floor for no particular reason at all. Perhaps to just avert my eyes from his. "Are the doctors thinking it will work? The radiation, I mean. Is it...will you..." but I cannot finish the sentence.

"They're thinking it could work," Stephen says. "Good chance of it."

I nod. A good chance of it. He may live. He may die. That's what he is saying.

"You don't have to stay in the hospital, do you?" I ask.

"No." His voice brightens a little. "Actually, if I don't have a black out spell today, I'll go home tomorrow. The radiation therapy is outpatient stuff. I'll start tackling this the first part of next week, most likely. I'm getting a referral for an oncologist who specializes in brain tumors. This hospital speaks really highly of him."

"Oh. That's good," but my comment sounds absentminded, even to me.

"It *is* good, Alexa."

I look up when he says this.

"Look," he says to me when our eyes meet. "This isn't what I wanted to have happen, but I can't stop it by wishing it away. And I know God is watching over me, looking out for me. I have been in worse straits than this, Alexa. A lot worse."

"What could be worse than this?" My voice is a whisper.

"Lots of things."

I study his face. He isn't being cocky or naive. He looks anxious, but not fearful. Stephen does not look as though he feels the way I felt when I learned I had a tumor under my arm that could easily have been malignant. Could easily have killed me.

"How can you not be afraid?" I whisper, and my eyes are misting over. For all kinds of reasons.

"Who says I'm not afraid?" He laughs nervously.

"You don't look like you're afraid."

"I don't want to be dead, Alexa, and I don't want it to hurt, but…but I am really not afraid to die. Just afraid of how it might happen."

"I don't want you to die." It's out of my mouth before I can decide if I really want him to know I feel this way.

"Come here," he says to me, soft and gentle, the way a father might speak to a frightened child.

I obey. I stand and close the distance between us. He reaches for my hand with his good arm. I almost smile at the thought that his good arm is reaching for my good arm. I extend it and our hands meet. He closes his fingers around mine.

"You don't have to go down this road with me, Alexa," Stephen says. "I wouldn't mind it a bit if you did, but I would never ask you to."

My heart is racing at the sensation of his touch. And I feel breathless. As though I have just sprinted across miles of sandy beach. Did he say he wouldn't mind it a bit if I did? Is he saying what I think he is saying? He would never utter such a thing if he didn't already suspect I was falling for him. And he must likewise be feeling something similar toward me. It's exhilarating, embarrassing, and alarming all at the same time.

"I…think maybe it's a little too late for me to turn around," I say, and I feel color rising to my cheeks.

"No, it isn't," Stephen replies quickly, and I realize he's giving me an out, a way of escape. He's holding the door open for me, the door that leads back to where I was before I met him. He's holding it wide-open, gentleman that he is. I also realize that I'm torn between whether or not to take advantage of it. It would be easier to walk away now, before Stephen meets up with whatever awaits him. But I'm not so ignorant that I don't know there are things we relinquish when we choose the easy way.

I wonder how long he will hold this door open for me. And to my horror I realize that I have actually said this aloud, for he says, "As long as you want."

Embarrassment washes over me as though I've been hit in the face with a pail full of water. But Stephen doesn't notice or doesn't seem to care. "What about your job? Won't the radiation make you ill?" I say, trying very hard to cover up my shame with a good question.

"I'll probably have to take a few months off. And yeah, it will probably make me ill, but that's just the way it is."

"How will you...I mean, who will be there to...um, what if you need help?"

I'm sure I sound like an idiot, but I think he is touched by my concern.

"I belong to an awesome church. I know they'll be there to care for me. I had some visitors this morning, and people are already praying for me."

My face must reveal that while I'm relieved to hear he has a support group already in place, I'm feeling out of place. Unnecessary, perhaps. In the way. He strokes the top of my hand with his thumb.

"But you can never have too many friends when you're facing tough times, don't you think?" he adds, looking intently at me.

I nod. I have this incredible urge to embrace him. No. To *be* embraced. To feel his arms around me the way I did on Tuesday when I barely knew him and he carried me into my house. I think of that moment now, and I remember confiding in him how frightened I had been when I thought perhaps *I* had cancer, that perhaps *I* was in for the ride of my life, that perhaps *I* would not survive. And that I felt as though there was no one I could tell how scared I was.

"Can I call you to see how you're doing?" I ask.

"Of course. Give me a scrap of paper and I'll give you my number."

I drop his hand, reach into my purse, and search for something for Stephen to write on. I find a receipt from a grocery store and hand it to him along with a pen. Stephen takes them, and I watch how he writes. Long, skinny letters. Legible, but wiry and wild. He hands the pen and the receipt back to me. On the back side of the receipt he has written his cell phone number, his home phone, and his address. It's an invitation to do more than just call, I think. As I fold the receipt and place it back in my purse, Ivy returns.

"Hello, Alexa," she says, and her voice and manner betray that despite Stephen's positive outlook, she, too, is not ready to imagine a life without him in it.

Small talk seems out of place. I find a way to politely leave five minutes later.

I spend the rest of the afternoon driving mindlessly around Balboa Park and downtown San Diego. I really don't expect to see Rebecca standing on a street corner toting her pink suitcase, but it gives me something to do with my mind and body. Before heading back home to Mission Beach, I stop by the Falkman Center. Pauline hasn't heard anything regarding Rebecca's whereabouts. No one has.

I make a cursory search of Rebecca's room, looking for anything that would suggest where she has gone, but I come up with nothing. Before I leave, I grab the shoe boxes on her closet

shelf and carry them out to my car. Perhaps the thing I'm supposed to know about and don't is buried inside one of them.

When I get home, I carry the boxes to my room and set
them on the floor by my closet. I open one of them. It is filled
with pictures of houses. All kinds of houses, all torn from
the pages of magazines and newspaper articles. Rebecca must
have been collecting these for years. The sight of them makes
me wonder if she truly loved living at the Falkman Center
as much as I thought she did. The thought of sifting through
the contents of even this one box is exhausting. I'm about to
attempt it anyway when the phone rings. Serafina is asking
me to join her and Jorge for empanadas. I drop the lid on the
box and head next door for a home-cooked meal and comforting company.

Sunday passes by interminably slow. I attend church with
Serafina and Jorge in the morning, feeling the need to be somewhere where God is. I offer a prayer for Rebecca's safety and
Stephen's healing that I feel is somehow better worded because
I am on my knees in a church. Then I enjoy lunch with them
and their extended family at a Mexican restaurant near downtown. I stop off at a grocery store and pick up enough staples
for Priscilla and me to get through the week, although I know
she will want to eat out. Often.

When I get home, I head to my computer and my e-mail
inbox. Sure enough, the note from Priscilla is there. She will
arrive at 10:04 AM tomorrow morning. I e-mail Mom right away
to tell her Priscilla is coming, and then I call the Falkman Center
to see if there is any news of Rebecca. There isn't. I call my dad, as
I said I would, and there is no answer at his place. I could leave

a message, but I don't. Lynne, his second wife, would probably be the first one to hear it. It's not that I don't like Lynne; I just don't feel like leaving a message pertaining to my dad's old life that his second wife will hear first.

Later, as I'm getting ready for bed, the phone rings. When I answer it, I hear my mother's voice on the other end. It takes me by surprise. I haven't heard her voice over a telephone line in a long time. She rarely takes the initiative to borrow someone's phone, but I can guess what drove her to do it tonight.

"What's this about Priscilla coming home?" She sounds unconvinced.

"She'll be here ten o'clock tomorrow morning, Mom. No joke."

"How can you girls plan such a thing and not include me!" She nearly roars.

"Mom, this was Priscilla's last-minute idea. I called her to tell her about Rebecca and she decided to come over."

"She's coming because of Rebecca?"

"Yes and no." I have no idea if whatever news Priscilla has to share is news she will also be sharing with Mom. "I mean, she has vacation time that she will lose if she doesn't use it right away."

"If I had known I could have had my guest room bedspread dry-cleaned," Mom begins.

"Mom, I asked Priscilla to stay with me. I begged her to. Okay?"

"With you?"

"Yes, but I promise we will come and see you as often as we can."

"When?"

I'm tempted to say, "Well, if you had a phone, we could call before we come," but there's no point to having *that* conversation for the millionth time.

"How about tomorrow after lunch? Okay?" I say instead.

"I insist you girls stay for dinner."

"Well, I'm sure that will be okay."

"All right." She pauses for a moment. "Did you call the Falkman Center today?"

"Yes."

"And?"

"They haven't heard from Rebecca, Mom."

Another pause.

"I'm going to hang up now."

"Okay. I'll see you tomorrow."

She hangs up without saying goodbye. Another one of her quirks.

I don't sleep well, no surprise there. My incision is itchy and my head is full. I awake in the morning feeling a little dazed.

I call the hospital where I work first. I'm not exactly lying when I tell my supervisor it's too soon for me to come back. I *do* still have stitches under my arm. My supervisor is a little peeved that I didn't tell her on Friday that I needed another week, but she tells me they will make it without me. I thank her profusely.

Then I call the Falkman Center to ask about Rebecca. There is nothing new to report.

While the phone is still in my hand I call Sharp Hospital and ask to speak to Stephen Moran in Room 304, and I'm told he was discharged yesterday.

So he is home.

At a little after nine, I head out to San Diego's airport. It's only a ten-minute drive away, but if Priscilla's plane is early or if the customs line is short, I don't want her waiting.

I'm sitting in a chair by the baggage claim carousels at half-past ten when I see Priscilla begin to descend the escalator amid a crowd of other travelers. I can't stop the smile that spreads wide across my face. It's been four years since I've seen her, but yet in some ways I see her every morning when I look in the mirror, trite as that may sound. Her sandy blond hair is styled better than mine; her tailored clothes fit her better than my denim capris fit me, and her makeup is expertly applied, but underneath her glamorous style Priscilla is still my twin. The smart half of me. I rise to meet her at ground level. And as I do, I notice that a little girl with curly brown hair is standing next to her. My mouth drops open a little when I see that Priscilla is holding the little girl's hand. Priscilla sees me, and she smiles also, but it's a stunning smile—not like the ridiculous grin I have on my face.

When her feet meet the ground, Priscilla walks swiftly toward me. The little girl, who looks to be no older than three, is still holding tightly to my sister's manicured hand.

Priscilla reaches me and hugs me gently with one arm, mindful of my incision. "Hello, Lex," she says effortlessly.

I'm crying and unable to say anything; I'm so happy to see her and so perplexed by the sight of the little girl who stands between us.

"Lexie, you look terrific," Priscilla says in her acquired British accent. "Doesn't she, Isabel?"

I look down at the little girl, who is smiling up at me with eyes that resemble my own. She's holding a picture book and a stuffed animal that looks like a sequined seahorse.

"Lex, I'd like you to meet your niece, Isabel. Isabel, this is your Aunt Alexa."

Shock, wonder, and astonishment sweep across me.

I have a pretty good idea I have just been told Priscilla's news.

7

A brilliant San Diego sun is shining down all around us as we make our way to my car in the airport's short-term parking lot. My mind is exploding with questions I cannot ask. It's not as though Isabel is an infant who can't understand human language. She is fully conversant and appears quite able to understand sentences like "How could you keep such a thing a secret from me, Priscilla! Why didn't you tell me you had had a child? Who is the father?" and "What else haven't you told me?" I cannot ask the questions my befuddled mind really wants to ask. On top of this, I'm aware that I'm as wounded as I am surprised.

Priscilla didn't tell me she had had a baby. A baby who is now at least three years old. For three long years she has kept this from me. I could never have done such a thing to her. But even as I mentally wrestle with these fresh wounds, I don't want her to know how much she has hurt me. She might decide to stay in a hotel after all, and I don't want her to.

I see now why she didn't want to stay with Mom, why she had to be talked into staying with me. She knew she would be bringing a child with her. Her child.

Isabel.

I look down at the little girl as we walk across the hot pavement. She's petite, with a mass of brown curls on her head. Isabel is wearing a smocked, white cotton dress and pink sandals with socks. Clutched to her little bosom with one hand are the picture book and the seahorse. Isabel has Priscilla's eyes. Dad's eyes.

My eyes.

Isabel looks weary from the long flight, but she is chattering away nonetheless as we walk, commenting on the height of the parking lot's swaying palms in a British accent even more pronounced than Priscilla's.

"Are there monkeys in those trees?" she asks her mother.

"What do you think, Lex? Think there are monkeys in those trees?" Priscilla looks at me. Her eyes are communicating that it would be best for all of us if I just chat with her daughter as if I've known her and loved her since the day she was born. I get the feeling Isabel has known about me for a long time. A lot longer than fifteen minutes.

I look down again at my little niece. She is beautiful. Innocent. Engaging. Worthy of being loved.

"Well, Isabel," I say, trying out her name for the first time. It sounds melodic off my tongue. "If there were, they would have a very hard time finding any bananas, I think."

"That's because bananas don't grow on those trees," Isabel says. "Pineapples do. But I don't think monkeys eat pineapples."

"I don't think they do, either," I reply, grinning as I try to picture pineapples growing on a palm tree.

"I like pineapples. Do you like pineapples?"

"Yes, I do, Isabel. I like pineapples very much."

Priscilla smiles at me. It's not the stunning smile at baggage claim. It's a simple one of gratitude.

The drive to Mission Beach is short, giving us time only to discuss the flight, the weather, and the current status of Rebecca, which is "missing." When we get to my apartment, Isabel sees a glimmer of blue from the driveway as we step out of the car, a glimpse of the sapphire vastness of the Pacific.

"Can we go see the ocean? I want to see the ocean," she says.

"Later, Izzy," Priscilla replies. "You promised me you'd take a nap after we arrived."

"But I'm not tired!"

Priscilla shuts the car door and begins walking calmly up the pathway to my front door, pulling her suitcase. "Isabel, we talked about this. You promised."

"I'm not sleepy," Isabel says, frowning and following her.

"Well, you can just lie on Aunt Alexa's bed and think of ways to stay awake, then."

I unlock the door and we are inside.

I serve a light brunch of croissants, sliced cheese, and a fruit salad, all of which I had picked up premade at the grocery store. Despite Isabel's claim that she's not tired, she is rubbing her eyes when we finish. I take our dishes to the sink and Priscilla and Isabel head to my bedroom. When I join them a few minutes later, I see that Priscilla has unpacked a soft yellow blanket that Isabel is now clutching along with the mint green stuffed seahorse. The child is propped up against my bed pillows and the shades are drawn.

"But I want to read it again," Isabel is saying, pointing to the book she was carrying when they arrived at baggage claim.

"Can't I read you another story, Izzy? Please?" Priscilla says wearily. "How many times must I read it?"

"I want that one."

Priscilla takes the book and then looks up at me.

"Want to read this book to her? She can't get enough of it, and I'm about to go crazy with reading it."

"You want *me* to read it?" I ask. I haven't read a book to a child since my babysitting days in high school.

"Would you please?" Priscilla says, lifting it to me. "I can't read it one more time today, Lex. Six times on the plane. Twice while waiting at Heathrow. Twice while waiting for the taxi to take us there."

I take the book and look at its cover. *A Seahorse in the Thames.* "I don't think I've ever heard of this book. What's it about?"

"It's about Clement!" Isabel says, holding up the bejeweled stuffed seahorse.

"It's new." Priscilla lifts her body off my bed and takes the stuffed chair next to it. She motions for me to take the place on the bed she has just vacated. "It's based on a news story from a few years back when this fisherman found a seahorse in the Thames Estuary. It made all kinds of headlines because there hasn't been a seahorse in the Thames in twenty or thirty years."

Priscilla yawns and continues. "Some author decided to write a children's book about it, fictionalizing it. The writer gave the seahorse a name, Clement, and it's currently a bestseller in the U.K. They even have toys and lunch boxes and such. It's Isabel's favorite book in all the world."

This last sentence Priscilla says with a smile, as though deep down she likes the fact that Isabel is in love with a book about a seahorse.

"I suppose I could give it a try," I say, taking the spot on the bed.

Isabel settles down onto the pillows. "Don't skip any pages, Aunt Lexa," she says.

I smile at her and cast a glance at my sister as I open the book and then begin to read. It's a simple story, really, about a seahorse named Clement who lived in the English Channel but who longed to see London. He left all that was familiar and went to the mouth of the Thames, following it to where the city lay. But when he got to the city of his dreams, the water there was dark and dirty and nothing of grace or beauty was to be found. Clement wanted to go back to his old life, but he couldn't tell which way to go, so he simply stayed, hoping things would get better. He stayed for many, many days. Clement was unaware that above him on the banks of the river, there was a sad fisherman who was tired of living in the big, noisy city. The fisherman wanted to escape to a peaceful, beautiful place, but there was no place like that in the bustling city. Then one day on the banks of the river—on a day when the fisherman was the saddest he had ever been—he saw a tiny shimmer of loveliness in the shallows. He very nearly walked away from it because he wasn't expecting to find anything of beauty in the dark river, but then he knelt down and peered into the water. Tangled in the slimy weeds in the shallow water was a beautiful seahorse. It was Clement. The fisherman was so enchanted by Clement's magnificence that he sat and just gazed at him. Clement was the most wonderful thing the fisherman had ever seen; a sliver of splendor in the darkest of places. And he had almost missed it.

The fisherman reached in with his net, removed Clement from the smelly seaweed, and put him in his bucket. He told all his friends and all the newspapers. Even the queen heard that a beautiful seahorse had been found in the filthy river. Though he loved the seahorse, the fisherman gave Clement to a London aquarium. Now Clement lives in a crystal clear tank with two friendly hermit crabs, in the heart of the big, bustling city, as a reminder to everyone to look close, bend down, and watch for beauty. The fisherman visits him every day.

And he is not sad anymore.

I look up when I'm finished and Isabel is fast asleep. I have no idea when she drifted off. I had been captivated by this story she loves. I feel as though I have just participated in something grand and remarkable. I feel as though I could grow to love this story the way Isabel does, though I'm not exactly sure why.

Isabel holds Clement close to her chest and her breathing is slow and even. Her brown curls frame her pretty face as she sleeps.

"Why didn't you tell me, Pris?" I'm still looking at my sleeping niece.

A few seconds of silence pass before Priscilla answers me.

"There were many times I wanted to, but I kept putting it off. It's only been lately that I have felt it was time you knew. That everyone knew."

"But, Priscilla, couldn't you have at least told me on Saturday when you decided you were coming instead of just walking off the plane with her?"

"Come on, Lexie. What would have been the good of that? All you would have done is lie awake at night until I got here wondering why I hadn't told you before. It's better this way for both of us."

Perhaps she's right, but this isn't what troubles me the most. It's that Priscilla hid Isabel from me. "Why did you want to keep her a secret?"

Priscilla sighs. "Don't take this the wrong way, Lex, but I just didn't want to have to share her with anyone at first. I didn't want her to be a part of my old life. It was easy to keep her separate from all that by not telling you. Because if I told you, I would have to tell Mom. And if Mom knew, then Dad would surely find out. I just wanted to avoid all of that."

"All of *what?*" I turn my head toward her. "What would have been so bad about us knowing you had a child?"

"Because then Isabel would cease to be just *my* daughter," Priscilla says, first looking at me and then looking back at Isabel. "She would be your niece. Mom's grandchild. Dad's grandchild. For the longest time I just wanted her for myself. She was the proof that I had made a new life for myself in England. A charmed life. Better than the one I left."

I can't help but feel as though I'm a big part of that unbearable life she ran from. When she moved to England and shook the dust of her old life off her feet, I was part of what fell away.

"Was it really so bad, Priscilla?" I feel my eyes are glazing over with tears. "I know you and Dad had your differences, but was life with Mom and me and Rebecca in it so terrible that you had to move so far away? That you came home only once in seven years? That you chose to not invite Mom or me to come to see you in all that time? That you couldn't tell at least me that you had a baby?"

Priscilla takes a breath and lets it out. "This really isn't about you, Lex. It's about me. It's what I did for me. All my decisions might look like mistakes to you, but I don't regret what I did.

I don't want to live here in San Diego with you and Mom. I want to live in London. That's my home now. And since having Isabel, it's been impossible to invite you or Mom over to visit me because until now I haven't been ready to share her with anyone."

There is a momentary lull in our conversation as I try to piece together what she's telling me. "Do you absolutely hate it here?" I ask a few seconds later.

"I don't hate it here; I hate what happened here. And it's not just about Rebecca and her accident. It began a long time before that."

"What? What began a long time before that?"

Priscilla looks at me the way she did all those times when we were young and she had figured things out way ahead of me. She is only minutes older than me chronologically, but she has always seemed like my big sister. The older one. The one who knows more.

"Let's just say I didn't like the way Dad treated Mom. I didn't like the way they treated each other. And us. It nearly drove me crazy. And I don't like what they let Rebecca's accident do to them."

"What about what you let it do to you?" I hope it sounds as though I'm accusing her of having been irreversibly affected as well. We all were.

"That's precisely why I moved to London, Lex. It's where I learned how to dig my way out."

"And did you? Did you dig your way out?"

"Yes. I'm very happy there. I have a wonderful job, a beautiful home, terrific friends, and my lovely Isabel."

"And...Isabel's father?"

"Isabel's father is no longer in my life or hers, and that's for the best."

"So you…you haven't missed…haven't missed me," I ask and I know how it must sound. Juvenile and self-serving.

"Of course I've missed you, Lex. It's why I decided to come home for this visit. Why I decided it was time you and Isabel met."

"You didn't come home because of Rebecca, did you?"

"Not entirely. I came for me. And for you. And for Isabel. I really do want her to know you. And to meet the rest of her family."

"Dad too?" I can't help but ask.

Again Priscilla takes in a breath and lets it out slowly.

"Yes, I think I'm even ready for that as well."

Priscilla's words amaze me.

For the first time since I don't know when, I feel that something good is about to happen to my family. And yes, we are still a family. I can't help but wonder that this sleeping child may be the very thing that will prove that to all of us.

We are both looking at Isabel sleeping peacefully on my bed when Priscilla leans forward in her chair.

"You know, Lex," she says, almost in a whisper. "I never understood how devastated Mom and Dad must have been when they lost Julian and then nearly lost Rebecca…until I held Isabel in my arms. I was finally able to imagine what a broken heart would be able to do to you. And through you."

I look over at Priscilla, amazed at her candor. And a bit jealous, too, that she has something so rare and precious in common with our mother. This understanding of mother-love.

The heavy moment passes and Priscilla laughs. "Mom's going to flip."

"Mom's going to love her," I say in return.

"She'll never let me forget what I've done," Priscilla says now, and she's no longer laughing.

"Priscilla, Mom is going to *love* Isabel. I know it."

"Yeah. I know it too."

I think I hear evidences in her voice that Priscilla is still a bit afraid to share Isabel with Mom.

"Mom wants us to come over this afternoon and stay for dinner," I tell her. "More like she insists. She actually borrowed someone's phone to tell me this."

A grin returns to Priscilla's face and she shakes her head. "I figured as much. It's all right. I need to get it over with."

An easy silence falls between us. Then she turns to me.

"So, Alexa. This man Stephen. Do you have news?" she asks.

Stephen has not been on my mind the last few hours. It startles me to hear his name. And then, of course, I'm instantly reminded of what I know.

"He…has a brain tumor. Inoperable. But he's going in for radiation treatments and then chemo, if necessary. His doctor says he stands a good chance of beating it."

I say these sentences as though I'm back at work, advising family members of the medical condition of the person they love. But inside I'm trembling. Priscilla misses nothing.

"And what about you? Are you in love with him?"

It's easy to be honest around Priscilla. She's my genetic equal; how could it not?

"He's not like any man I've ever met," I reply. "I know it sounds crazy. I have known him only a week. Seven days. But… there's something about him, about the way he *is* around people that I find…" I search for the right word.

"Attractive?" Priscilla offers.

I find it.

"Irresistible," I say, knowing I have nailed it.

"Then stop trying to resist it," she says calmly.

Her practical side still amazes me.

8

As we drive across the Coronado Bay Bridge on our way to Mom's, Priscilla and I formulate a plan. Isabel, whom we had to wake at three o'clock, is singing to herself in the backseat. Clement is at her side. She doesn't appear to be interested in what we're talking about.

We decide that I will drop Priscilla and Isabel off at the city park. I'll continue on to Mom's a few blocks away and share Priscilla's news. I won't tell Mom where Priscilla and Isabel are, nor will I bring Mom to them until I'm sure she's ready to embrace them both. Or at least not strangle Priscilla.

"She's going to hate you for this, you know," Priscilla breathes as she helps Isabel out of the car when I stop the car at the entrance to the park.

"For a couple hours, anyway," I say.

Priscilla smiles and shuts the door. Isabel, seeing swings and a slide, is already scampering off, holding Clement by his curly tail.

Within minutes I'm at Mom's. Her front door is open, and

I can hear the soundtrack of *Madame Butterfly* blaring inside. I rap on the screen door.

"Mom, it's me," I yell.

She's at the door in an instant. "Where have you been? I've been waiting all afternoon." She's looking past me to my empty car. "Where is Priscilla? Did she miss her plane?"

"No, Mom. She didn't. Can I come in?"

"Well, then, where is she?"

"Let me in and I'll tell you."

Mom holds the door open for me and frowns as I walk past her. She follows me in and walks briskly over to her stereo. She grabs the remote and presses the mute button as though she's firing off a round.

"What is all this about?" she asks impatiently.

"Have a seat, Mom. I need to tell you something before you see Priscilla." I sit on the couch in the same place I sat on Friday, and the dogs run in from the kitchen to jump on my lap.

Mom's eyes are wide with apprehension as she sits in the chair across from me.

"Mom, it's nothing bad, okay?" I begin. "In fact, it's really rather wonderful news, but it will surprise you. It will probably even make you a little angry."

"For the love of God, Alexa, *what is it?*"

Well, here goes.

"Mom, Priscilla didn't come alone. She brought someone with her."

"So?" Mom says, annoyed.

"She has a little girl. Priscilla has a daughter. Her name is Isabel."

Mom's expression is all that I thought it would be. She is surprised beyond belief. "Priscilla has had a baby?"

Wait till she hears what I have to say next.

"Actually, Mom, Isabel turned three in May."

Mom explodes off her chair. Margot and Humphrey jump off my lap and both start barking.

"How could you not tell me something like this!" she roars.

Humphrey and Margot chime in with a chorus of yaps.

"I didn't know! Mom, she didn't tell me, either! I found out today. Just like you. Okay? She didn't tell anyone!"

Mom begins to pace the living room. Margot and Humphrey run to the front door to continue their concerto, assuming, no doubt, that something amazing must be happening outside and that's why their mistress is yelling. "I don't believe this! I *do not* believe this. How could she do this? How could she do this to me?"

She's not really speaking to me—yelling at me, rather—she is appealing to Reason, asking for an explanation. I attempt to provide it.

"Mom, I don't like what she did, either, but I think I understand why she did it."

"You would take *her* side!" Mom yells, turning to me in mid-stride.

I stand then too. Margot and Humphrey turn their heads and bark in my direction.

"I'm not taking a side, Mom. I just know that she did what she did because she felt she had to. She did what she did because she had to find a way to get over what happened to us. To our family."

"And this was her solution! It's absolutely ridiculous, that's what it is. Of all the selfish…"

But I stop her.

"You think your way is any better, Mom?" I interrupt, and my voice is also raised.

Yap, yap, yap.

"What do you mean *my* way!"

"I mean, you retire ten years early, you dump your entire inheritance into this tiny house on this little island, you visit Rebecca only every blue moon, you spend every waking moment absorbed with those dogs, you make absolutely no attempt to ever go see Priscilla, and you refuse to have a telephone in your house! *That* is your way!"

Yap, yap, yap.

Then there is silence. I'm appalled at what I've said. So is my mother. And I guess the dogs are too, for they have ceased barking and are both looking at my mother, awaiting her response.

But she says nothing.

"Mom, I'm sorry, " I say, coming to her.

She feels for the back of the chair behind her and sits down. I kneel next to her. "Mom?"

"It's never going to end," she whispers.

"Mom," I say, trying to get her to look at me. "Mom?"

She finally turns her head and our eyes meet. "It's never going to end," she says again.

I lock my eyes onto hers. "I think this is actually the beginning of something wonderful, Mom. Isabel is a beautiful, sweet little girl. You're going to love her."

Mom blinks, takes in a breath of air, and lets it out slowly.

"You want to meet her?" I ask, smiling.

A few tears escape Mom's eyes as she nods.

We head out to my car.

I park near where I let Priscilla and Isabel off. As I get out I can see my sister off in the distance sitting on a bench with one leg resting over the top of the other. She has an arm draped over the back of the bench and her eyes are trained on a little slip of a girl playing on a merry-go-round. Isabel. Clement is on my sister's lap.

I come around to the passenger side and watch as Mom slowly gets out of the car. She is watching Priscilla watching Isabel. When I close Mom's door, Priscilla's head turns toward us. Priscilla hesitates a moment, and then she stands and begins to walk toward us with Clement in one hand. As Mom begins to also walk toward her, I feel the sudden impulse to stay back. To let the reunion take place as a bystander. I see that Isabel has stopped spinning the merry-go-round and is also watching.

When the distance closes between Mom and Priscilla, they share a few words with each other that I can't hear, am not meant to hear. Their hushed conversation lasts several minutes. Then their arms slowly entwine, and I watch as they embrace. That same moment, Isabel begins to run to her mother, and when she reaches Priscilla, my sister bends down to her daughter. She touches Isabel softly on her back and tells her something. I'm sure it is something like, "Isabel, this is your grandmother." Isabel looks up at my mother, and I can't see Mom's face because her back is to me. But then I see my mother drop to her knees— something I can't recall seeing in a very long time—and she sweeps the little girl into her arms.

I stand there transfixed.

We leave Mom's a little after nine. I can see that jet lag is finally catching up with Priscilla, and Isabel, despite her long nap, is yawning and looking drowsy.

Mom doesn't want us to go. She wants to know when we can come over again.

I have an idea.

"Look, Mom," I say, reaching into my purse. I grab my cell phone and extend it to her. "Why don't you take my cell phone for the next few days. Then you'll have a way of calling us, and we'll have a way of calling you."

Mom stares at the phone in my hand as though I'm holding out illegal narcotics.

"You don't have to turn it on, Mom, until you want to use it, okay?"

She reaches for it. "Can you just let me call you?" Her voice is laced with hesitation. "I mean, please don't call me. Yet."

I let it slip from my hand to hers. "Sure, Mom."

"I'll call you in the morning, then."

"Sounds good."

We say our goodbyes, Mom hugs little Isabel, and we head for Mission Beach.

Later, as Priscilla is putting Isabel to bed—after having read *A Seahorse in the Thames,* of course—Priscilla notices the pile of old shoe boxes by my dresser.

"Cleaning out your closets?" she asks as she nods toward the pile.

"No. They're from Rebecca's room. I brought them home with me. I thought maybe I would come across whatever it is she wants me to find and get rid of. Or maybe I'll figure out where she was headed. She tends to save everything."

Priscilla hands Isabel the yellow blanket and helps her

snuggle into the covers on my bed. She bends down and kisses Isabel. "Night, love," she says.

"Good night, Mummy," Isabel replies. "Good night, Aunt Lexa."

"Good night, sweetie," I say.

"Bring them out," Priscilla says as she rises from the bed.

I look at the boxes. "Really?"

"Sure. Bring them out. Let's look."

"You're not too tired?" I ask.

"I was earlier, but I think I'm getting my second wind. Make us some tea. Let's look."

"All right."

We each grab two boxes and take them out to the living room.

Minutes later I'm setting two mugs of herbal tea on the coffee table. Priscilla is looking at the pictures of the houses.

"Good Lord, there must be a hundred pictures in here," she says, reaching for her cup.

"I know. I had no idea Rebecca was collecting those. It almost seems as though she's been wishing for a house of her own."

"It sure does," Priscilla says. After a pause she adds, "I can't say as I blame her. The Falkman Center is nice, but it's not a house. It's not really a home. And, of course, it's where she met Tim."

I haven't heard Tim's name mentioned in a long time. Hearing it now makes me cringe. Tim was a mentally disabled man who came to live at the Falkman Center five years after Rebecca moved in. Rebecca had taken a tremendous liking to him, and it wasn't long before the unbelievable happened: She began to call him her boyfriend. And his affection for her was just as evident, scary, and—according to the Center's staff—

inappropriate. Mom had a fit, and though I was only seventeen, I was worried too, as was Priscilla. Tim's embarrassed
and outraged parents moved him out as soon as they learned
of their son's overboard attraction to Rebecca. And they refused
to let him stay in contact with her, which Mom thought was
best. Rebecca had taken it hard, throwing temper tantrums one
minute and then lying on her bed practically catatonic the next.
Her therapist suggested the Center let her have a pet in her room
to give her something upon which to lavish her love. She was
provided with two female chinchillas that she promptly named
Tim. Both of them. It took nearly a year, but Rebecca eventually waded out of her despondency. Four years later, when the
chinchillas died within a month of each other, Rebecca grieved
for a while, but not as long as I feared she would, thank God.
I have not thought of Tim in a very long time.

"Alexa, you will be all right if you don't find her right away,
won't you?" Priscilla continues, interrupting these thoughts,
and I am only too happy to whisk them away. "I mean, she's
not really your responsibility. She never has been. She'll contact
you when she's ready. I'm sure of it."

I sit down on the floor next to Priscilla and reach for my own
cup without answering.

"Lexie?"

"What?"

"Pardon my bluntness, but I think the sooner you realize
she doesn't need you like you thought she did, the better off
you'll be."

Priscilla's words hit me in a place where I feel surprisingly unprotected. I haven't thought about my dependence
on Rebecca for providing a purpose for my life in a long time.
The funny thing is, the minute Priscilla says this, I know she's

right. Since Rebecca's disappearance four days ago, I've been wrestling with the notion that my need for Rebecca's company has always exceeded her need for mine. And now Rebecca has proved it true by packing a bag and leaving without a trace of a trail. I guess my way of dealing with the disintegration of my family has been no less peculiar than Mom's or Priscilla's.

"Lex?"

"Yes?"

"I'm *really* glad you have fallen in love with someone."

I know what she means. This growing attraction I have for Stephen, even though his future is uncertain, could not have come at a better time.

"Me too."

We each take a sip of tea and then turn back to the boxes. I open one that I carried out of my room. Inside are promotional fliers from the museums at Balboa Park, a dozen or so movie stubs, a nest of Laffy Taffy candy wrappers, and some recipe cards. There are also postcards from friends who live at the Center as well as a Ziploc bag full of letters. I reach into the bag and pull out a handful of envelopes, each with a foreign stamp. My breath catches in my throat when I see the return addresses.

"Why, these are from you!" I say, astounded.

Priscilla looks up from the floor plan of a Tudor-style house. "Oh, she keeps those, does she?"

I'm still taken aback. I had no idea Priscilla had been writing to Rebecca. The postmarks span the years she's been gone.

"I didn't know you were writing to her."

Priscilla looks not the least bit nonplussed. "Should you have known?"

"Well, I mean, Rebecca never mentioned it."

"Probably because it's not such an odd thing to have your sister write to you," Priscilla says, looking back at the pile of house pictures. I can see that she's annoyed that I assumed she has ignored Rebecca in the years she's been away.

"Sorry, Pris," I mumble. "I just...I thought..."

"I can see what you thought," she says, not looking at me. "Don't worry about it, Lex. I only wrote her a few times a year. It's not like we were pen pals."

I'm trying not to worry about it, but I can't stop. Guilt is a hard thing to wish away. "Did she ever write back to you?"

Priscilla tosses a pile of house pictures back into the box. "Sometimes. There's nothing in here." She means there are no clues in the "house" box; she also means she wants to move on. I'm not quite ready.

"Did you tell her about...." but Priscilla doesn't let me say Isabel's name.

"Of course I didn't, Lex. Are you crazy?" Priscilla puts the lid on the box and grabs another one.

End of discussion.

I place the letters back in the bag and place them back in the shoe box. There are no clues in that box, either. I grab my second box. It's the oldest one of the bunch. Inside are the swimming medals from high school, a prom corsage, her address book, and several smaller boxes of high school mementos.

There certainly can be nothing in here that relates to Rebecca's current whereabouts. From the bottom of the box, I lift a thin, white gift box held closed by two rubber bands that break when I touch them. I peek inside the box to see what Rebecca has hidden away. I see a couple cards from her nineteenth birthday, some photographs from her freshman year at UC Santa Barbara, and a broken charm bracelet. Nothing earth-shattering, to say the least. I toss the little box onto the coffee table. This has been a completely fruitless search.

"Well, I don't think we're going to find anything here." Priscilla stands and stretches. "And I think that second wind I had was just a second breeze. I'm going to go crawl in bed with Isabel. Want help with the mugs?"

"No, go on ahead. Good night, Priscilla. I'm really glad you are here."

"I'm glad too, Lex." She turns and starts to leave the living room. "Thanks for what you did today at Mom's, for me and Isabel. I don't know what you told her, but whatever it was, it was the right thing."

Priscilla heads down the hall as I take our mugs to the kitchen and wash them quickly. It's after ten, but I feel the urge to call Stephen, to hear his voice, to tell him the news that I have a niece. I stand and look at my kitchen phone for several moments as I summon the bravery to call him. Then I reach into my purse and pull out the grocery receipt that bears his phone number. I look at those numbers for long moments too. Then I punch in the number, hoping it's not too late.

He answers on the second ring.

"Stephen?"

"Alexa! Hi."

He recognizes my voice.

"So how was your first full day at home?" I ask, settling into a kitchen chair.

"I managed to shave, make coffee, and work the TV remote with one good hand and one good leg," he says. "How was your day? Did Priscilla arrive?"

Within those few seconds we are off the subject of him and onto the subject of me. He lets me rattle on for nearly twenty minutes as I tell him about Isabel, about my mother's and Pris-cilla's reunion, and about my realization that I've been using Rebecca as a way of finding purpose in my life for the past seven years. It's amazing how easily I open up to this man.

It's nearly ten thirty before I realize the conversation has been drastically one-sided.

"I'm sorry, Stephen," I say, covering my face with my free hand, even though I know he can't see this. "I didn't call to talk about me."

"It's okay. I asked. I wouldn't have asked if I didn't want to know."

"So, you are doing okay? Really?"

"Today I am doing okay. Really."

"When do you see the oncologist?"

"Thursday."

"Do you have someone to take you?"

"Yes, Alexa, I do."

"Oh. Okay."

"Were you going to offer to take me?"

I can't tell by his voice if he's smiling or not. And thankfully he can't see that I'm fidgeting like a kindergartner in my chair. What the heck.

"Well, yes, I was."

"That's really kind of you. But you have Priscilla visiting you. I wouldn't dream of it."

We spend the next thirty minutes talking about virtually nothing. It's just the kind of conversation two people have when they first meet and there's attraction between them.

"I'd better let you get to bed," I finally say, when it's a little after eleven.

"I'm really glad you called, Alexa. It's been great talking

with you. And now that you're on my caller ID, I can call *you* sometime."

"Okay," I respond, smiling and toying with my hair.

"Alexa, I want you to know some friends and I are praying for Rebecca, that she will be kept safe wherever she is. I hope you don't mind that I told a few people."

His compassion for me and for Rebecca intrigues me. No, I don't mind at all.

"Thanks. I mean, that's really nice of you."

"Well, good night, then," he says.

"Good night, Stephen."

I hang up the phone and sit for several long minutes in my quiet kitchen. When I rise from the kitchen table, images of Stephen are crowding my thoughts. I see him on my porch pulling boards, in my living room listening to me confess my deepest fears, in my kitchen drinking lemonade and talking about God. And now I see him in a circle of friends, praying for Rebecca, someone he's never met, someone for whom life dealt a heavy, unexplained hand.

Amazed, I lean down to put the contents of the last shoe box away. I pick up the little box with the broken charm bracelet inside, but I lose my grip and the box and its ancient contents fall to the carpet. It's as I am replacing the tissue paper that lined the bottom that I see the yellowed envelope that must have been at the very bottom of the little box, probably underneath the tissue paper. I pick it up and scrutinize it. It's sealed and there's nothing written on it. I hold it up to the light, and I can see that something is inside—a piece of paper. It has the size and look of a check. It is highly unlikely that an old check will offer a clue as to where Rebecca is, but I turn the envelope over anyway and slide my finger across the seal. It crackles open.

I look inside and I see the back of a typical bank check. I pull it out, turn it over, and gasp.

It is a check for $50,000. Made out to Rebecca a month before her accident. Signed by Gavin O'Neil.

Leanne's father.

9

Morning clouds fat with moisture hang over the surf at Mission Beach, but Isabel doesn't seem to care in the least. She is walking barefoot at the water's edge, picking up shells, poking at bits of seaweed with a stick, and turning to Priscilla and me every now and then to let us know what she sees.

My sister and I stand a few yards away, each holding a caramel mocha from the Starbucks down the street. We are watching Isabel, but our minds are busy with contemplations.

I had shown the check to Priscilla the moment she got up this morning. Her reaction mirrored mine; it was one of utter astonishment. Even now, nearly an hour later, I cannot think of a reason why Rebecca would have a check made out to her from Leanne's father for that amount of money.

It can't be that Gavin wanted to help with Rebecca's medical bills. The check is dated a month *before* the night of the accident. That means it can't be related to the accident in any way.

So why does Rebecca have it? What was it for? Why did

she not cash it? Why did she keep it? If she wasn't planning on cashing it, why didn't she just give it back or rip it up and throw it away? Is this the thing she couldn't find? Could this be the item she had practically begged me in her note to quietly dispose of?

And why is the check for so much money? Fifty thousand dollars! Why would Gavin McNeil write out a check for that kind of money to his daughter's best friend? Granted, it probably wasn't a ton of money to him, but to nineteen-year-old Rebecca it must have seemed like a million dollars. It made no sense.

Priscilla is now looking past the frothing, breaking waves to where calm water meets sky.

"I really don't think this has anything to do with why Rebecca left, Alexa," she says. "We should just put it back and forget we saw it." I can tell by her tone that she wishes I had not opened the envelope, that she wishes we didn't know what we now know.

"I can't forget I saw it, Priscilla. I know it might not have anything to do with why she left, but..."

Priscilla interrupts me.

"I'm quite sure it doesn't. The envelope was sealed, and you said the rubber bands disintegrated at your touch. Rebecca probably hasn't touched or had a conscious thought about that check in years."

"Then why did she keep it?"

"Why does Rebecca keep anything?" Priscilla asks, turning to me. "Why does she have a hundred pictures of houses?"

But the minute she says it, I can see in her eyes that Priscilla knows there is a reason why Rebecca has been cutting out pictures of houses. I'm already beginning to see the reasons.

"Besides," Priscilla continues, "Rebecca's memory of that time is locked away. She no doubt kept it because she doesn't remember why she has it."

"Her memory of the accident is locked away, but not her memory of that *whole year*, Priscilla. How do you know she doesn't remember how she got that check? How do we know this isn't the very thing she knew she had somewhere in her room but she couldn't remember where?"

"Well, if it is indeed what she was referring to in her note, then you should respect her wishes and destroy it."

But that's not what I want to do. Sometimes Rebecca asks for things that aren't in her best interest, and my gut tells me this is one of those times. Something is very wrong here. If Rebecca was trying to escape from something, and if the last thing she wanted to do before she left was to destroy this check, then it was certainly possible the check is mixed up in this.

Priscilla is looking past me to the ocean and to her little girl, who is running like a nymph across the sand. When I say nothing in return, she turns to me

"What are you going to do with it, Lex?"

I think for a moment. I haven't really had time to form a plan of action, but I know I simply can't throw the check away and pretend forevermore that I didn't see it.

"I don't know," I say. "I haven't decided. Maybe I'll give Gavin McNeil a call."

"For heaven's sake, Lexie, please use your head!" Priscilla says, turning her attention back to me. "Why would a rich man give his daughter's best friend fifty thousand dollars! Think about it!"

"I don't know."

"I can think of just two reasons why a man like Gavin McNeil would do that. And if you stopped to put two and two together, you would see it too!"

My mind wants to obey Priscilla, but the minute I try I'm besieged with images of Rebecca being involved with something illegal. Or, at the very least, unethical.

"A bribe?"

"Or blackmail," Priscilla says, making eye contact with me, forcing me to look at her. "If you go poking around in this, you may unearth things that ought to be left where they lie."

I'm considering her words when it suddenly occurs to me that I know now why Gavin and Kevin McNeil came to see Rebecca so often after her accident. I had chalked it up to compassionate sensitivity or a desire to know what really happened the night of the accident. But Gavin probably just wanted to know what happened to the check. He had written it a month before, and Rebecca had not cashed it. He no doubt wanted to know where it was. Was it safe? Had she destroyed it? Was she planning to cash it? Had the memory that she even had the check been swept away along with her memory of that night? And if so, then where was the check?

I then remembered how Gavin and Kevin had asked if they could be alone with Rebecca whenever they visited her at the house and that I had thought nothing of it. I wonder now if my parents had thought that was strange. My mother never said anything if she did. She no doubt also wanted to know why Leanne had driven off the road, and if Gavin McNeil could pry it out of Rebecca's wounded brain, well, then so be it.

But Gavin never got what he wanted.

And Rebecca had the check all along, in a shoe box in a sealed envelope buried beneath her high school swimming medals. If the reason had indeed been blackmail, then Rebecca knew something or had seen something that could have ruined Gavin McNeil in some way. And she had then capitalized on her knowledge with extortion.

Impossible. I remember Rebecca being opinionated and self-centered before the accident, but not devious and conniving. It couldn't possibly be blackmail.

But a bribe? Was it possible Gavin McNeil was buying something from her? Silence, perhaps? Cooperation?

For a moment my mind flutters to the possibility that Gavin McNeil was paying Rebecca for sexual favors, but I whisk these nauseating thoughts away as quickly as they come. I can't conceive of Rebecca selling her body to her best friend's father. And Gavin certainly never seemed the type to have committed something so grotesque and immoral.

He was no doubt paying Rebecca to do or not do something, to say or not say something. But what?

My mind takes me to the night of the accident. Rebecca had been moody and short with everyone that day. Mindy had called, and they had had some kind of argument over the phone. Then Leanne had come over, but she hadn't come up to the door. She had just honked the horn at the curb. Two hours later Leanne was dead and my sister was near death. Did the check have something to do with the events of that night?

"Alexa?" Priscilla says, rousing me from these thoughts.

"What?"

"Do you hear what I'm saying?"

"Priscilla, I don't think it was blackmail. I think it was a bribe. Gavin McNeil was paying Rebecca for her cooperation. And I bet it had something to do with Leanne."

Priscilla says nothing. She waits for me to continue.

"Do you remember how Gavin and Kevin used to come visit Rebecca after the accident?"

"Yes," Priscilla says slowly, and I can see she is tracking with me.

"Don't you think now that that was kind of odd?"

"I always thought it was odd."

"Priscilla, I think Gavin paid her for something," I say. "It was some sort of deal they had made. A deal *he* had made, anyway. But I'm thinking Rebecca was having second thoughts about the deal. She hadn't cashed the check. And then she was in the accident, and Gavin was afraid someone would come across it. He was afraid that with her injuries, Rebecca might not remember she even had the check. He needed to get it from her. But he never did. He finally gave up."

Priscilla is considering my theory. I can see that it makes sense to her, but even so, she's still not convinced we should do anything besides put the check back and take Isabel to the zoo.

"That was seventeen years ago, Lex," she says. "I'm sure he has come to believe the check no longer exists. I don't think calling him to tell him that it does will accomplish anything. It will probably just make him angry. And it won't get you any closer to finding out where Rebecca is."

"But, Priscilla, I think this check might have something to do with what happened to Leanne and Rebecca. Don't you ever wonder why Leanne lost control of her car? The roads were dry. There were no other cars involved. Something caused her to go off the road, Pris. What if she and Rebecca were arguing? What if it had to do with this check?"

"What if it did?" Priscilla asks briskly. "What good is there in knowing why Leanne went off the road!"

"What good is there in not knowing?"

Priscilla turns her head from me to gaze at Isabel chasing a seagull.

"It won't help you find her," she finally says.

I pause to let her words penetrate. She's probably right, but I can't live with endless speculation about this check.

"Maybe it won't," I reply. "But maybe it will help me understand why she left. I thought she was happy at the Center, Priscilla. I thought because all her physical needs were being met she had to be happy. But what if all this time she's just been waiting for the right time to spring free? What if she remembers just enough to regularly find herself at the edge of wanting to break away from it all?"

"If you feel you must understand why she left, that you won't be able to rest until you do, then you must do what you must. Surely you know that I, of all people, understand that," Priscilla says.

Yes, I am sure she does know what it's like to feel you simply must do a certain thing or go mad.

"So will you help me?"

"You don't need my help to look up Gavin McNeil, Lex. Just open the phone book. And if he's still in San Diego and you plan to go see him, no, I will not go with you. I have Isabel to think about. And you might want to consider your own welfare. It may not be either smart or safe to dredge this up with him."

"You think it's a dumb idea."

"It's not a dumb idea if it brings you peace, Lex. But gaining peace at the expense of the peace of other people is something I don't highly recommend. I know all about that too."

I say nothing and she continues.

"You might also want to consider how exposing the truth about this will affect Rebecca. You're more than her little sister.

You're her closest friend. She obviously thinks she told you about it. She asked you to keep it secret. She asked you to get rid of it."

What Priscilla says makes sense, but I still feel that something is amiss here. Greatly amiss. And has been for seventeen years. I'm not afraid of the truth. It surprises me that Priscilla, my shrewd and reasonable twin, seems to be. I don't want Rebecca to be hurt by this, either, but the plain fact is that Rebecca is not around right now to be wounded.

"I'll be careful," I say simply.

We stand there for a few more minutes, and then Priscilla calls for her daughter.

We really are taking Isabel to the zoo today.

By four o'clock jet lag and the excitement of seeing so many animals has taken its toll on Isabel. Priscilla carries her to the car, and we head over to Coronado to visit and have supper with Mom. Isabel is sound asleep in the backseat when we get to Mom's house, so while Mom takes the dogs out into the backyard, Priscilla carries Isabel in to the guest room and lays her on the bed. She puts Clement in the crook of her arm. We tiptoe out and join Mom on her backyard patio.

Priscilla sits down by Mom and bends down to pat Margot and Humphrey. They begin to chat, and I feel as though they probably need some alone time together.

I ask my mom where my cell phone is, and then I excuse myself to make some calls. Priscilla watches me leave but says nothing. I have no intention of telling Mom anything about the check or my suspicions. At least not yet.

I find my cell phone on Mom's dresser where she said it

would be. I walk with it over to her desk and bend down to the stack of phone books, catalogs, and AKC journals she has neatly stacked on the floor beside it. I pull out the San Diego white pages and flip to the M's. I haven't thought about the McNeils in a long time. I have no idea if they stayed in our Mount Helix neighborhood or if they are even still in San Diego.

My heart falls when I see that there is no listing at all for Gavin McNeil, but then it skips a beat when I see that there is a Kevin McNeil, and that his address is the street over from our old street in Mount Helix. It's the same address. The McNeils have not moved away. At least Kevin McNeil has not.

I stare at the telephone number listed.

There is no doubt in my mind that this is Kevin, Leanne's older brother—the same one who came and visited Rebecca with Gavin, as well as at least once by himself. He surely must have known something or why else had he come with Gavin? What exactly did Gavin tell him? Was Kevin in on it? And where is Gavin? Has he died?

My mind is filled with questions, and I know I'm not able to have an intelligent conversation with Kevin McNeil at the moment, but I turn on my phone to store the number and also jot it down on a yellow sticky note, which I then shove in the pocket of my shorts. I expect I will have the courage and the composure to try it later. I truly would not know what to say if I called him now. I have not seen him since I was twelve.

When I turn on my phone, I see that Dad has called and left a voice mail. I quickly punch in the phone number for Kevin McNeil, and then I press the button to hear Dad's message.

"Hey, Lex, it's Dad, and it's Tuesday morning about nine-ish. Just calling to see if there's any word on Rebecca. You didn't call back. Give me a call." I click the phone off and I put Mom's phone book back.

I will call Dad later, after I can talk to Priscilla alone.

Isabel is fast asleep after her long day, and Priscilla and I are sitting on the porch, enjoying the sounds of Mission Beach in the pleasant evening. Serafina and Jorge have just left after visiting with us for a little while.

And Patrick has also left after a five-minute chat, deciding no doubt, that he hasn't a chance with Priscilla.

"Are you going to call Kevin?" Priscilla asks me when we're alone again.

"I think I might drive by the house first and just look at it," I answer. "I want to see if I can tell by the outside what Kevin has turned out like. I wouldn't mind seeing our old house, either. I haven't been over there since Mom moved out. Would you like to come with me? I promise I won't do or say anything to upset Isabel."

"Thanks for the offer, Lex, but I really have no desire to see our old house. Why don't you just let Isabel and me sleep in in the morning and go do it then. By the time you get back, we'll be ready to take you out to lunch. I've been in the mood for fish tacos."

"You really don't want to come?"

Priscilla smiles and shakes her head. "No. I really don't."

Her tone makes me wonder if my timing might be really bad, but I have to ask her about Dad. He will be expecting me to return his call.

"Priscilla? Dad called and I'm supposed to call him back."

She turns to me and her expression reveals nothing.

"It will be very hard for me not to tell him you're here," I continue. "But if you insist on it, I will."

She waits for a second before answering me. "I don't insist on it," she finally says.

"So I can tell him?" I ask, and I am smiling.

"Yes."

"Would you like to see him?"

She pauses again. "Yes, Alexa."

"Really?"

"Please don't act like it's the strangest thing you've ever heard."

"Sorry!" And I am sorry, but I can't help it. I feel that an ugly chasm that has been open for years is finally about to close. And it's surprisingly not taking any victims with it.

"I'll go call him right now," I say, jumping out of my chair.

"Lex," Priscilla says.

"Yes?"

"Let him have the opportunity to make the first move."

I don't know if it's kindness or stubbornness that motivated her to say that, but I don't stay long enough to find out. I step into the house and head to the kitchen phone to dial my dad's house.

My half-brother, Laird, answers the phone. With my dad living an hour away in San Juan Capistrano, I don't see Laird very much, but he's a decent ten-year-old kid. Quiet. Shy. I feel kind of sad that his father—our father—is 64 years old. When Laird is my age, Dad will be in his eighties.

"Laird, it's Alexa. How are you?"

"I'm okay."

"Great. Say, is Dad home?"

"Yeah. Just a sec," I hear him walking through the house calling for Dad.

It's Alexa, I hear. Then my dad's voice.

"Lex! It's about time. Where've you been?"

"Sorry, Dad. I did call Sunday morning, but you weren't home."

"Why didn't you leave a message?"

"I don't know. I just didn't."

"Well, I've been wondering if there's news about Rebecca."

I so want to say, "Well, did you call the Falkman Center and ask?" But I don't.

"No," I say instead. "There's no news about Rebecca. But I do have some other news for you."

"Really? What?"

"Dad, Priscilla is here."

There is a momentary pause. "Are you serious?" he asks.

"Yes. It came about rather sudden. I called her to tell her about Rebecca, and she decided to come over. She had some vacation time coming to her, and she needed to use it."

"So just like that she came?"

"Yes. And Dad? She has a little girl. I know that's going to come as quite a shock, but her daughter is three. Her name is Isabel, and she's the most precious little thing."

"I don't believe this," he says, but I know he does. It's just something you say when you are completely astounded.

"Dad, Priscilla never told anyone about Isabel, so please don't think Mom or I have kept this a secret from you. We just found out too."

"Why in the world would she do such a thing? Keep a secret like that!"

"She did what she did because she felt it was best. Please, Dad. Don't dwell on this. Isabel is a beautiful little girl."

"They're both here?"

"Yes."

"For how long?"

I take that to be interest in perhaps seeing Priscilla. And Isabel.

"They leave on Sunday."

He pauses.

"What am I supposed to do?" he finally says, but he hardly frames it like a question.

"What do you *want* to do? Do you want to see them?"

He sighs. "What difference does it make whether or not *I* want to see them?" he replies harshly, and I can tell I've hit a nerve. I also finally understand. He doesn't get it.

"Dad, it makes all the difference in the world. All the difference. She wants you to want to see her."

He doesn't answer right away. And I let him take all the time he wants.

"How? Where?" he says.

"Why don't you invite us for dinner on Thursday. We can eat at your place or go out."

"Will she come?"

"I think she will if you invite her."

"All right. I'm inviting her. Will you tell her that? Will you tell her I'm inviting her?"

"I'll tell her."

"Okay," he says, and he sighs again. How can the prospect of seeing his own daughter be so fraught with difficulty? "I will have Lynne and Laird go visit her parents in Burbank," he adds.

I recoil at the notion that the battle lines are still drawn. "Is that really necessary?"

"Don't be ridiculous, Alexa," he replies, as though the idea of Lynne and Laird actually being at the house when we come is as preposterous as the concept of life on Mars. "Will six o'clock work?"

Fine. I'll play his way. "Six is fine. We'll see you then."

We say our goodbyes, and then I head out to the porch to tell Priscilla what I promised him I would tell her.

That he invited her.

10

I awaken Wednesday morning early, before the sun, and I can't fall back asleep. I finally get up off the sofa bed and make coffee. I take a mug out to the porch and wait for the paper and the sun to arrive.

Priscilla didn't have much of a reaction last night to my telling her Dad has invited us for dinner on Thursday. She just nodded her head and looked away from me.

Then, still looking away, she had asked, "Will Lynne be there?"

I could strangle the two of them sometimes. She draws a battle line at the same place he does. It drives me crazy.

I had slid back into my chair and told her no, Lynne wouldn't. I said it in a way that I hoped communicated how childish I think it is that Priscilla and Lynne can't get along. Actually, they have never tried. No, make that Priscilla has never tried. Lynne made a feeble attempt in the beginning, but she was met with a disdain that was practically three-dimensional in its depth.

Priscilla hated her from the moment Dad told us, four months after he moved out and the divorce was final, that he was getting married again. To a woman named Lynne.

To be honest, I was utterly shocked. *Who gets married just four months after a divorce?* I had wailed inside my head. I know now, of course. A man gets married that soon after a divorce when he is already in love with a second woman. I remember crying when he told us. We were at a restaurant, in a booth near the back. Mom wasn't with us and neither was Rebecca. It had been two years since the accident and two days after Priscilla's and my fourteenth birthday. Priscilla sat there like stone. She said nothing when Dad told us his news. It was as though she knew already. Or as though she hadn't heard a word he said.

Priscilla had already stopped talking to him by then; she did that before he moved out. Her communication with Dad consisted of a yes or no here and there and occasional nods or shakes of her head. Visitation with Dad after he moved out was laughable. He would take us to a movie every other Saturday and then out to a crowded restaurant before bringing us home. Imagine the level of intimacy you can have in a movie theater and then a noisy restaurant. It wasn't until I was much older that I realized Dad was making Priscilla's silence seem like a by-product of the things we did, instead of a result of something he did: leaving our mother. It was the last straw for Priscilla, our dad leaving Mom. After Rebecca's accident and while Rebecca was still home, Priscilla slowly withdrew into a place where even I couldn't penetrate. Plus, I had my own troubles. My parents' heightened bickering, Rebecca's never-ending therapies, and the advent of puberty collided on us both. Priscilla retreated into silence, and I ran for cover under the umbrella of Rebecca's recovery needs.

When Rebecca moved to the Falkman Center, everything changed for me. I felt suddenly unsure of my place in the family. My parents were at odds with each other, fighting over the most mundane things, including the forced absence of phones in our house. They barely noticed they still had two daughters at home. Priscilla had attached herself to a new circle of friends that I was not invited to be a part of, nor did I really want to be. Her new friends were older—most of them were driving already—and they scared me. And Rebecca was gone, living her semi-independent life on the lovely grounds of the Falkman Center. I don't ever remember feeling more alone and bereft of love. When I look back on it now, that year—my thirteenth—was the worst. Worse than my twelfth, when Rebecca nearly died, and worse than my fourteenth, when my dad remarried and moved away.

Dad invited Priscilla and me to his wedding. We didn't get an invitation in the mail or anything. He just invited us one afternoon, a few months after he told us he was remarrying. We were at a pizza place after a movie, and while we were eating, he said the wedding was in two weeks—on his next visitation Saturday—and if we wanted, he would arrange to have us picked up for the ceremony. Priscilla hadn't even looked at him when he said this, but he wasn't looking at her anyway. He was looking at me. Even at fourteen, I knew it was foolishness to think Priscilla would consider going to Dad's wedding. Did my dad really think I would come alone?

I had told him we'd get back to him.

He had then said something like, "Sure, I understand." And then he said it would be several weeks before he could arrange for weekend visits again because he and Lynne were moving to San Juan Capistrano.

"Okay," I had said.

"Maybe you girls would like to take the train up for visits? You can catch it downtown or at Del Mar. It's a beautiful ride. You could stay overnight and then take the train back on Sunday. I'm sure your mother wouldn't mind taking you to the station."

I know he meant well, but when he said "your mother," even I bristled. Priscilla nearly sprang from her seat in rage. It was the wrong thing to say somehow. As though he had no history with Mom. She was simply "mother" to us and nothing to him.

I had waited a second or two before responding with, "Yeah, maybe," knowing full well that Priscilla was seething next to me. I didn't think she was going to say anything, but she did. Oh, she did.

Priscilla had first leveled her eyes at me, and then she turned to Dad, looking at him full in the face as she opened her mouth to speak. "I will not come to your house," she had said. "I will not come to your *wedding.* I will not sleep in your guest room. I will not share meals with that woman you are marrying. And I would like to go now."

It was the most Priscilla had said to Dad in nearly a year. I know my mouth dropped open. I saw Dad's fall open too. But he looked bewildered only for a moment. As his mouth slowly closed, the countenance of his face changed too. I think it was at that moment he realized he'd had it with Priscilla's hostility and her refusal to accept that our parents had divorced and that he was in love with someone other than our mother.

What he said next pulled the last frayed thread from the fabric of our unraveling family.

"You may not like the choices I've made, Priscilla, but I'm a grown man, not your son or your employee or your slave. You don't decide what I do. I may not be your mother's husband anymore, but I'm still your father whether you like it or not. If you choose not to have a relationship with me, then obviously you're making a choice I'm going to have to learn to live with. Just like you're going to have to learn to live with my choices. Got it?"

I remember wincing when he said those last two words. I wish he had not said them. It would have been slightly easier for Priscilla to swallow his reprimand if he had left off the cocky "Got it?" at the end. He was angry and hurt. But so was she. And she was the child, after all, not the adult.

Priscilla had stood up then, calmly. It scared me how calmly she stood and then turned and walked away from our table.

I waited for Dad to stand up and go after her, but he didn't.

"Dad! Go get her!" I had whimpered.

He was watching Priscilla walk away, and he looked nervous and mad. I could tell he didn't know what to do.

"She'll be back. She just needs a few minutes to herself, I think," he said uneasily.

"Dad!" I whispered.

"Where's she going to go, Alexa? It's five miles to home!"

I got up then and followed after my sister. I found her at the front of the restaurant, using a pay phone.

"Priscilla, come back to the table. Please?" I had said.

She looked at me but said nothing. Then she turned her head as she spoke to whomever she had called.

"I need you to come and get me," she said into the receiver. "I'm at Giuseppe's, but I'm going to start walking to the intersection. Right. Thanks."

She hung up and began to walk out of the restaurant. I followed her.

"Priscilla! Where are you going? What am I supposed to tell Dad?"

"Tell him whatever you want, Lexie," she said, and her voice was void of emotion. She stepped out into the sunshine and the restaurant parking lot.

"But where are you going? Who did you call?" I asked, squinting into the late afternoon sun.

"I called a friend."

"Priscilla!"

She had stopped then and turned around to face me. My mirror image.

"You really want to know what to tell Dad? You tell him this. You tell him I will not 'get it.' I won't. All right, Lex? You tell him the answer's *no*."

She walked away, out of the parking lot and toward the intersection, where a friend would soon pick her up. I stood there, crying, until she was a far-off figure on a busy street corner.

When I got back to the restaurant, Dad was paying the bill.

"Where have you guys been?" he asked, annoyed.

I told him my version of what had happened, not Priscilla's.

He had shoved his wallet back into his pants pocket and stormed outside to the parking lot, cursing under his breath. We got into his car, left the parking lot, and headed to the intersection.

But Priscilla was already gone. Dad took me home—dropped me off, actually—and I had to go inside and tell Mom that Dad and Priscilla had had an argument and Priscilla was now out with a friend. My sister didn't come home until nine o'clock that night.

Mom said nothing to Priscilla about any of it. I believe Mom was secretly glad that Priscilla had walked out on my dad.

That happened fifteen years ago. To my knowledge, Priscilla and Dad haven't spoken to each other since.

I did make the train trip up to see Dad and Lynne a few times, but I hated going alone and Priscilla wouldn't come with me. When I turned fifteen, I stopped going to see Dad, and he didn't put up much of a fuss. It was as though he believed his rift with Priscilla extended to me because we were twins; as though he assumed that if we shared the same DNA and the same clothes, we surely shared the same opinion about Lynne. He was probably wondering why I came at all that first year of his second marriage.

To be truthful, I don't particularly care for Lynne, and I'm sure the feeling is mutual. From the beginning, it was easy to see she resented having to share my dad with what surely seemed like baggage from his past. There were a few times when Dad came to visit Rebecca that Lynne came along with him, but it didn't happen very often. Most of the time when Dad came— usually just a couple of times a year—he came alone. Then, when he and Lynne had Laird, his visits trickled down to once a year, if that.

But I still call my father from time to time; I still drive up to see him on Father's Day. I still send Laird Christmas presents, and I spend New Year's with Dad and his new family if I have no other plans.

My mother rarely speaks of Dad anymore. It's as though she wants to forget she ever knew him.

And until now, Priscilla was the same way. But her sudden interest in seeing Dad makes me think she came back home for a second reason besides introducing Isabel to her American relatives. I'm starting to believe that the old adage that time heals all wounds may actually be more true than false.

The paperboy is now turning onto my street, just as a rosy-gold spray of light begins to tint the sky. He tosses the paper in my direction, surprised and perhaps self-conscious at my presence on the porch at dawn.

I take the paper and my empty mug back inside. I refill my cup before sitting down at the kitchen table. I try to read the news of the day, but my thoughts wander. I can't keep my mind from trying to process all that's swirling about inside it. I'm amazed and somewhat intimidated by Priscilla's boldness in coming home with a daughter in one hand and an olive branch in the other. It's as though she's taking the initiative to finally fix a priceless, broken vase, one that's been in pieces for fifteen years. It's such a forward action. And it suddenly occurs to me that this is exactly what Rebecca has done. She has done something very forward. She made a very conscious act of her will when she packed her bags and left. I don't know why she did what she did, but I think Rebecca planned her escape. She made it happen.

I think of Stephen, this man who has tumbled into my life and whom I am inexplicably drawn to. I think of Rebecca's escape. I think of that check I found and how much I want to know why Rebecca had it. None of these events are things I planned; they happened while I was leisurely recovering from minor surgery. But now that they lay before me, what will I do about them? What conscious acts of the will shall *I* make? What are my choices? What will I make happen?

It's just a few minutes after seven, but I have a sudden urge to hear Stephen's voice. I feel that I will burst if I do not. How rude is it to call someone you have known for just nine days at seven in the morning? Stephen does not seem the type to be annoyed by someone in need. If I'm wrong about him, then I'll surely know it when I call and rouse him from sleep. Before I can change my mind, I walk over to my kitchen phone, grab the grocery receipt that lies next to it, and press the numbers.

When it begins to ring on the other end, I begin to pace.

What in the world am I doing?

But it only rings twice. He answers.

"Alexa? Is everything okay?"

My first reaction is mute shock. He knows my number. He knew it was me on his Caller ID. He knows something is troubling me, or I wouldn't have called so early in the morning. He doesn't sound sleepy. He sounds wide awake.

"Alexa? Is that you?"

"Y-yes, Stephen, it's me. I'm so sorry to call you this early, but…"

"Don't worry about it. I'm up. I usually get up at six every morning, so you don't need to apologize."

"Six every morning?" I repeat with a nervous laugh. "You didn't tell me you were a morning person."

He laughs too. "I wouldn't exactly say that, but I like having the time to read and pray and sort my day before it really starts. I usually have a pretty good day when I do. And now I just wake up that early whether I want to or not."

Again the lure of his relationship to God draws me. "I'm sorry to interrupt it, then," I say.

"I'm done. I'm just sitting down with a bowl of Lucky Charms and the latest *Sports Illustrated*, so you've interrupted nothing. What's up? Is it about Rebecca?"

I sigh. "Kind of." I decide to take him into my confidence. I tell him about the check, about Gavin McNeil, about Priscilla and Dad and our upcoming dinner.

I stop when it occurs to me I'm not sure why I need to tell him all this.

"Well, I think it's great that it looks like Priscilla and your dad are going to patch things up, especially after so many years, but I have to say I'm worried about you asking about that check."

His tone surprises me. He sounds…like an older brother telling me to watch out.

"How come?" I ask, somewhat startled.

"Because it could be dangerous. It's quite possible that the check is related to a bribe of some kind. This McNeil guy might not like you asking him about it. Especially if he thinks that check has long been out of the picture."

"Yes, but I can't help but think that check is somehow related to what happened to Leanne and Rebecca, that Gavin McNeil is somehow mixed up in what happened to my sister. It's not right what happened to those girls. It shouldn't have happened."

"But it was ruled an accident, right?"

"Yes. I'm not saying Gavin killed his daughter and maimed Rebecca. I'm just saying if there hadn't been a check, maybe there wouldn't have been an accident."

"Hmm," he says. "Okay, but just think with me here a minute. If Gavin was involved in something unethical and Rebecca knew about it, then we have to assume it was also something criminal, if not corrupt. That makes him dangerous, Alexa."

"But Gavin McNeil isn't like that."

"You really can't know what Gavin McNeil is like, I don't think. Am I right?"

I sigh again because I have to admit it is possible I don't know Gavin McNeil much at all. I remember him being rich, always busy, and quick-tempered. And that's about it.

"But it's not right what happened," I counter. "I can't just bury this. It would be like saying lies are better than the truth."

"Look, I understand what you're saying, Alexa, but you're not a cop. And you don't have the protection of the police. I want you to promise me that if you do end up talking with this guy that you do it in a public place and that you have someone with you."

I stop to think for a moment as to whom I might ask. I have a couple of friends at work I could call, but involving my co-workers in this doesn't appeal to me. Serafina would come if I asked her, but she wouldn't like the circumstances. Patrick would come if I begged him. He would probably like it if I begged him. That *really* doesn't appeal to me. And I already know Priscilla won't come.

"Would Priscilla go with you?"

"I don't think so. She doesn't like this idea."

"Then I will come."

His offer floors me. "Stephen, I couldn't ask that of you. You are recovering from surgery. You have a...a..."

"A brain tumor, yes. But that doesn't mean I can't come with you if you decide to meet this guy. In fact, I insist."

"Really? You would come?"

"I said I insist."

"Wow. Thanks, Stephen."

"You're welcome."

A second of silence passes between us.

"So are you feeling okay?" I ask.

"I've felt better, but it's tolerable."

"Elbow and ankle sore?"

"Oh, yes. I'm reminded every time I sneeze, cough, and blow my nose that I have broken bones that are mending."

"And the headaches?"

"What about them?"

So they have returned.

"Did you get some more Tylenol?"

"Actually, I was sent home from the hospital with some pretty powerful stuff, but I try not to take it too often. Makes me loopy. I wake from a stupor to find that I'm watching *SpongeBob SquarePants* and actually enjoying it."

I can't help but laugh.

"So you get your stitches out today?" he asks.

I'm touched that he remembered. "Yes."

"And then?"

"I'll just drive by my old neighborhood. I don't plan to get out and ring the doorbell at the McNeil place. I just want to look."

"Please be careful."

"I will, I promise."

"And you'll call me if you make plans to meet Gavin?"

"I promise that too."

"Okay, then. I'd better go. The brown bits in my Lucky Charms are getting soggy."

"All right. Bye, Stephen."

"Bye. And Alexa?"

"Yes?"

"I'm glad you called."

I hang up the phone to get ready for my doctor's appointment. You'd never guess by the smile on my face that I'm dreading having those stitches pulled.

11

I leave my place a little before nine, peeking in on Priscilla and Isabel on my way out. Both are in deep sleep. Isabel's curly head is just touching Priscilla's right shoulder. Clement's head is under Isabel's chin, eyes open, of course, as if he's staring at the ceiling.

Having the stitches removed hurts less than I thought it would. Dr. Chou seems pleased with how my incision is healing. He tells me I can now start doing very simple range-of-motion exercises. Small arm circles at first with my elbow bent, then larger circles with a straight arm. He also tells me what he has told me before: He wants to see me at three-month intervals for the next year to make sure the tumor does not make a reappearance.

I leave the clinic feeling very unworthy of such a trouble-free prognosis. This is so very different than Stephen's. It doesn't seem fair. Stephen seems like such a nice man. He doesn't deserve what is happening to him. But then, who does deserve cancer?

The drive to Mount Helix takes only twenty minutes. Traffic on I-8 is manageable at 10 AM, and I'm soon winding my way up the hills of my old neighborhood. I haven't been up here since I helped Mom move out the summer I graduated from college. The trees seem a little taller, but other than that, the neighborhood hasn't changed all that much.

Arriving at the curb of my old house fills me with a sense of nostalgia that surprises me. I loved this house. It's set at an angle with an inviting curved drive lined with Italian cypress trees and verbena bushes. A tall jacaranda tree still commands attention at the center of the smallish lawn. Peach-toned bougainvilleas shade the west side, and the little rose garden Priscilla and I created when we were eleven is still thriving on the south side.

It was a house of many happy memories. I think sometimes Priscilla, my mom, and even my dad forget this because the sad ones were so extreme.

My parents bought this house when Rebecca was about a year old, moving here from San Bernardino, which is where they are both from. Dad had started a new job with an electronics company that had just landed several multimillion dollar contracts with the Department of Defense. The new job was quite a step up for my dad. I think it nearly doubled their income. For a creative outlet, Mom got a part-time job as an event planner for the convention center downtown. They began attending a local Methodist church, though not regularly. When Rebecca turned three, my parents learned Mom was expecting another baby. Julian was born three weeks early, but with no visible complications until the cord was cut and he was expected to manage

his own circulatory system. His tiny heart was impossibly malformed. A heart transplant probably could have saved him, but
he died before one could be located.

Mom and Dad hardly ever spoke of Julian. The knowledge I possess of Julian came from Grandma Poole, my father's
mother, whom I saw once or twice a year while growing up,
when she came from Tucson to visit us. I don't think my mom
and Grandma Poole got along very well. It's hard for me to
know for sure because Grandma died when Priscilla and I were
nine and my memories of her are sketchy. But it seems to me she
felt my mother had treated Dad badly when Julian died, and
this angered her because her son, my dad, was hurting as much
as my mom was.

I know my parents' marriage was severely tested during this
time. I think they even separated for a few months, but they certainly must have moved past their grief and reconnected emo-
tionally because four years later, Priscilla and I were born. My
parents were hoping for a boy, were probably secretly convinced
it was a boy, so it was quite a shock when two girls emerged
from my mother's body. Mom has told us how surprised she
was. They didn't even have a girl's name picked out. Then suddenly she and Dad had to come up with *two* names.

When we were older, and after Priscilla's falling out with
Dad, Priscilla told me she thought our parents had given us
ridiculous names. I had told her that was nonsense. I thought
our names were beautiful. Elegant.

"C'mon, Lex. Alexa Ariana Marguerite. Priscilla Giselle
Antoinette. What kind of names are those?"

I had been flabbergasted at first. I hadn't known how Priscilla felt about our names. I thought having two middle names
was unique and wonderful.

"They're lovely names," I had said, defending our honor.

"They are preposterous names," Priscilla had argued.

"Priscilla, how can you say that?"

"Because it's true, Lex. You know they wanted a boy! And what did they get? Not one girl, but two. Two girls! So what do they do in response to this twist of fate? They choose names that no kid would want announced over a loud speaker at their high school graduation."

I had hotly disagreed with her, but in the end we simply had to stop talking about it. Priscilla was full of textbook teenage angst, and I perhaps was too, but her personality flaunted it and mine hid it. At our high school graduation ceremony two years later, Priscilla insisted her name be read off as "Priscilla Poole." No middle names. Not even the initials. There was nothing I could do except ask that my name be read off the same way. "Alexa Poole."

We had that conversation about our names inside the house I'm now gazing at. It's one of those memories I don't enjoy. We never talked about it again. I have no idea if Priscilla still feels this way.

I chase away this memory and sort through the others, the ones that make me happy. I think of sitting on Rebecca's bed when she was a teenager and Priscilla and I were still young girls, on those rare occasions when she let us into her room. I remember the time when we were nine and Rebecca was sixteen, and she had let us in so that we could watch her put on her makeup. It was a Saturday night and she had a date. Rebecca was in advice-dispensing mode that night. It was one of the infrequent times when she wasn't picking on Priscilla or me or ignoring us or bossing us around.

The door was closed and she was putting on eye shadow the

color of lilacs. She was preparing for a date with her then-latest boyfriend, Mike Somebody.

"This is how you kiss a boy," she was saying in my memory. "Don't pucker up your lips like they do in movies. Nobody does that. That would be like kissing an old, shriveled up potato."

Priscilla and I properly grimaced at the thought.

"You tip your face up a bit and open your mouth just a little, like you're going to say the word 'egg.'"

Priscilla and I had tried it out. "Egg," we had said.

Rebecca had turned around to face us. "Don't really say it!" she rebuked us. "*Like* you're going to say it."

We had shut our egg-saying mouths in embarrassment.

"Then you wait until he comes close to you. You don't close your eyes until you see him closing his."

On the bed, Priscilla and I practiced slowly closing our eyes.

"When his lips touch yours, you have to move your head to the side a little bit or your teeth will click together and that's just tacky."

Priscilla and I tipped our heads to the side in obedience.

"Then, if he puts his tongue in your mouth…"

But Rebecca had not finished because I had doubled over with disgust and yelled "Yuck!" Priscilla had just sat there, her face contorted with revulsion too, but I could see in her eyes that she was thinking, *So, that's really how it's done?*

"Wait till you're my age, and then we'll see if you think it's gross," Rebecca had said, slipping on a huge hoop earring.

I'm smiling as I remember this, Kissing Lessons on Rebecca's bed. Then it occurs to me, as it usually does when I conjure up this memory, that by the time we *were* Rebecca's age, she was twenty-three, living in a group home, and not being kissed by anyone. This is why it's hard to come back to this house, why Priscilla probably had no desire to come here this morning. As good as some of the memories are, the bad ones always find a way to work themselves in.

I don't know who lives here now. I suppose if I walked up to the front door, rang the bell, and asked whoever opened the door if I could just peek inside this house that used to be mine, I would probably be invited in. But I don't want to look inside it. I like remembering how it was. I really don't want to see how it is now.

I drive away, turning on the next street and passing five houses before I pull up alongside the house where Leanne lived.

I notice first off that it's no longer off-white. It has been painted a soothing shade of coral. The red tile roof looks new. The evergreens in the front yard have been removed and a trio of palm trees that stand in their place is encircled by a kind of grass cover that I know hardly ever needs mowing. The garage is open, and I see a Lincoln Navigator parked inside. I also see several bikes; two of them look as though they belong to children. Then a little dog strolls out from the garage, a Scottish terrier, and a little boy walks out after it. He looks as though he's about six.

The front seat windows are down on my car, and the dog immediately senses my presence. He takes a guard stance and begins to bark in my direction.

"Gizmo!" the little boy yells. But then he notices me too, and he just stares at me. Instinctively, I put my hand on the key, which is resting in the ignition. The dog trots across the front lawn to bark more thoroughly at my unwanted presence, and I hear a woman's voice from within the garage.

"Chase, what's up with Gizmo?"

Then I see a slender, brown-haired woman come out from the shadowy, open garage and into the sunlight. My hand freezes on the key. For a moment we stare at each other: the woman, the boy, and me. The dog continues to yap furiously.

"Can I help you?" The woman walks toward me, asking the question with enough volume so that it easily meets my ears as I sit inside my car. Her words are kind, but the underlying tone is one of suspicion. "Are you looking for someone's house?"

Well, here goes. "Uh, actually, I was looking for this house," I call out to her.

Her eyes widen at my answer.

"My name is Alexa Poole. My sister Rebecca and Leanne McNeil were best friends in high school. Leanne McNeil lived in this house. Are you...are you married to Leanne's brother, Kevin, perhaps?"

"Oh my word!" she says, stunned. "Yes, I am. My name's Lisa. And this is Chase. Would...you like to come in?"

I think of what I promised Stephen earlier this morning. I told him I was just going to drive by the McNeil house, but I didn't promise him I wouldn't go in. I just promised him I would be careful.

Which I plan to be.

"Thank you," I say in response. "That's very kind." I get out of my car and make my way to Lisa McNeil. She reaches down to grab the little dog, whose barks have now increased in quantity and decibels at my approach.

"Hush, Gizmo," Lisa says. "Chase, take him into the backyard, okay?" She hands the little dog to her son. Chase grabs the dog and walks off with him toward a gate at the side of the house.

"Please, come in," Lisa says.

I haven't been inside the McNeil house in I don't know how long. Leanne was Rebecca's friend, not mine. I came here once for a party, Leanne's high school graduation reception. If we had gone to Leanne's funeral, we would have come back here for refreshments, but Leanne's funeral was four days after the accident and doctors had not yet said that Rebecca would survive. Leanne's graduation party was probably the last time I was here.

We step inside.

"Have a seat," Lisa says, motioning me to a little room off the entry that is full of books, heavy cherry wood furniture, and big, comfy chairs. I remember this room. It used to be Gavin McNeil's study. "Can I get you something to drink? Some coffee?" she asks.

"Sure. Coffee would be great," I say, sitting on one of the big chairs. I take in the room while I wait. By a bay window I see a long table with photographs displayed on it. There is a wedding photo of Lisa and Kevin. He looks very much the same in the photo as he did when he was twenty-one and visiting my sister after the accident. There is a family photo of Lisa, Kevin, Chase, and two other children, a boy who looks about eight or nine and girl a couple years older than that. Next is a photo of Gavin and Lenore McNeil. Gavin is wearing a suit and Lenore, a soft pink double-breasted dress. She is wearing a corsage. Gavin looks the same. Lenore looks the way she did after the accident. There, but not there. There's also a photo of a younger Gavin in a karate uniform with a black belt around his waist. He's holding a young boy in his arms; Kevin as a child, most likely. Last, I see Leanne's senior picture from high school. She is wearing a white tailored blouse and diamond earrings. She looks as though she's ready to take on the world.

At that moment Lisa returns with two steaming mugs and offers me one. Then she takes the chair opposite mine. "So, how is your sister doing? Kevin has told me she survived the accident," she says.

"Rebecca is doing well," I say, unsure of how much to say. "She lives in a group home near Balboa Park. It's a great place, really. It gives her some measure of independence, but also lots of assistance with the things she can't manage on her own."

"Yes, I think Kevin may have mentioned the place to me once, " Lisa says. "So are you in town for a visit, then?"

"No. I still live in San Diego. I just haven't been up in this neighborhood in quite a while."

"Oh."

Lisa seems nice enough. She's the mother of three kids. She knows how to express kindness. I decide to trust her.

"The thing is, Rebecca ran away from the Falkman Center last Friday night," I tell her. "No one has heard from her, and I've been trying to find out where she might have gone."

"Oh my! I am so sorry to hear that." Lisa seems genuinely concerned.

"I've been going through the things she left in her room to see if there's a clue as to what her plans were, and I came across something I think would be of interest to Gavin McNeil."

"Really? To Gavin! Kevin's father?" Lisa is astonished. "Well, what is it?"

I instantly decide I want to leave Kevin with the impression that I can be discreet. I'm trusting that he'll find my discretion comforting.

"I wish I could tell you," I say, "but I don't think I should say

at this point. I was wondering if you could just give that message to Kevin for me. That I've found something. And perhaps
he could relay it to Gavin. Gavin is still living, isn't he?"

"Yes...yes," Lisa says, stammering. "He and Lenore live in
Palm Springs."

Poor thing. I've probably ruined her day.

"Could you just ask Kevin to call me at home? I live in Mission Beach. And here is my number." I take out a scrap of paper
from my purse and write my telephone number on it. I hand it
to her.

"Is this about Leanne?" Lisa ventures, taking the piece of
paper from me.

"To be truthful, I really don't know. I think it probably is."

"All right. I'll give it to Kevin."

I sip my coffee. "It's nice to see your family living in this
house," I say.

She smiles weakly. "At first I didn't want to move in here.
For the first couple years of my marriage I hated coming here.
Gavin was so preoccupied with his work, and Lenore slipped in
and out of depression so much I never knew what she was going
to be like when we came to visit. But Gavin really wanted us
to have the house when he retired. He bought a condo in Palm
Springs about five years ago and moved Lenore out there. He
thought maybe getting away from this house and the memories
would be good for her, but she just took it all with her. All the
grief. She packed it as surely as she packed her good china..."
Lisa trails off, realizing she's sharing more than she meant to. "I
beg your pardon," she says quickly.

"No need to. I know the road you've been on."

"Yes. I bet you do," she says softly.

"Thanks for the coffee," I say, rising from my chair. "I'll be home tonight if Kevin wants to give me a call."

"Are you sure there's nothing else you can tell me?" she asks.

"I don't think it's my place to," I said. "I'm sorry."

"Okay," Lisa says, shrugging her shoulders and rising too.

"Thanks again for the coffee. And for inviting me in," I say as I open the front door.

I walk out to my car, get in, and drive away, glad to have met Lisa McNeil. She's kind and thoughtful. Normal. I don't know what Gavin McNeil was up to seventeen years ago when he wrote out a check to my sister for $50,000, but I feel that Lisa is someone who might take my side, if sides ever need to be taken.

I get back on the Interstate and head west for the beaches. Priscilla will no doubt be up by now. If she's still in the mood for fish tacos, I'll take her and Isabel to Seaport Village at San Diego's harbor. While we eat, Isabel can watch the people who bring their kites to the grassy knoll by the yacht club to fly them, seemingly without a care in the world.

12

When I get back to the triplex in Mission Beach, Priscilla is sitting in a lawn chair in the backyard watching Isabel blow bubbles. A cat that belongs to the retired couple that lives on the other side of our backyard is chasing the bubbles, much to Isabel's delight.

"Mom called," Priscilla says when I reach her. "She'd like to take us out to dinner tonight."

"Well, I hope you don't mind if we make it an early one. I need to get back here before the evening gets too old."

"You expecting company?" she says, looking up at me.

"I'm expecting a call."

"From?"

I look away, watching Isabel frolic. "From Kevin McNeil."

I turn my head back to her, and I see that Priscilla regards me with a mixture of awe and disapproval. It's as though she's proud of me for taking such a bold step as contacting Kevin

McNeil, but she still has reservations about my poking around
in this at all.

"Kevin McNeil," she says.

"I met his wife today, Priscilla. I wasn't planning on it. It
just happened." I quickly tell her about being invited in by
Lisa McNeil and my belief that she seems to be someone I can
trust.

"Well, I guess it can't hurt to have someone else in the loop,"
Priscilla says, turning her head back toward her daughter.
"Someone who can vouch that you were alive and well on
Wednesday morning."

"Priscilla, you don't really think I'm in any kind of danger,
do you?"

She shakes her head. "No—I don't know. I just wish you had
more than an uncashed check to go on; something that would
let you know if you should go to the police with this or just let
it go."

"But that's what I am doing. I'm finding out which I should
do."

We are quiet for a few moments.

"Are you still in the mood for fish tacos?" I ask.

"Yep. Let's do it."

Priscilla calls for Isabel, and she runs to us with the open
bottle of bubbles. Some of the liquid sloshes onto her hand and
wrist.

"Uh-oh!" Isabel hands Priscilla the little pink wand she holds
in her fingers.

"Let's get washed up, love. We're going out to eat."

"I want an Orangina!" Isabel declares.

"I don't know if they sell Orangina in America, Izzy. You can
have a Sprite instead."

They begin to walk inside.

"Is it orange?" Isabel says.

"No."

"Is it fizzy?"

"Yes, love. It's fizzy."

Their voices taper off as they head down the hall to the bathroom to wash the bubble liquid off Isabel's hands. A few moments later they return, and we start to head out the door to my car.

"Wait!" Isabel suddenly yells as we begin to file out. "I forgot Clement!"

She runs back to my bedroom and reappears seconds later with the shiny seahorse in her hands.

"He's a regular fixture, isn't he?" I ask softly.

"Don't I know it," Priscilla whispers.

We head for Seaport Village, talking about lots of little things. But Priscilla never asks me more about my morning, such as what does our old house look like now, and I don't volunteer to tell her.

We're at Mom's by two thirty, and she reluctantly agrees to an early supper so that I can get home by seven. I don't tell her whose call I'm expecting, only that I need to be home for an important call. I believe it's on the tip of her tongue to ask me who will be calling me, but I think her aversion to telephones in general wins out. She does not ask.

Isabel asks to see the ocean again, so we pack a few beach chairs, a blanket, and cans of soda and head back into my car. We drive the few miles to Silver Strand State Beach, a thin peninsula of land that connects Coronado Island with the mainland just a few miles north of the Mexican border.

Kite-surfers are spread out over the tumbling waves, enjoying the ever-present gusts on the Strand. Isabel is transfixed by their almost ballet-like acrobatics. She begs for Priscilla to walk her closer to the shore so she can watch them. They start to walk away, and then Isabel runs back to me, dropping Clement in my lap.

"Can you hold him?" she asks, but she skips away before I can answer.

I finger the delicate sequins on Clement's stuffed body and I decide this is a good time to tell Mom that we'll be going up to see Dad tomorrow evening.

"Priscilla and Isabel too?" she says, a trifle perturbed.

"Well, yes, Mom."

Mom frowns a bit, and then her features soften somewhat. "I suppose it's best that they bury the hatchet. I never would have dreamed your father and Priscilla could have kept up this war for as long as they have."

"Me neither."

"I used to be flattered by Priscilla's hostility toward your father's leaving me for another woman, but it seemed a little over-the-top after a while."

"They have both been incredibly stubborn."

"Yes. A Poole trait I have tried to forget I once found intriguing."

We sit in silence for a few minutes as we watch Priscilla and Isabel a hundred yards away, hand-in-hand, at the water's edge.

"I wonder what made her change her mind about your dad,"

Mom says, rather absently, as though she's not expecting me to answer.

"I think maybe it's because of Isabel. I think she wants her daughter to grow up with a family," I venture.

"Even one as flawed as ours?"

Mom kind of smiles when she says this. It makes me smile.

"I guess so," I say.

"Alexa, would you let Priscilla and Isabel stay with me Friday and Saturday night? They leave on Sunday, and I feel that…that I…I want that little girl to know her grandma."

I, too, feel the pull of Sunday, knowing it's the day Priscilla and Isabel will fly back to London. My first response is to say I don't like this idea. But that would be selfishness talking. "Sure, Mom," I say.

We turn our attention to the kite-surfers and the two figures far off that are also watching them. Clement sparkles in my lap as the sun catches his spangled fabric.

Priscilla agrees to the plan to stay with Mom Friday and Saturday night, though I think she does it more for Isabel's sake than her own. It's comforting to think she would rather spend the last two nights with me.

The three of us head back to Mission Beach after eating crepes at a sidewalk café near the Hotel Del Coronado, a place that—to Isabel's delight—has Orangina on its menu.

When we get back to my place I check my answering machine. There's nothing from Kevin McNeil. Nothing from the Falkman Center, either.

Priscilla, Isabel, and I spend the next hour looking at photo albums from my childhood, books I put together the year I turned fifteen, when I began to finally understand the family I grew up with was gone. Isabel recognizes a few of the pictures.

"Mummy! You have this picture!" she says of a photo of Priscilla and me wearing matching Minnie Mouse outfits, taken one Halloween when life was still relatively normal at our house.

She turns the page. The 8 x 10 photo on this page is a JC Penney shot of Rebecca, Priscilla, and me. Rebecca is ten and Priscilla and I are three. She is holding us both in her lap, one on each side.

"Who's that?" Isabel asks, pointing to Rebecca.

"That's your Aunt Rebecca when she was a little girl," Priscilla says.

"Oh. Aunt Rebecca. I know her. She's visiting friends, right, Mummy? I'll see her next time we come."

I look over to Priscilla and she just shrugs. It's as good an explanation as any. Isabel turns the rest of the pages quickly. When she gets to the end of the book, Priscilla tells her it's time for a bath and then bed.

I put the photo albums away, and just as I close the cabinet door where I keep them, the phone rings. I nearly run to the kitchen to pick it up.

"Hello?" I say.

"Is this Alexa Poole?"

A man's voice.

"Yes."

"This is Kevin McNeil. I understand you were at my house today."

He sounds a bit peeved.

"Yes. Yes, I was."

He waits. And so do I.

"Well, are you going to tell me what this is about?" he asks curtly. "My wife says you found something in your sister's room that you think would be of interest to my father."

"Yes, I did."

"Well?"

I swallow. He sounds *very* peeved. I don't like it. "Kevin, I think maybe you know what I found."

Silence.

"I really have no idea what you're talking about," he finally says.

I can't tell if he's lying or not. My guess is he's lying. I wonder if Lisa is listening to how he's talking to me.

"Okay, I found a check," I say calmly, though I don't feel calm. "Do you want me to tell you how much it's for and who signed it?"

"Now you listen to me," he says after a moment's pause. "I don't know what game you and Mindy are playing here, but I won't play it. You understand me? My father was a fool for falling for your tricks, but I won't play the fool's game. So you'd better just watch it!"

Mindy? Leanne's and Rebecca's other high school chum and college roommate? What has she got to do with this check? What tricks?

"Okay, now I don't know what *you're* talking about," I say, trying to match his angry tone. "What does Mindy have to do with this?"

"I told you, I will not be played a fool."

"And I'm telling you I don't know what you're talking about!" I say and I find that I'm shaking a little.

"Are you making this call for Rebecca?" he says evenly. "Is she with you? I want to talk to her."

"My sister Rebecca is missing," I say, and I find that I'm pacing. "She's been gone for five days and no one knows where she is. I found an uncashed check, Mr. McNeil, in her room at the Falkman Center, dated one month before the accident, in the amount of fifty thousand dollars, signed by *your father*. I want to know why she has it. That's why I came to your house today. I want the truth. You either tell me why my sister had this check or I will call the police. I swear I will."

A few seconds of silence follow, and I'm glad for them because I'm trembling with anger and fear. I hadn't planned on threatening to go to the police. I'm not even sure they would bother to look into this. There's nothing illegal about writing a check, even one for $50,000, to your daughter's nineteen-year-old best friend.

"Who else have you talked to?" he finally says.

My heart begins to race. It sounds like a threat.

"I've told a number of people," I say. I don't know if Stephen and Priscilla count as a "number of people," but I feel safer with him thinking there are several people who know about the check.

"And have they advised you to go to the police?" he asks, challenging me.

"That's none of your business," I reply hotly.

"And neither is this any of yours. This conversation is over."

The phone clicks in my ear. He has hung up on me.

I hold the phone for several seconds before replacing the handset in the cradle. When I do, I notice that Priscilla is standing at the entrance to the hallway by the bathroom door with her arms crossed over her chest. I'm sure she has heard every word I've said.

"Guess that didn't go over very well, did it?"

"No. He's furious. But, Priscilla, he *knows*. I can tell he knows. Whatever deal Rebecca made with Gavin McNeil, Mindy Fortner was also in on it. And I think Mindy kept after McNeil, asking him for more money. I think maybe she moved on from accepting a simple bribe to blackmail."

"Lex…"

"I can't just let it go, Priscilla. I still think if Gavin McNeil hadn't written that check, Leanne and Rebecca never would have been in the car that night."

"You can't change what happened to them."

"But maybe if we can understand *why* it happened, it'll be easier to live with the fact that it did."

"Or it might make it harder. Did you stop to consider that?"

"Priscilla, what could be harder than this? The way we have all ended up? Don't you think knowing the truth, hard as it is sometimes, is better than believing a lie?"

"Sometimes it is, sometimes it isn't." She turns and walks back into the bathroom, leaving me to ponder which of us is right.

13

I spend the night tossing and turning on the sofa bed, my mind filled with unanswered questions. I finally fall asleep sometime after three in the morning. I awaken a few minutes before eight, groggy and with a sizeable headache. I head into the kitchen to make coffee, pouring in an extra measure of grounds with hopes that the padded caffeine level will chase away the pounding in my head. There's no sound from the bedroom. Priscilla and Isabel are presumably still asleep.

I'm halfway through my second cup when the phone rings. I catch it after the first ring, hoping it hasn't awakened my guests. I answer, unable to keep myself from hoping it's the Falkman Center telling me Rebecca has come home. But it's not the Falkman Center.

It's Stephen.

"I didn't call too early, did I?"

"No, no. I'm up," I manage to say. I'm surprised to hear his voice.

"I had to know how your day went yesterday," he tells me. "Did you go over to your old neighborhood? Did you drive by the McNeil house?"

I have a feeling he's on to me. That he suspects it's quite possible I did more than just drive by. I don't see how he could know this, though. My meeting Lisa McNeil in her driveway was coincidental. I didn't plan it.

"Well," I begin, wondering how he'll react to what happened. "I did go to my old neighborhood. And I did drive over to the McNeil house."

"And?"

"And I sort of met Kevin McNeil's wife."

A second of silence hangs between us.

"You did?"

"I didn't expect I would. I was just sitting in my car at the curb. She saw me from her garage and came out to see if I needed help finding someone's house. And so we met."

"So did you tell her anything?"

"Just that I was Rebecca's sister, that she had run away, and that I had found something in her room I thought would be of interest to her father-in-law. He's still living, by the way. He and his wife live in Palm Springs."

"And how did she react to that?"

"She was very nice, Stephen. She asked what it was I had found, but I apologized and told her I didn't think it was my place to say. I gave her my number to give to Kevin, and I told her to tell him I would be home in the evening if he wanted to give me a call."

"Did he call you?"

For some reason I don't want to tell Stephen how the conversation went with Kevin McNeil.

Well, it's not "some" reason. I know why I don't want to. I think he'll be bothered by it. I like that. And I don't like it.

"Yeah, he called me."

"And?"

"I think he knows about the check. He kind of got defensive about it, first telling me he had no idea what I was talking about and then telling me it wasn't any of my business," I answer, trying to sound nonchalant about the whole conversation. "And he accused me of being in cahoots with Mindy Fortner, like she and I are up to something. I haven't seen Mindy since a few weeks after the accident."

"Who's Mindy?" Stephen asks. He sounds a little upset.

"She and Rebecca and Leanne were all high school friends who roomed together at UC Santa Barbara their first year," I answer. "But like I said, I haven't seen Mindy since a few weeks after the accident. She transferred to Pepperdine afterward. I don't think she wanted to go back to Santa Barbara after what happened."

"So I take it you're not going to meet with him?"

"I doubt there will be a meeting anytime soon. He practically hung up on me."

"What are you going to do?"

While staring sleepless up at my living room ceiling last night I had come up with a plan. I share it now with Stephen.

"I'm going to try and locate Mindy."

Stephen pauses for a moment. "Are you sure that's what you should do?"

"What is the harm in talking with her?" I ask, realizing I haven't actually told Stephen I suspect that Mindy got a check of some kind too. And that she didn't stop with just one.

"Perhaps none at all. But just keep in mind that people

sometimes do crazy things when they feel cornered, Alexa. I'm a little worried for you, that's all."

I smile in spite of feeling that I'm being mothered.

"I promised you I'd be careful," I say.

"I'm going to hold you to that," he answers right back, and I like the way it sounds.

I may have not had much luck with men the last few years, but if I'm not mistaken, Stephen is as interested in me as I am in him. It's a wonderful, scary feeling. The minute I contemplate this, though, I remember I'm falling in love with a sick man.

"You have your appointment with the oncologist today," I say, changing the subject.

"Yep. At ten thirty."

"How are you getting there?"

"Mom drove up last night and stayed with me. She wants to come to this first appointment. She's probably afraid I'll leave out any juicy details if she doesn't get to talk to the doctor herself. Besides, I'm not supposed to drive because of the medication I'm on. So I guess it's meant to be that she drives me there. At least for this first one. I'm going to have to make some other arrangements when I start treatment, though."

I'm secretly wishing I didn't have to go back to work on Monday. I wouldn't mind taking Stephen to his treatment appointments.

"I wish I could help you out there," I say, "but I have to go back to my job on Monday."

"It's okay. I didn't mean to sound like I was fishing for favors," he says quickly.

"No, I mean I really *do* wish I could take you to some of them, Stephen."

He pauses for a moment. "Thanks. That's nice to know."

Then he changes the subject. "If it's not too late for you, why don't you call me when you get home tonight and tell me how things went with your dad."

"Okay." I can't help smiling.

"Well, I'll catch you later, then."

"Bye, Stephen."

I hang up and see that Priscilla is walking toward me in her pajamas.

"Prince Charming?" she asks effortlessly, grabbing a coffee cup from the dish drainer.

I nod my head, realizing as I do that the headache has all but disappeared. "Yup."

She pours a cup and sits down across from me. "I suppose you were up all night speculating."

"I couldn't help it, Priscilla."

"So?"

"So I'd like for us to go to the Falkman Center this morning and get something out of Rebecca's closet."

"The Falkman Center?" Priscilla says, eyeing me, wondering what I'm up to.

"You can show Isabel where Aunt Rebecca lives," I say, getting up to pour myself some more coffee.

"Mmm," Priscilla says, watching me.

At that moment Isabel appears in the living room and makes her way to the kitchen.

"*Bonjour, mon ange,*" Priscilla says. "*Tu as bien dormi?*" And I can't help but be in awe at how lovely her French sounds.

"*Oui, Maman, mais j'ai faim. Je veux des oeufs,*" Isabel says, a little choppy, but still amazing for a three-year-old, even one as bright as Isabel.

"You're teaching her French," I say.

"Well, why not? *Eh, chérie?*" Priscilla pulls Isabel onto her lap. Then she turns her head toward me. "Do you have any eggs?"

"Sure," I say. "Coming right up." I walk over to the fridge and pull out a carton of eggs.

"So what's in Rebecca's closet?" Priscilla says as I take a skillet out of one of my cupboards.

"I'm pretty sure Mindy Fortner got married quite a number of years ago. I need to know her new last name if I am going to look her up."

"So..."

"So Rebecca's closet is where I'll find her married name."

Priscilla hasn't been to the Falkman Center in a long time. And the last time she was there, she spent no time looking in Rebecca's closet. She doesn't know Rebecca has kept all her old wedding invitations, and that they rest on her closet shelf, bound by a silver ribbon.

Frances looks up in surprise from the resident she's speaking with as Priscilla, Isabel, and I walk into the Falkman Center. She has never met Priscilla, and I suppose she doesn't think very often about the fact that Rebecca is the older sibling to a set of twins. She excuses herself from the resident and comes to us.

She hesitates just for a second before addressing me first.

"Alexa! Good morning," she says, and then she turns to Priscilla. "I'm Frances Newkirk, the day manager. You must be Rebecca's other sister, Priscilla." She holds out her hand and Priscilla takes it.

"Nice to meet you. This is my daughter, Isabel," Priscilla says, and I can see that Priscilla's faint British accent also surprises Frances.

"You're visiting from England, then?"

"Yes. Just a short visit. We leave Sunday."

"Oh, so soon? We've heard nothing from Rebecca, I'm afraid," Frances says. "We would have called you, Alexa, if we had."

"I know that, Frances. We didn't come here expecting to see Rebecca or even that you would know where she is. There's something I need to get from her room."

"Oh. Of course."

Frances starts to walk with us down the hall to Rebecca's room. "Alexa," she says and I detect uneasiness in her voice. "Your sister's account is paid up through the end of the month, but if she doesn't return by then, you might want to think about..."

Frances is having a hard time completing her sentence. She doesn't want to say, "You might want to think about moving her things out." But I know she's thinking it.

"I know, Frances. I just don't want to think about that yet," I say. I can't imagine giving up Rebecca's room at the Falkman Center. I doubt she would get back in. The waiting list is enormously long.

"I do understand," Frances says. "We can talk about it another time. I'll leave you, then." And she walks back to the lobby.

We step inside Rebecca's room. Marietta is not here; she's no doubt in the work shed sitting at a loom. I see right away that Rebecca's fishbowl is now sitting on Marietta's dresser. And Cosmo the fish appears to be thriving. I had forgotten all about him. The only instruction Rebecca left is the first thing I completely forgot. Well, it's not exactly the *only* instruction. She also told us not to worry.

"So is this Aunt Rebecca's bed?" Isabel is asking.

"Yes, love," Priscilla says.

"Are these her books?" Isabel asks, pointing to a woven basket filled with books of all shapes and sizes.

"Yes, Izzy."

I turn to the closet, open it, and reach up on tiptoe to the top shelf where the little bundle of wedding invitations rests by itself because the shoeboxes are all at my house.

I hear Isabel ask Priscilla about a book she has found in the basket.

"That's Rebecca's baby book," Priscilla answers.

"Is this Rebecca's baby?" Isabel asks. She has placed the open book on Rebecca's bed, along with Clement, and is looking at a photo of Rebecca as a wrinkly, week-old infant.

"No, love, that's Aunt Rebecca when she was a baby."

Isabel continues to turn the pages, and I undo the ribbon on the stack of invitations. There are probably eight or nine of them, all of them dating back at least a dozen years, back when her high school and college friends still kept in touch. Mindy's is near the bottom of the pile. I peel it away. Inside the invitation is the yellowed newspaper announcement from the wedding itself.

The wedding announcement includes a picture of Mindy and her then new husband Ronald Bettendorf. Mindy Bettendorf. The last line on the announcement reads: The happy couple resides in Redondo Beach.

Perfect.

I have a name and a city. It's possible she no longer lives in Redondo Beach, but at least I have a place to start.

"How come there's nothing on this page?" Isabel is asking.

"Lex," Priscilla says.

I turn to my sister. Priscilla is looking at the page in the baby book. I look at it too. In scrolled gold lettering the page headline says: *Baby's Birth Certificate*.

But there's nothing there besides empty black photo corners.

Rebecca's birth certificate is gone.

Minutes later I'm sitting in Frances' office with the baby book. Priscilla has taken Isabel outside to the landscaped grounds in the back.

"So Rebecca didn't give you the certificate for safekeeping?"

"No, she didn't," Frances replies.

"And no one from the Center would have taken it and put it in her file?"

"Alexa, we would never take a resident's personal belongings without their knowledge."

"Can you just check, please?"

Frances stands and heads over to a file cabinet. She opens it and skims across file tabs, stopping at one, reaching in for it, and looking at its contents.

"It's not in here," Frances says.

I sigh in frustration. I have no idea how long the birth certificate has been gone, but it concerns me that it is. I think of how easy it is to steal someone's identity with a just a copy of a birth certificate and a Social Security number. Rebecca always carries her Social Security card with her. It's the only important card she carries in her wallet and she knows it. It's why she insists on having it there.

So I picture her now out in the wicked world, with a Social Security card and a birth certificate in tow, naive as Goldilocks.

"We have always stressed to our residents and our residents' family members that it isn't wise to keep valuables in their rooms," Frances is saying.

"I know it's not your fault," I say quickly, rising from my chair. "Thanks, Frances."

I leave her office and make my way to the lobby and then to the double doors that lead out to the back lawns and gardens, where Priscilla is waiting for me.

I see her standing next to a man with pruning shears in his hands. Isabel is near them, peering into the goldfish pond and talking to Clement, whom she holds in one hand. The man and Priscilla appear to be in conversation with each other. When I reach them, Priscilla turns to me. I see something like shock or alarm in her eyes.

"Lex," she says and she sounds troubled. "This man's name is Manuel. He's a gardener here at the Center. He's new. This is only his third day on the job."

So what? I'm thinking. "Hi. Nice to meet you," I say rather absently.

Priscilla continues. "Manuel got called in by the contractor for the landscaping company that the Center uses. They had a guy who quit last Friday because he was leaving the area. The guy who quit worked here for three years. Lex, his name was Cosmo."

I know my face is being drained of color. I can feel it happening. In spite of having heard everything Priscilla has just said, I utter one word: "What?"

"The guy who quit on Friday is named *Cosmo*," Priscilla says.

Cosmo. My mind somersaults with images. First of the blue-and-silver fish. Then of two chinchillas named Tim. Then of Tim himself, the disabled man from long ago, whom Rebecca had begun to love and who was snatched away from her. Cosmo! She named her fish Cosmo! Am I crazy to be imagining what I'm imagining right now? That the gardener named Cosmo knew Rebecca? That she knew him?

No, I'm not crazy. Priscilla, the rational one, is thinking the same thing. I can see it in her eyes.

I had never asked Rebecca why she named her fish Cosmo. It didn't occur to me to ask. I never once imagined she had named her fish the same way she had named her chinchillas. Cosmo! My gut is telling me Rebecca did not run off alone. Rebecca has run away with a man. A gardener named Cosmo.

Oh, Jesus! It feels just like a prayer when I whisper the name. *Keep her safe, keep her safe, keep her safe!*

"Do you know where they are? I mean, where he is?" I ask Manuel, finding the words after seconds of numbing shock.

"No," he says, shaking his head. "I never met him. I heard some of the guys say he has family in Chicago, but they were not talking to me."

"We've got to talk to Frances," I say to Priscilla, and I turn to run back to the Center. I sense that Priscilla has reached down to Isabel and taken her hand. They follow me.

"Thank you, Manuel," Priscilla says over her shoulder.

I'm barely able to string two intelligible words together when we get inside to Frances' office. Priscilla does most of the talking. When I'm sure Frances understands that we think Rebecca has run away with the Center's gardener, I explode.

"How could you let this happen!" I yell.

Frances' eyes grow wide, but she maintains control. "Alexa, the residents are on a first-name basis with all of our hired staff, including the gardeners. I knew Rebecca and Cosmo were friends, but Cosmo was friends with all the residents. Do you hear me? *All* of the residents. I never would have expected that he...that Rebecca...that they...When the contractor called me Monday to say he was assigning a new gardener because Cosmo was moving away, it never *once* occurred to me that his leaving had anything to do with Rebecca's disappearance."

"I can't believe this!" I exclaim. "How could you not see it?"

"How could *you* not?" Frances asks me. "You were here every week! You spent most every Sunday with her. You probably spent more one-on-one time with her than anyone aside from Marietta!"

Her words cut me to the quick. I can think of nothing to say in response. Priscilla comes to the rescue.

"Frances, can you give us the name and number of the owner of the landscaping company so that we can talk with him?"

"Yes, of course," she says, shaking off her anger. She pulls out a piece of paper from a memo pad and flips through her Rolodex. She writes the number down. "We can call him right now if you like."

"That would be nice," Priscilla says.

Frances pushes in the telephone number, and I continue to stare in mute disbelief. Priscilla has Isabel in her lap. I look at Isabel's face, and I see that she's staring at me wide-eyed and holding onto Clement as though he's a life preserver. I want to cry.

"Sorry, Isabel," I say. "I lost my temper. I didn't mean to scare you."

She nods at me.

"Yes, I need to speak to Mr. Hooper, please," Frances says into the phone. "Hi, Tony, it's Frances Newkirk at the Falkman

Center. Yes. I just need to know if you know how I can get in contact with Cosmo DiMarco, our last gardener. We think maybe one of our residents has left town with him…No, I'm not holding your company responsible in any way. It appears our resident left willingly and deliberately. We would just like to see if we could contact him. The resident's family is concerned. They just want to make sure she's all right…None at all? What about any family here in San Diego? Do you know where he lived?"

Frances waits for a second and then writes something down.

"Well, if you do happen to hear from him, would you please let us know? Or tell him we would like to speak with him? No, I don't think he has broken any laws. At least none that involve the resident. Unless, of course he has harmed her in some way… No, I agree. Cosmo seemed like a wonderful person. I can't picture him being unkind to anyone, either. Yes. That would be very much appreciated. Thanks, Tony."

Frances hangs up the phone.

"Cosmo left no forwarding address. The owner said he came three years ago from the Chicago area. He may still have family there. He gave me his address here in San Diego. If you want it, here it is."

Frances extends her hand and I take the slip of paper.

"Do you happen to know where this address is?" Priscilla asks.

"Well, I can run it through Mapquest and find out," Frances says.

She retrieves the slip of paper and turns to a computer on a credenza. While she types in the street number I clear my throat.

"So, you really can't picture this Cosmo being unkind to anyone?" I ask her.

"I really can't," Frances answers. "All the residents liked Cosmo. Every single one. He's very gentle, kind, helpful, and polite. I honestly have never seen him say or do an unkind thing."

She prints out a map and hands it to Priscilla.

I rise from my chair. "Thank you, Frances," I murmur. "And I'm sorry about my little outburst. I just wasn't prepared to deal with this. I shouldn't have blamed you. I'm really sorry."

She smiles at me. "Please don't worry about that, Alexa. I know how much you love your sister. I wish all our residents had family who cared for them the way you do."

Priscilla, Isabel, and I walk out of the Center and head to my car. I carry with me Mindy's wedding announcement and Rebecca's baby book. I feel as though I've been run over by a truck.

"Want me to drive?" Priscilla says.

The minute she says this, I picture my sister—who has been driving on British roads the last seven years—careening into oncoming traffic, and I turn in utter amazement to chastise her for suggesting something so ridiculous.

She winks at me. She's joking.

The grin that spreads across my face, as tiny as it is, feels pretty good.

14

"I can't believe she did this," I say to Priscilla as I back out of a parking space in the Falkman Center lot.

"It's not the end of the world, Lex," Priscilla says, ever the rational one.

"It's crazy!"

"Lexie, if she ran off with a man, it's highly probable she did it because she's in love. Don't pretend you don't know what that's like. We both know you do."

I feel my face color as I wait at the lot entrance for traffic to clear. "But if he is such a nice guy, such a polite and kind gardener-of-the-year, why did he sneak off with her like this?" I pull out and head toward the address Frances gave us. *Nice guys don't run off with vulnerable women!*

"You are assuming sneaking off was his idea," Priscilla says casually. "How do you know it wasn't Rebecca's idea to run away in secret? How do you know he didn't try to talk her out of it, but she insisted? Do you really think she has completely forgotten what happened the last time she fell in love with someone? Turn right here."

"Tim wasn't…Tim couldn't…that situation was hopeless, Priscilla."

"Well, maybe it was, but it broke her heart just the same."

I sigh as we drive through a busy intersection. "I just wish she would have told me."

"I think Rebecca probably thought she would not have been taken seriously if she told you or anyone else she was in love with the Falkman Center's gardener," Priscilla says. "More than likely, Cosmo would have lost his job. She wouldn't be able to see him anymore. And I suppose she figured none of her adult caregivers would be happy for her, not Frances, not Mom. I guess not even you. Next left."

For some reason Priscilla's words prick me.

"Don't you want to know that she's okay?"

"Of course I do. But if she's happy, I don't for a minute wish she was back at the Falkman Center with no one but Marietta to share her life with. I think you're hoping you can bring her back."

"I just want to make sure she's okay," I mumble.

"As do I." Priscilla pauses. "I think we're lost."

We're entering an upper-class neighborhood above Mission Valley where manicured lawns, million-dollar homes, and luxury cars abound. It doesn't seem like the kind of neighborhood where a gardener named Cosmo would live.

"This can't be right," I say, agreeing with her.

Priscilla consults the map. "We've made all the right turns. Maybe he gave his employer a bogus address."

"That just makes me feel all warm and snuggly inside," I say, feeling renewed alarm welling inside me.

"If this address is correct, it should be that brick house right there," Priscilla says. The house she's pointing to is a huge brick home with four white columns supporting an enormous roofed porch. Black shutters frame every window. Massive oak trees shade the expertly trimmed lawn.

"I have to use the loo," Isabel says from the back.

I had nearly forgotten about her.

"Hold tight, love," Priscilla says. "I don't think we'll be long here."

We stare at the house for another long minute, and then I press my foot on the accelerator and turn into the curved driveway.

"I have to ask," I say.

I leave the car running and head for the porch. The doorbell chimes inside as I press the button. A moment later the door opens, and a silver-haired woman stands before me.

"Yes?" she asks sweetly.

"Hi. I think I might be lost. I'm looking for the home of a man named Cosmo DiMarco. I don't suppose this is it?"

"You found the right place," the woman says.

"I did?" I know my eyes have widened to a ridiculous size. "Is he here?"

"No, I'm afraid he just moved from here this past weekend. He was our gardener. He lived in a cottage around back, so technically this was his address."

"Did he leave a forwarding address? Or do you know if there is any way I can get ahold of him?"

"Is something wrong?" the woman asks, concern etched in her face.

"I don't know. Perhaps. I think maybe you could help me, though."

"Would you like to come in?" She opens the door wide for me, but her voice betrays a certain hesitancy.

"Would you mind if my sister and my niece came inside as well? They are waiting in the car."

"Oh. Of course."

I motion for Priscilla and Isabel to come join me. I see Priscilla reach over to turn the car off. Within seconds they are at the door.

"My name is Alexa Poole, and this is my sister, Priscilla, and her daughter, Isabel," I say to the woman.

"I am Thelma Murdock. Won't you please come in?"

"Mummy, I have to use the loo!" Isabel says again. She is holding Clement by his tail. His pointy nose is nearly dragging on the ground.

Thelma Murdock smiles. "Second door on the left," she says as we follow her into her marble-tiled entryway.

"Thank you very much," Priscilla says, taking Isabel's hand.

"Why don't we sit in here?" Thelma asks, motioning me to a room just off the front door. It's a living room of some kind, perhaps not Thelma Murdock's formal living room, but it's nonetheless elegantly furnished. The sofas and chairs are upholstered in a dusty yellow. Oriental carpets cover the floors. Books in recessed shelves line the walls. Fresh flowers in lead crystal vases are everywhere.

"Please," she says, offering me the sofa. She takes the chair across from it. "Now, how can I help you?"

"Mrs. Murdock..."

"Please call me Thelma."

"Thank you. Thelma, Priscilla and I have an older sister

named Rebecca who lives at the Falkman Center near Balboa Park."

"Oh, yes. I know that place. It's one of our favorite charities. Lovely place. Cosmo worked there."

"Yes. Yes, he did."

Priscilla and Isabel come into the room, and Priscilla sits on the couch next to me, pulling Isabel onto her lap.

"Thelma, we think—that is, Priscilla and I—think Rebecca and Cosmo became friends at the Center. Good friends. Rebecca ran away last Friday. And we think maybe she ran away with Cosmo."

"Oh! Oh, my!" Thelma says, and she stiffens in her chair. "Are you sure?"

"Well, pretty sure. That's why we came looking for his house. We're looking for him. We just want to make sure Rebecca is all right."

"Oh, dear," Thelma says, shaking her head. "I had no idea that he…oh, dear!"

"Thelma, do you know where Cosmo is? Did he tell you where he was going?"

Thelma shakes her head. "No, no. He just came to Peter and me on Friday—Peter is my husband—and said he was getting married and moving. His mother is ill, I think. He was going to go to her."

"Married!" Priscilla and I both echo this word. She whispers it, and I nearly shriek it.

"That's what he said. He said he was getting married and moving. He didn't exactly say where. I think his mother lives in Italy somewhere. Cosmo was a very good gardener and a true gentleman. We hated to see him go."

"Italy? Are you sure his mother is in Italy?" Priscilla says. As usual, I'm shocked speechless.

"Well, I think so. He seemed genuinely sad to be leaving us, but he was also extremely happy. I've never seen Cosmo so happy."

"Did he say anything about the woman he was marrying?" Priscilla continues.

"Well, Peter and I asked about her, and he just said she was an angel sent by God, beautiful and kind. We asked if we could help him with the wedding. We even told him he could have the ceremony here at the house, but Cosmo said they wanted to be married right away because of his need to get home to his mother. They were going to go to Las Vegas and get married the next day."

I close my eyes as this new bit of information assaults me.

Rebecca. Married.

"Peter and I didn't know the woman was a resident at the Center," Thelma says, almost apologetically. "Honestly, we didn't."

Rebecca is married. That's why she took her birth certificate. She's not coming back to the Falkman Center. She's not coming back at all.

"Cosmo is a very good man," Thelma says now. "He will be a good husband. I'm sure he would give his life to protect the woman he loves. I'm sure of it."

"Can you tell us anything more about him?" Priscilla asks. "How old he is? Anything?"

"Well, he's Italian, you know. His English is very good, but it's not his first language. I think he is forty-six, maybe forty-seven. He sends money to his mother every month, and he goes to church every Sunday. I think he has some cousins in Chicago.

He had some family here too, but they moved away the same year he came. He's been with us almost three years. He worked part-time for us and part-time for the Falkman Center. He was married once a long time ago, but his wife got sick and died. That's about all I know."

I finally find my voice. "Is...would there be any point in looking in the cottage for the address of his family in Chicago?"

"Our housekeeper has already cleaned out the cottage, I'm afraid. But he had left none of his personal belongings."

Priscilla starts to get up and I numbly follow. "Thank you so much. You've been very helpful," Priscilla says, taking Isabel's hand.

"Just one moment," Thelma says, and she gets up from her chair and walks over to a large, Queen Anne escritoire at the back of the room. She opens a compartment and takes something out. She walks back to us with a 4 x 6 photograph in her hand.

"You can have this. It's a double," she says, extending the photo toward me. "This was taken last Christmas."

I look at the photo. I see a mustached man of average build with black hair turning silver at the temples, olive skin, and a wide smile. He's standing next to a roundish woman, who is also smiling broadly.

"That's Cosmo," she says, pointing to the man. "And the woman is our housekeeper."

I stare into the eyes of the man named Cosmo, the man who is most probably now married to Rebecca and my brother-in-law. His eyes look kind, his smile, genuine. He doesn't look like a serial killer or a wife-beater or a raving lunatic.

"So you hated to see him go," I say, kind of tenderly.

"Yes, we did," Thelma says, touching my arm.

"Thanks for the picture."

"You're welcome."

We head back into the late morning sunshine, wiser. Thelma watches from her lovely porch as we drive away. I honk a farewell.

Many minutes pass before Priscilla and I speak. She comes up with something first.

"Lex, just let her go. I'm sure she will not just drop off the face of the planet. When she's ready, she'll let us know where she is."

I'm not so easily swayed.

"All we know is what we *think* happened. We don't know for sure they went through with it. What if Rebecca chickened out and is sitting in Las Vegas by herself wishing one of us would come and get her?"

"Come on. You know you don't believe that."

"I don't know what I believe. I just know I'm not going to *just let her go*; like, just forget about her. That's not something I'm good at doing."

I don't mean for it to sound like a chastisement for how easily Priscilla largely ignored her family for the last seven years, but I think it comes across that way. Maybe deep down, I wanted it to sound that way.

We ride back to Mission Beach in silence.

We stop at a pizza place on the way home and bring with us a pepperoni-and-black-olive pizza for lunch out on my patio. Rafael is visiting Serafina and Jorge, and he is playing with a remote control car on Serafina's side of the patio. As soon as Isabel eats a slice, she runs off to watch him.

"So when do we tell Mom and Dad?" I ask.

Priscilla takes a long drink of her Diet Coke with lime. "I don't see much point in waiting to tell them. May as well tell Dad tonight. Mom will be ticked that he found out first, but she told us not to call her, and I don't feel like driving over to the island this afternoon, do you?"

"Not especially."

"Well, then. We'll just tell Mom tomorrow when you take Isabel and me over there."

"Yeah. Okay." But I'm wondering how Mom will react. How this might affect her. It surprises me how powerfully it's affecting me. I'm frowning, deep in thought, and Priscilla notices.

"What is it, Lex?"

"I just can't get over the fact that Rebecca is married. I mean, more than likely married."

"Why not? None of her disabilities prevent her from being married. She just can't be the one to balance the checkbook or make the Thanksgiving turkey or drive the kids to soccer practice."

"Priscilla, I just can't imagine her in bed with a man!"

"Lex..."

"What if she had no idea what she was getting into? What if when she ran off with Cosmo, she was figuring it would be like running away with Marietta?"

"Lex, Rebecca didn't write me very often, but when she did, she never gave me any indication that she was clueless as to the way of men with women. I know she often responds and reasons like a child, but that doesn't *make* her one."

"I just hope that he—that Cosmo—is gentle with her. Patient. I hope he knows the kind of person he married."

Priscilla takes another long drink and then says, "He sounds like a great guy, Lexie. A perfect gentleman. I'm practically jealous."

We're silent for a few moments.

"Priscilla, what happened between you and Isabel's father? Can I ask?"

She offers a weak smile. "You just did."

"Well, will you tell me?"

Priscilla pauses for a moment. "His name is Bernard Rousseau. I meet him four years ago at a trade show in Paris. He is Parisian and was quite the first date. Spoiled me rotten the three days I was there. I didn't sleep with him then, by the way."

She takes a drink and then continues. "He came to London often after that, and we would get together whenever he did. After five months, he was practically at my place every weekend. I *was* sleeping with him by then. In fact, it wasn't long after that that I found out I was pregnant. I didn't mean for it to happen, and he certainly didn't. He was quite put out. Mad, actually. It was this reaction to something he was equally at fault for that clued me in as to what he was really like as a person. I lashed out by telling him I wasn't even sure if he was the father. And you know what? He visibly relaxed before my eyes. He didn't care a whit that that would've meant I had been sleeping around on him. And it took me a few seconds to realize that he didn't care because *he* was sleeping around on me."

She stops for a second, and I can see that thinking about this still pains Priscilla. She takes a sip of her Coke and then continues.

"So I told him to leave my flat and my life and I would not

trouble him again. I told him the child was indeed his, that I had been with no one but him, but that I was ending our relationship and he would not have a need nor was he invited to have anything to do with the child's life. He left. And I have not seen or heard from him since."

"I'm sorry, Priscilla," I say.

She shakes her head. "I'm not. He was a jerk. I was a fool to let him woo me. Isabel is mine alone. She has my last name, not his. She knows she has a daddy in France, but she also knows he doesn't want to be a daddy because no one ever showed him how to be one. She pities him, actually."

We both watch Isabel chasing after Rafael's car as a few moments of silence again fills the air between us.

"Think you'll ever find love that really lasts?" I ask.

"I'm counting on it," she says with ease. "But no imitations the next time around. It's the real thing or nothing."

"Yes, the real thing," I say, musing. Stephen is on my mind, of course. "How will you know when it's real?"

"I'll know," she says confidently. "I knew all along Bernard wasn't my soul mate. I just let myself get carried away by his good looks and temporary affections. And it wasn't the first time. So I know what the fake stuff feels like. The real thing will be completely opposite."

Serafina comes out onto the porch and tells us she and Rafael have a date with the beach and would we like to come? A few hours lazing on the warm sand will help us prepare for the evening ahead with Dad. Priscilla and I both know this. We accept.

Minutes later, Priscilla and Isabel have changed into swimsuits and Rafael is at my front door with a wagon full of plastic sand castle-building equipment. I have changed into my suit as well, but there's something I want to do before I lose myself to the caress of the sun.

"Go on ahead," I tell Priscilla as Isabel dashes out to see what Rafael has in his wagon. "I just want to make a quick call."

"Oh?" Priscilla says, inviting me to confess my plan.

"I want to see if I can find Mindy. If I can't locate her within a few minutes, I'll be right out."

Priscilla nods and follows Isabel out the door. She doesn't even try to talk me out of it. I think she knows by now it would be useless. I'm determined to unravel at least this one mystery regarding Rebecca.

When they're gone, I head to my computer first to do a name search. I try searching for a Ronald and Mindy Bettendorf in Redondo Beach, but I only come up with one Ron Bettendorf in California, in Costa Mesa. I write down the phone number and take the slip of paper to the kitchen to give it a try.

The phone rings twice and then a woman answers.

"Mindy?" I say.

"Who is this?" The woman sounds immediately annoyed.

"This is Alexa Poole in San Diego. Is this Mindy?"

"No, it's not. If this is some kind of joke..."

"I beg your pardon?"

"Are you her lawyer?"

"No, I'm not."

"Well, you've got the wrong number. Mindy does not live here, okay?"

I'm starting to get the idea perhaps Mindy is no longer married to Ronald Bettendorf. "Do you know how I can find her?" I ask.

"You want her phone number?" the woman replies, but not in nice way.

"Yes, I would."

"Fine. I will give it to you. And then you give *her* something. You give her this message. You tell her to get a life, okay? You tell her she's not getting another penny from us."

"And you are…"

"I am Mrs. Ron Bettendorf now. That's who I am. Do you want that number or not?"

"Yes. Yes."

She rattles off the number and then hangs up before I can thank her, if indeed I would have been so inclined.

I look at the numbers I've written. The area code is in San Diego County. Mindy is somewhere close by. I press in the numbers.

It takes four rings, but finally there is a voice on the other end.

"Hello." If it is Mindy, she sounds sleepy or ill.

"Mindy?"

"Yeah. Who is this?"

"Mindy, this is Rebecca Poole's sister, Alexa."

She lets an expletive slip off her tongue, but she's not angry. She's surprised.

"Mindy, I know you and Rebecca haven't kept in touch, and I apologize for intruding on your day like this…"

But she laughs and interrupts me. "Intruding on my day? Intruding? That's a good one. Very funny. Hey, who gave you my number? It's unlisted."

"Oh. I got it from…" I have no idea what the new wife's name is.

"I'm just messing with you. I know who probably gave it to you. Darla hates my skinny guts. She's probably hoping you're from the IRS. You're not, are you?"

"No, I'm not. I…"

"Good. Well, well, well! I haven't seen Rebecca since…since my joke of a wedding. So is she still living at that place?"

"Actually, Mindy, that's why I've looked you up. Rebecca's run off. We think she may have eloped, and…"

"Really? Eloped? Wow! Well, go figure."

"And I've been trying to figure where she went. I found something in her room, Mindy, and I have been at a loss to figure out what it means. I thought maybe you could help me. Someone who knows about this mentioned your name. I don't know if it will help me find her, but I feel like it will help me understand what was going through her head."

Mindy, for a blessed moment, is at last silent.

But then she speaks and her voice is suddenly charged with curiosity. "You found something?"

"Yes, I…"

"Something small and flat and made of paper?"

I pause for a second before saying, "Yes."

"Oh, I know what you found," she says rather slyly. "You found the check."

15

Priscilla is not overly thrilled when I join her on the beach and tell her I not only found Mindy but that we're also going to stop and see her in Carlsbad on our way to Dad's. Her first concern is that Isabel will be with us, and she doesn't want her daughter overhearing troublesome talk. I quickly assure her that I've arranged to meet Mindy at a city park. Isabel can play on the playground while we chat. I also tell her that Mindy has a child of her own and will most likely bring him.

"She knows about the check, Priscilla," I tell her as I sit in a beach chair next to her. "She mentioned it before I did. As soon as I told her I had found something unexplainable in Rebecca's room, she knew it was the check."

Priscilla nods and looks out toward the shoreline where Rafael and Serafina are building a sand castle. Isabel is near them building one of her own, a monolithic-looking thing that will surely topple within minutes.

"I hope we're not stirring up something Rebecca would rather we had left to lie still," Priscilla finally says.

"I can't help but think Rebecca was pressured into doing something she later wished she hadn't done. And you know what else? I think Mindy got a check too. But Mindy cashed hers and Rebecca didn't. I think Gavin McNeil owes us an explanation, if nothing else. Don't you wonder why Leanne just honked at the curb the night of the accident? And why Mindy and Rebecca had had an argument on the phone earlier that evening? And why Gavin and Kevin McNeil kept showing up after the accident to visit with Rebecca?"

"Actually, Lex, no...I really haven't wondered about those things. What's done is done. Nothing Mindy can tell you will change what happened."

I pause for a moment. "I know that, but I look at how that night changed us all, and I can't help but think we deserve an explanation. Our family was never the same after that, Priscilla. It altered Rebecca's life in countless ways. It drove you away from Mom and Dad—and even from me—it made Mom a paranoid wreck, and it destroyed our parents' marriage."

Priscilla bolts up from her beach chair. "I don't want to discuss this anymore, Lex. You want to see Mindy, we'll go see Mindy."

She walks away from me just as Isabel's creation folds in on itself.

"*Ne t'inquiéte pas, chérie,*" Priscilla says in French as Isabel lets out a cry of frustration. "Just build another one," she adds in English.

I stay where I am, watching as Priscilla clears away the "rubble" so Isabel can start over.

We leave at three thirty, freshly showered and somewhat mentally prepared. Isabel has fallen asleep in the back when we arrive in Carlsbad. I park near the children's playground as Mindy suggested. If Isabel wakes up, she will be able to stay close to us. Priscilla opens all the windows and we get out of the car to sit at a picnic table a few yards away.

A few minutes after four, a silver Honda Accord pulls up, and though the years have changed her, it's obviously Mindy at the wheel. Next to her on the passenger side is a boy who looks as though he's about ten. They get out and the boy immediately heads for the play structure. Mindy walks up to us, holding a can of Dr Pepper and a pack of cigarettes. She's visibly startled at seeing Priscilla and me. She verbalizes an expletive that's really not needed.

"I forgot how much you two look alike. It's scary!" She walks over to us and sits down at the table. Priscilla and I had stood when she arrived, but now we sit also. Mindy is lean, tanned, and just beginning to wrinkle, and her sandy blond hair is dry and brittle. She's wearing a sleeveless black top and white capris. Several toe rings decorate her feet.

"Which one of you is which?" she asks, tossing her pack of cigarettes onto the wooden tabletop.

"I'm Alexa. This is Priscilla," I say.

Mindy looks around. "So one of you has a kid?"

"Isabel is asleep in the car," Priscilla says, almost coolly. She and Mindy never did get along.

"Is that accent for real?" Mindy asks, clearly amused.

Priscilla bristles beside me and I quickly answer. "Priscilla has lived in London the past few years. Is that your son?" I nod with my head to the boy who had been in her car and is now swinging with all his might several yards away.

"Yep. That's Cole. He's the only good thing that came out of my marriage. Well, him and child support." She turns away from looking at Cole and addresses us. "It's not enough, though. Not for Southern California. I wonder if those judges ever tried raising a kid on their own with what they order fathers to pay."

I have no desire to discuss Mindy's financial woes, which appear to be many. I clear my throat. "So, Mindy, about what I found..."

"Can I see it?" Mindy interrupts.

"If you mean the check, no. I didn't bring it," I answer.

"Why not?" She seems disappointed.

"Because you obviously know what it's for, and I felt it best to keep it in a safe place."

Mindy smiles. "I can't say as I blame you there," she says, winking. "That check may turn out to be worth a lot more than $50,000, if you know what I mean."

Priscilla stirs beside me. If we were still kids, Priscilla probably would have hauled off and slugged Mindy by now. I want to be finished with this conversation as much as she does. But first, I want answers.

"Can you tell us why Rebecca has it?" I ask, masking my growing dislike for Mindy's personality.

"Oh, can I!" she says, clearly enjoying herself. "I thought for sure Rebecca had torn that thing up. Lucky for her she didn't."

"What happened? Why did Gavin McNeil give it to her?"

"Because he is a lying..."

Mindy then proceeds to describe the kind of liar Gavin is with language that I don't use or care to hear.

"Was it a bribe?" I ask, struggling to maintain a civil tone.

"You're darn right it was a bribe! And it wasn't nearly enough for what he expected us to do for him!"

"What did he ask you to do?"

"You really want to hear the whole thing?"

"Yes."

"Okay, but if you're going after Gavin, I want to be in on it. We split it fifty-fifty. Half for you two, half for me."

Priscilla stiffens beside me. "Lex," she says through her teeth.

"Just tell us what happened," I say.

"Okay, okay," Mindy says. "Well, it started with Leanne and this loser of a guy she met at the library our freshman year at UCSB. He was a poet or an artist, I don't know which, but he was certainly a bum. He lived in someone's backyard; he slept on a chaise lounge, if you can believe that, and I know he only came to the library to meet rich college girls. His name was James Leahy.

"Okay, so one day he meets Leanne, and he likes her, of course, 'cause her dad is rich, and he starts writing her poetry and stuff and laying it on thick, like he's Don Juan. Well, Leanne falls for it, and pretty soon she decides she just has to marry the guy. Rebecca kind of thought he was cute and harmless, but I could see right through him. I knew he went after Leanne for the bucks.

"Anyway, Leanne comes home one weekend and tells her parents she has met the man she's going to marry and that she wants to bring him home the following weekend so they can meet him. Well, as soon as Leanne tells Gavin that James is an unemployed poet living on someone's patio furniture, he has a total fit and tells her there's no way she's marrying him, that a guy like that is only interested in one thing: her money. Leanne comes back mad and hurt, 'cause, you know, she thought her dad was saying she wasn't pretty or nice because he said all James wanted was her money. She tells Rebecca and me she's going to run off and elope. She calls her parents and tells them that's what she's going to do if they don't change their minds, and Gavin tells her he'll see James dead before he lets him have one cent of his money.

"Well, Leanne is head over heels in love with the bum, so she hangs up on Gavin. And she and James start making plans. The very next day, guess who calls Rebecca? Gavin McNeil. He tells her he loves his daughter and doesn't want her to throw her life away on this scoundrel. He tells Rebecca that as Leanne's best friend, he knows she doesn't want Leanne to throw her life way, either. He says he has a proposition for her. Bring the poet down to San Diego without Leanne's knowledge so that he can have a word with him. He tells Rebecca that he knows that the guy just wants money, and Gavin is prepared to give some to him. He just needs a few minutes of his time. And he will pay Rebecca to do it.

"So Rebecca tells Gavin she won't do it alone. And Gavin tells her to bring me along. He will pay us both. So that's what we did.

"That Thursday morning, when we knew Leanne had classes all day, Rebecca and I skipped our own classes, drove over to this house where James was, you know, 'staying,' and we told him Leanne's father had asked to speak with him and that we would take him and bring him back.

"Well, the guy comes with us and the whole drive down he's talking like this is the opportunity he's been wanting: a chance to talk to Leanne's parents himself because he really loves Leanne, blah, blah, blah. And Rebecca, I can tell, kind of likes this guy, and she's starting to think maybe he's really not interested in the money after all.

"Anyway, we get to Leanne's and it's midday. Kevin is there, but Lenore is not. We're told to wait in the kitchen while the men talk. Gavin and Kevin and James go into Gavin's study. Well, I didn't drive three hours to listen to the fridge go on and off, so I sneak over to the study door to listen and Rebecca follows me.

"It doesn't take long for Gavin to get all hot and bothered. He starts to raise his voice because James isn't accepting any of his offers. So they start yelling at each other, cursing and stuff. And then Gavin says, 'You're making a huge mistake by messing with me. I know what you're up to.' And then we hear someone fall or something and Kevin yells his dad's name. And then there are more shouts and we can hear those two fighting, slugging each other, and stuff breaking and Kevin yelling the whole time. I'm surprised all the neighbors didn't hear it. Then suddenly it got real quiet.

"Rebecca and I are lookin' at each other, wondering if they knocked each other out. Then we hear Gavin say, 'Get up and get out of my house!' And Kevin says something like, 'Dad, he's not coming around.' And Gavin curses and tells Kevin to go get some brandy.

"Okay, well, right then the door opens and Rebecca and I get caught with our ears practically glued to it, but Kevin just walks past us. We can see inside the room. James is lying on the floor and his face is all bloody and his nose is, like, all flat. And Gavin is yelling at him to get up. Then Gavin leans down and pulls James by his shoulders, shaking him and that's when we see James' eyes. They are rolled back in his head. Open but not open, you know what I mean? Kevin comes in with the bottle of brandy and he sees James' eyes too. Gavin lets James fall back on the floor and there isn't a sound from him. No moanin' or nothing. He was *dead*. I knew he was."

"My God." The words are out of my mouth before I can

make them a true appeal to the Almighty. I can hardly believe what I'm hearing, but I have no doubts that Mindy is telling the truth. Or at least what she believes is the truth.

"Yeah. Well, get this," Mindy continues. "Gavin turns to Rebecca and me in the doorway. Rebecca is crying. First he tells Kevin to get us out of there. Then he stands up and comes to us and says James is just knocked out. He'll come around. And when he does, he will pay him and send him on his way. We don't have to worry about it. But he's not fooling me for a second.

"I ask him what are we supposed to tell Leanne? And Gavin says, 'You tell her nothing. She's not going to ask you how come James isn't sleeping on someone's patio anymore. For her own sake, tell her nothing. Tell *no one anything.*' And I looked at him and I said, 'That's a big secret to keep, Mr. McNeil,' 'cause I knew what he was asking us to do. I knew James was dead. And that weasel looked at me and said he would make sure Rebecca and I were both well compensated for protecting Leanne from a money-hungry bum. That's what he said. Well compensated."

Mindy pauses. My mind is reeling with images. I can scarcely picture Rebecca witnessing all of this. Partnering with Gavin in this horrible charade. Priscilla is silent next to me. I can see her chest rising and falling, but she makes no sound.

"So he paid you each fifty thousand dollars for your silence?" I whisper.

"That's right," Mindy says. "He paid us fifty grand to pretend we didn't see him kill a man."

"And you're sure James was dead?"

"Oh, he was dead all right."

"I don't see how a simple fist fight could…" I begin, but Mindy cuts me off.

"That's 'cause it wasn't a simple fist fight! Gavin had a black belt in karate, remember? He struck James in the nose with the heel of his hand in a fit of rage. All those bits of bone at the bridge of the nose slammed into James' brain. He was dead as soon as he hit the floor, I'm sure of it."

Priscilla moves slightly next to me. "How do you know this is possible?" she says.

"Because I took Tae Kwon Do in high school, sweetie. You can do the same thing with a well-placed elbow strike if you hit hard and fast enough."

"Rebecca." I say my sister's name for no other reason than to express my horror at what she saw. And what she agreed to do.

"Oh, she was a mess," Mindy says at the mention of my sister's name. "I had to drive us back to Santa Barbara. And I had to convince Leanne that Rebecca had a terrible case of the flu to explain the shell shock. By the next day Leanne didn't seem to care Rebecca had such a nasty case of the flu 'cause she was already lamenting the sudden disappearance of the bum."

"And what happened to James?" I say, finally understanding the hell Rebecca went through.

"Who knows? My guess is Gavin disposed of the body somehow. Probably took him out on his sailboat and dumped him in the ocean."

"No one ever came looking for him?" I ask.

"Why would they? He was a drifter. No one else around the campus was surprised he just up and left. He was a bum. That's what bums do."

"And Leanne?"

"Well, Leanne took it harder than I thought she would. Three weeks later when the semester was over and we all moved home for the summer, she was still miserable. It was pathetic. And it was driving Rebecca nuts."

"Did she think James was dead too?"

Mindy shifts in her seat. "I dunno. We didn't talk about it. She didn't want to."

"She never cashed the check," I continue, though the three of us already know this.

"No, and *that* was driving Gavin nuts. It was actually driving me nuts too. Rebecca started wanting to tell the truth to Leanne, and I told her that was a stupid idea. It would ruin their friendship and probably Leanne's relationship with her dad. But Rebecca kept saying it was wrong what we did. She just wouldn't let it go. On the day of the accident she told me she couldn't live with it anymore. She was going to tell Leanne the truth, that Gavin was responsible for James' disappearance. I was furious with her, but she wouldn't listen to me.

"I honestly don't know when or how she did it, but I suspect when Leanne came to your house that night to get Rebecca, Leanne already knew something was up with me and Rebecca and her dad and that it involved James. Rebecca had told her that much. Unless you know something I don't, no one knows what happened after Rebecca got into the car with her. Rebecca told me when she was still in the hospital that she didn't remember the accident at all. I think Leanne went suicidal when she found out, that's what I think. Anyway, before I left for Pepperdine, I went to visit Rebecca one last time, at Gavin's request. I asked her about James. She said she didn't remember taking James down to see Gavin. She said she didn't remember anything about a check."

I'm fairly certain that Rebecca *did* remember the check, at least that she had it and that it represented something terrible.

I'm certain she had been lying to Mindy and the McNeils when they questioned her about it, using her terrible injuries as a cover-up. I'm also certain Mindy came back to Gavin at some point for more money.

"I take it you didn't stop at fifty thousand," I say.

Mindy looks a little startled.

"Kevin accused me of being in partnership with you," I continue. "He seemed to think I was planning to extort money from him."

Mindy tosses her head. "Look, I'm not the one who's guilty here," she says hotly. "Gavin is the one who killed James. He's the one who bribed us to play his dirty little game. It's not my fault!"

"I think we need to go. We'll be late," Priscilla says coolly. She has been silent this whole time.

Mindy looks to Priscilla and then back to me. "Late for what? Are you meeting with him? 'Cause if you are, remember I'm in on it. That was the deal."

Priscilla rises from her place at the table. Isabel is still asleep, but she walks to the car and gets in, slamming the door.

"What's *her* problem?" Mindy asks me.

"Thanks, Mindy," I say, ignoring her question and standing up myself.

"Hey! What about my half?"

"I never said I was interested in making any money off this. What happened to Leanne and my sister and James ought never to have happened, but I'm glad to finally know the truth. It needed to be told. I appreciate that."

I start to walk away. Behind me I hear Mindy curse.

I get into the car and start the engine. Mindy is standing by the table with her hands on her hips watching us drive way. She looks livid.

I drive off and am two blocks away when Priscilla says, "So now you know."

"Yes."

"And?"

"I'm glad we know the truth, Priscilla. I'm glad to know that Rebecca regretted what happened, that she felt remorse over what she agreed to. I'm glad she wasn't like Mindy. And I think she kept that check because she *did* remember that she had it, but for some reason she couldn't bring herself to destroy it. That's the only explanation that makes sense. And I think when she left with Cosmo, she really wanted to be free of it at last. That's why she wrote the second note."

Priscilla doesn't argue with me.

I have to believe it's because in spite of her earlier misgivings about my wanting to find out the truth about the check, she knows I'm right. Not only does knowing the truth help us understand what probably happened in Leanne's car that night, it shines a whole new light on what Rebecca was like before the accident robbed her of so much. Yes, she was independent. Yes, she was headstrong. But she had a compassionate heart. And an honest one.

We say little as we drive the rest of the way to Dad's. Priscilla is no doubt lost in troubling thoughts just as I am, not the least of which is what we are supposed to do with the knowledge that a man named James Leahy very likely died in the McGavin house seventeen years ago from a lethal blow to the face.

16

As we take an exit off Interstate 5 for San Juan Capistrano, I sense Priscilla is breathing differently. I'm trying to imagine what she must be feeling, but it's hard to put myself in her shoes, even though she is my twin. Her extreme hostility toward Dad since he divorced Mom has always baffled me somewhat.

My father, Merrill Poole, is not the easiest person to get along with. Even before Rebecca's accident, Dad was a bit unapproachable. He was stingy with showing affection; at least, that's how I saw it growing up. He was passionate about his job, and I suppose he was very good at what he did—contract negotiations—but that passion kept him away from home a lot. When he was home, he seemed happy to be there, but most of the time he was exhausted from his schedule. He liked his solitude when he was home. I remember him losing himself to weekend sports on TV and the Narcolepsy Couch—my and Priscilla's name for the sofa in the family room. Dad didn't mind helping us girls with our homework or teaching us how to fix a flat tire or even

handing down discipline when we had broken a rule, but I think
he liked doing those fatherly things because he could perform
them at a safe distance. There wasn't a great deal of emotional
involvement in helping Priscilla and me understand fractions.

To be fair, I was mad at him, too, when he moved out. It was
as though he was running away from the family *he* had decided
to begin. Worse, he did what the rest of us also really wanted
to do and figured we couldn't: He escaped. I was mad because
I felt he was supposed to be the captain. The captain always
stays with the sinking ship. But Dad bailed, leaving his wife
and daughters to struggle to stay afloat on a boat that seemed
doomed.

I couldn't stay mad at him year after year, though, not the
way Priscilla did. I didn't have it within me. I saw what that
kind of bitterness did to her and to my mother, and I just didn't
want to live that way. I'm glad for Priscilla's sake that she's
decided she's had enough of it herself.

I pull into Dad and Lynne's driveway. It's a nice house in a
well-to-do neighborhood. Dad and Lynne both work in Irvine,
but they choose to live in San Juan Capistrano because the quaint
seaside town is slightly removed from the chaos of urban sprawl
that starts a few miles away in Mission Viejo and spreads north
to Los Angeles like a thick oil spill. Isabel has been awake for the
last fifteen minutes and is eager to get out of her car seat.

"*Un instant, chérie,*" Priscilla says to Isabel over her shoulder.
Then she turns to me. "You're going to keep secret what Rebecca
asked you to keep secret, right?"

As much as I wanted to know the truth behind that check,
I agree with Priscilla on this. I'm glad I was the one to find it,
and not Mom, and I'm even glad to know how Rebecca came
to have it. But Priscilla is right. Mom and Dad do not *need* to

know about it. Someday they may want to know, but this isn't the time. And it's not me who should tell them. This is Rebecca's story to tell.

"Of course," I answer.

"Good." Priscilla puts her hand on the handle of the car door. "Well, let's do this."

"It'll be okay, Pris," I say, wanting to encourage her.

"Just don't expect a miracle, Lex," she says, opening the door.

Priscilla helps Isabel out and the three of us walk up to the front door. Before I have a chance to ring the doorbell, it opens. Dad has been watching for us. He stands there, dressed in khaki pants and a silk camp shirt, with a look on his face that I don't see very often. I guess "apprehensive" describes it best.

His eyes seek out Priscilla first, but because I speak to him before she does, he quickly turns his face to me, unwillingly perhaps.

"Hi, Dad," I say, leaning forward and kissing him on the cheek. "We're here."

"Hi," he says absently, but his gaze has already wandered away from me. Again his eyes fall on my sister. "Priscilla," he says simply.

"Hullo, Dad," she says, and I can see my dad's eyes widen at the accented lilt in her voice.

Dad hasn't asked us in yet, and though I'm sure he will, it's awkward just standing there while he acclimates himself to the idea that Priscilla has spoken to him. He leans toward her, as though he wants to embrace her, but he stops short and lays his hand on her shoulder for just a moment. He quickly removes it and steps aside.

"Please come in," he says, and his voice sounds strange.

As we file past him, he seems to notice Isabel for the first time. "You must be Isabel," he says, in a slightly less nervous tone.

"And this is my seahorse," Isabel says, thrusting Clement up so that Dad can get a good look at him. "I'm three," she continues, holding up her free hand and extending three fingers forward like a fat lower case *w*.

"Very nice to meet you both," Dad says, a little awkwardly.

We've made it past the flagstone entry when Laird appears at the entrance to the open kitchen area.

"Laird!" I say in surprise. "You're here!"

I see Priscilla turning her head toward me, no doubt wondering if I've tricked her and that the next person we will see pop out of the kitchen is Lynne.

"Laird wanted to see you very much. And he absolutely insisted on meeting Isabel because she makes him an uncle," Dad says, laughing, but it's an anxious laugh. "Lynne is visiting her parents tonight. Laird, this is Priscilla, and this is her daughter—your niece!—Isabel."

"Hi," Laird says, looking at Priscilla uneasily. He has always known he has a half sister named Priscilla and that she's my twin, but it's obvious that actually seeing my genetic clone in the flesh is ponderous to his ten-year-old mind.

"I thought we'd eat out on the patio," Dad says. "I've ordered some pasta and it's already here, so why don't we head that way?"

That he so quickly gets us to the dinner table is proof that he's wishing to fill every moment we're here so that no uncomfortable pauses occur. I can't blame him, but rushing out to the patio after just arriving seems a bit poorly timed.

"I think Isabel may want to use the restroom first," Priscilla says.

"Oh! Oh, sure. Laird, why don't you show them where the bathroom is."

Laird takes off down a carpeted hall and Priscilla and Isabel follow. Dad brushes past me and makes for the kitchen. I tag after him.

"Is white wine okay?" he asks as he scurries about the kitchen grabbing napkins and glasses. "I have some red too. But it's Alfredo I've ordered. I got a pizza for the kids. They'll probably be happy with root beer, don't you think?"

"Dad," I say.

"What?"

"Just relax, okay? Slow down. You're making *me* nervous."

He halts his rushing around for a minute and looks at me. "Yeah. Okay. I'm just not used to this."

"Used to what? Eating?" I ask, grinning.

"You know what I mean," he says, turning and walking out to the patio.

I follow him. Within moments, Priscilla, Isabel, and Laird have returned, and we all take our places around a glass-topped patio table.

It's a beautiful evening and a slight ocean breeze keeps the flies away as we eat. Dad asks Isabel to tell him all about London, and she obliges by eagerly describing their flat overlooking the Thames, as well as her friend Gemma who lives down the hall from her and her distaste for Yorkshire pudding. Isabel's juvenile chatter mixed with Laird's occasional comments keeps the mealtime conversation light and casual. Priscilla answers questions as they're asked directly of her, but briefly and without a lot of enthusiasm. She lets Isabel carry most of the conversation.

As we eat cheesecake for dessert, I explain to Dad that Priscilla and I have a pretty good idea that Rebecca ran off to get married. We tell him about Cosmo and the likelihood that Rebecca married him last Saturday in Las Vegas. We also tell him we have no idea where they went after that, that it could possibly be Chicago or even Italy, but there are no guarantees.

"Wow," Dad says, absorbing the news pretty well. "Well, if he's as nice a guy as these people say, then I guess I'm happy for her. It's high time something nice happened to Rebecca. I wish they hadn't just run off, though."

"When I find out where she is, I'll let you know," I tell him.

"Yes, please. By all means." He pauses for a moment. "I guess that means she won't be moving back to the Falkman Center."

"I highly doubt it," I say.

He nods. "Think you will need help moving out her things?"

It's a charitable thing to say. He knows he won't be needed. Clothing, books, and knickknacks are Rebecca's only personal belongings at the Center, but it's nice of him to ask.

"I'm sure Mom and I can handle it," I say, "but thanks."

When the children are finished with their dessert, Isabel asks Laird if she can see his room and the two of them leave. Dad watches them go with an unmistakable pained look on his face. He's dreading being alone with Priscilla and me.

Come on, Dad. Don't blow it now, I say in my head. I mentally implore him to make the first move. It seems to take forever, but at last he turns to Priscilla.

"Priscilla, I'm so glad you decided to come," he says, and he does sound as though he really means it.

Priscilla doesn't say anything in return. She's probably thinking, *Well, why wouldn't you be glad? Should I have expected you'd be mad that I came?*

"And Isabel is a beautiful little girl," he continues, although somewhat apprehensively.

"Yes," Priscilla says. "She's the one completely wonderful thing that has ever happened to me. It surprises me to no end that God gave her to me."

Dad smiles as though he thinks he's making an inroad. I have my doubts, though. I know Priscilla a little better than he does. "Why would it surprise you?" he says.

"Because people like us don't deserve treasures like Isabel," she says calmly. Quietly. As though she's only speaking to him.

Dad fidgets a little. "Like us?"

"I know it wasn't the smartest thing to have kept you at a distance all these years, but closing that distance now doesn't mean I was wrong about you."

Oh, Priscilla. Can't you just let it go?

Dad says nothing for a second, but then he sits back in his chair. He looks angry, in a sad kind of way. "Why did you even bother to come if it's still going to be like this between you and me?"

"Because the way it is right now is not the way it was before," Priscilla says, and again I get the impression she is purposely speaking in low tones. Maybe I should excuse myself.

But I don't.

"It sure seems like nothing has changed." Dad sounds defeated.

"Before, you and I were not honest with each other. I'm now

being completely honest with you. I'd like for you to be honest with me."

"You call this being honest? For Pete's sake, I thought you were coming so that we could finally be done with all this, Priscilla!"

"That is indeed why I came, Dad. I do want to be done with it."

"Well, you sure don't seem like it."

Priscilla is completely under control. I think maybe she has had this conversation in her head a thousand times. She knows exactly what she will say no matter what comes out of Dad's mouth.

And I still am unable—or unwilling—to leave the patio.

"That's because you want to pretend the past never happened. And that's just not possible. You desire something that is impossible to have," she says. "To be done living in the past does not mean you pretend the past didn't happen. It means you learn to accept that it did. I'm choosing to accept the past because I want Isabel to know her family. My family is the only one she has. But my choosing this doesn't change who you are anymore than it changes who I am."

Dad throws up his hands, but his face looks different. It's as though he has been caught with his hand in the cookie jar. I'm not entirely sure what this means.

"People," Dad says, swallowing before he finishes, "can change, Priscilla."

"I'm sure they can, but the past doesn't change. It stays the same. And I'm telling you the past is not something you can ignore."

Dad sighs. "So it's going to be war between us for the rest of our lives?" he asks sadly.

"No," Priscilla says calmly. "It's going to be truth between us. I have made the first move."

Isabel comes running out of the house and onto the patio. "Mummy! Come see his lizard! Come see!"

"What does Laird have, love?" Priscilla asks with ease, turning to her daughter.

"He has a guana!"

"An iguana?"

"Yes, come see!"

"Excuse me," Priscilla says to Dad and me. She rises from the table and follows a prancing Isabel back into the house.

Dad watches her go and then turns back to me, shaking his head.

"She's so stubborn," he says.

"She's just like you," I reply.

"For crying out loud, it's been, what, fifteen years since the divorce? It's time she realized life isn't always perfect."

"Dad, we all dealt with what happened to our family in different ways," I begin, but he cuts me off.

"But you got over it! It didn't scar you for life!"

Well, that's not exactly true. I have my scars. Any child of divorce does.

"Dad, the accident and your leaving Mom hurt me too. In lots of ways."

Dad shakes his head as though he's annoyed with me. "I'm not talking about *that*. I'm talking about Lynne! It's not like I planned it."

Okay, I'm a little confused. "I thought we *were* talking about Lynne," I say.

"I'm not talking about Lynne *after* the accident. I'm talking about Lynne *before* the accident! I didn't plan that! I didn't want that to happen. It just did."

My mouth drops open. I feel my lips separate as the shock of what my father is saying envelops me. *Lynne before the accident. Lynne before the accident.*

"What are you saying?" I whisper.

"What?" Dad asks, looking at me. He had been talking to the air off to his left.

"What are you saying?" I ask again, a little louder.

"What do you mean, what am I saying?"

"What do you mean 'Lynne before the accident'?"

Now his mouth drops open as the same kind of nauseating shock envelops him.

He doesn't say anything at first, but he doesn't need to. I'm finally beginning to understand why Priscilla has held on to her bitterness for so long. Dad had been with Lynne *before* the accident. Somehow Priscilla had known this. She must have seen them together. And he had assumed, all these years, that Priscilla had told me, that she had ratted on him to me. He assumed I knew but that I had chosen to overlook his faults. He didn't know Priscilla had kept his horrible secret from me. Priscilla had let me think the worst thing my father had done was that he fell in love with another woman while mired in grief for his gravely wounded firstborn child.

It all makes sense.

It was why Priscilla had stopped talking to Dad a few months before he moved out. It was why Priscilla reacted the way she did in the restaurant when Dad told us he was marrying Lynne, when it seemed as though falling in love with her was something that had just happened within the last few months. It was why, just days ago, Priscilla refused to discuss with me why she had such a falling out with Dad all those years ago. It was why earlier today she had bolted from her beach chair when I said the horror of Rebecca's accident had destroyed our parents' marriage.

Priscilla had known that Dad was cheating on Mom *before* Rebecca got hurt. Dad didn't run into the arms of another woman because of the accident. He was already involved with Lynne when he got the call in Tokyo.

This is what Priscilla meant minutes ago when she said it wasn't war she wanted between herself and Dad. It was truth. She wanted them to be honest with each other. Honest about the past. And the truth was, Rebecca's accident wasn't the cause of the disintegration of my parents' marriage. It was just ordinary, age-old infidelity.

I can't stop the tears that are forming in my eyes.

"Oh, Alexa! She didn't tell you," Dad is saying, almost whispering it. "She never told you, did she?"

He leans forward and places his head in his hands.

He had been dead wrong about Priscilla.

And I had been dead wrong about him.

I'm still in a state of stunned shock when Priscilla, Isabel, and Laird come back out to the patio a few minutes later. I hastily get up under the pretense of wanting to take the wine glasses into the kitchen, but I've already caught Priscilla's attention. She's eyeing me, wondering what Dad said while she was in the house that has upset me.

I flee the patio with the glasses and hope with all my heart that she doesn't follow me. Wise Priscilla. She does not.

I spend several long minutes taking deep breaths and willing my trembling heart to be still. For the first time in a couple days my incision is pounding with pain.

Do not think about it now, I tell myself. *Do not! Do not!*

I want to leave. I want to get in my car and go home where I can take in this new knowledge on my own turf, but Priscilla and my dad are finally speaking to one another after fifteen years of silence. I can't suggest leaving until Priscilla is ready to go. I wash the glasses and place them in a drainer, focusing on the task and trying at the same time to cleanse my mind of troubling thoughts.

I turn from the sink and look out the patio doors. Isabel and Laird are playing on Laird's massive swing set. Priscilla and my father are still on the patio, standing a few feet away from each other. I see them talking. I see Dad shake his head. I see him lean against one of the posts that holds up the patio roof.

I can imagine their conversation.

All this time I thought you had told her. Dad

What would have been the good of her knowing? Priscilla

Does your mother know?

Do you really have to ask that? I kept your nasty secret just like you begged me to. But I'm done keeping secrets for you. And from others. It isn't fair to anyone, least of all Rebecca.

Rebecca!

You've let everyone think the stress of her accident and the extent of her injuries is what led to the failure of your marriage. That's a lie. And I won't live with it anymore. Neither should you.

Are you actually suggesting I tell your mother?

You should be asking yourself what you should be doing. You should be asking yourself what you're willing to live with.

They're silent now. I wait a few seconds to see if they will resume the conversation, but neither one says anything. I slide open the door and walk out to join them, and I can't look into the eyes of either one. I watch Laird and Isabel as they repeatedly go down Laird's curving slide.

Up and down. Up and down. Up and down.

Finally Dad speaks. "I'm sorry, Alexa. I thought you knew."

Words will not form in my mouth. I just nod.

Dad looks off toward his son and his granddaughter. Laird is pushing Isabel on one of the swings. "So is this what you wanted, Priscilla? To have it all out in the open? Because now it is."

I think it's on the tip of his tongue to add, "I hope you're satisfied." I'm so glad he does not.

"No, Dad. I didn't want it to be all out in the open," Priscilla says. "If I had wanted that I would have told Alexa a long time ago. And Mom too, for that matter. I want for you and me to be honest with each other about what happened."

Dad turns to her. "What do you want me to do, Priscilla?" he says. He sounds tired. I feel as tough I'm invisible, as though I'm not even here and my father and sister are having the conversation they should have had ages ago without me present.

"You lied to me about Lynne," Priscilla says calmly. "For two and a half years you lived a charade in front of me, buying my complicity with a promise I don't think you really ever intended to keep. You told me your affair with Lynne was a momentary indiscretion. And I was naive enough to believe you."

"Priscilla, I…" he says but Priscilla continues.

"But month after month after month you were living two lives. The one you let me think you were living and the one you really were."

Dad throws up his hands and paces a few steps. He probably has never used this lovely patio for confessions like this one. "Do you want me to tell you I'm sorry? Is that what you want?"

"Believe me, Dad, the last thing I want is an apology if you don't mean it. Let's not trade one farce for another."

"But I *am* sorry! I didn't want any of this to happen!"

"Oh, please, Dad! This did not *happen!*" Priscilla says, raising her voice just a fraction. "You chose it! And then you let the world believe that the mighty hand of fate that crushed Rebecca crushed your marriage as well. You and I both know that's not true. It's time we both acknowledged that."

They're both silent for a moment.

"So where does this leave us, Priscilla?" Dad says.

Priscilla regards him with a look that almost resembles pity. "It leaves us in the blistering light of truth, Dad. It's where I want to be. It's where I want to raise my daughter. And if you want to be a part of her life, you're going to have to meet us there."

The way she says this reminds me of that long ago day when we were at the restaurant and Priscilla was seconds away from fleeing the table. Dad had said, "If you choose not to have a relationship with me, then obviously you are making a choice I'm going to have to learn to live with. Just like you are going to have to learn to live with my choices." Only this time Priscilla is laying down the challenge.

I find myself praying to a God I'm just beginning to know better, thanks to Stephen. *Don't let him walk away like Priscilla did. Please, God. Don't let him walk away.*

I think maybe Dad also hears the echo from this aged conversation.

"Priscilla," he says, and at first he does not look at her. But then he raises his head, lifts his eyes to meet her eyes. "I'm really very sorry for what I did to you. I've always been sorry, but I didn't think you would ever forgive me."

For the first time Priscilla looks as though she's close to tears. I can see her willing the tears to stay put. "You never asked."

Dad closes his eyes and swallows. I'm sure it's very hard for him to wrestle with his pride and come out on top.

"Please forgive me, Priscilla," he says, and I can hear his voice breaking when he says her name.

She swallows too. They are so alike. "I'm learning to," she finally says.

A breeze stirs around us, picking up a stray napkin off the patio table. It takes flight and is whisked away to a bank of ice plant, but no one chases after it. The air seems charged with the physical weight of Priscilla and Dad's truce. No one says anything for several long minutes.

"She's a beautiful little girl," Dad says finally, gazing at Isabel.

"Yes, she is," Priscilla replies.

And we stand that way for a long time watching the kids play in the last rays of sunshine. Finally, Priscilla tells Dad that we need to get going. Dad asks when he will see her and Isabel again. Priscilla says perhaps she and Isabel will come over for a few days at Christmas. She doesn't promise and he doesn't insist.

At the door Dad and Priscilla share an awkward hug. Isabel plants a kiss on his cheek that brings a fresh round of tears to his eyes. When he turns to me, he can barely look at me.

"Alexa," he begins, but I touch his shoulder as if to ward off what he wants to say.

"We'll talk about it another time," I say. I need time to think.

To digest. It's enough for me at this moment to know that he and Priscilla are no longer at war.

We say our goodbyes and get into my car. Isabel holds up Clement at the open car window, nodding his head in farewell to Dad and Laird as they stand at the threshold. Clement's sequined body shimmers under the streetlight above us as we drive away.

17

Isabel chatters away for the first twenty minutes of our drive home. She finally nods off when we reach the open landscape of Camp Pendleton, a Marine Corps base and a long stretch of government land that separates Los Angeles from San Diego. Priscilla and I are finally free to speak to each other about our evening with Dad.

"Look, Lex," she says when she's sure Isabel is asleep. "I had really hoped to speak to Dad alone about all this. I never meant for you to find out that he had been having an affair with Lynne long before Rebecca's accident. This was something Dad and I had to clear up between us. I had to, if I was going share Isabel with him."

"But how did you find out?" I ask. Perhaps it's only out of morbid curiosity that I do, but she answers me anyway.

"I found them together. At our house. Rebecca had just gone back to college after Christmas break. Grandma Ardell was still alive, and Mom had gone up to move her into that assisted care

facility in Glendale. You were at play practice and I was supposed to be at a basketball game, but I came early because I had
cramps."

She pauses for a moment and I say nothing. I'm almost afraid
to hear what she will say next, even though my mind is already
playing it out.

"Dad had her upstairs in his bedroom, Lex. That's how I
found out. When they came into the kitchen after…afterward, I
was sitting there at the table, trying to pretend like I didn't know
what was going on.

"He was surprised to see me. He knew I had a basketball
game. He had even told me that morning he couldn't come
because of work. Then he wanted to know how long I had been
home—for obvious reasons. I had told him 'a little while,' which
made him even more nervous. He fumbled to explain away the
woman who was standing next to him, looking as guilty as he
did. He said Lynne was a co-worker and they were working on
a big project. He had forgotten something at home. Then she
had said something like, 'Well, I guess I'd better get back to the
office.'

"When she left I started to cry. Dad tried to pretend he didn't
know what had made me so upset. I really didn't know if he
thought I was just plain stupid or that twelve-year-olds don't
have a grasp on reality. I finally told him to stop it. That I knew
he hadn't been working on a project for work in his and Mom's
bedroom—and yes, I said Mom's bedroom.

"He finally admitted that he had a horrible lapse in judg-
ment, just that one time, and that seeing my hurt face had convinced him he had made a terrible mistake. He told me he didn't
want to hurt Mom or Rebecca or you, that it was bad enough
that he hurt me, so he was never going to do anything like that

again. He begged me to keep what I had seen and heard a secret so that we could save the family.

"And I agreed to it. Five months later Rebecca was in the accident, but I still believed he was keeping his promise. I had to believe it. Even while Mom and Dad fought and bickered over whether or not to have a phone in the house, I believed he was keeping his promise because of what we are all having to bear. And maybe for a while he did. But it didn't last. When he moved out, my little wall of denial finally began to crumble. And then when he told us he was marrying Lynne, I realized how foolish I had been. It had all been a lie."

Priscilla stops for a moment. I wonder if she has ever told anyone what she's telling me right now. I ache for her; that she had to bear so much and never told a soul.

"I didn't want you to know, Alexa," she continues. " I didn't want you to feel what I was feeling. But year after year, everyone kept looking at the accident and thinking that's what shattered our parents' marriage. You believed it. Even Mom believed it. But I knew better, and it nearly drove me crazy. That's why I moved to England. I had to get away from it, Lex.

"And for a long time I *was* able to escape it. I was able to completely distance myself from what happened here. I missed you, and Mom and Rebecca too, but the peace I felt for the first time since I was twelve felt too wonderful. I wasn't about to let it go. Then I had Isabel. For the first two years, I was so enamored with her, and there was nothing else I wanted except to be her mother and share her with no one. But Lex, it started to wear on me, my self-imposed exile. One day when I was coming home from work, a bus and a taxi almost got into an accident. I was one of several pedestrians in a crosswalk. We almost got hit. It suddenly occurred to me that I'm not going to live forever. I could die any moment, and who would take care of my Isabel?

"That feeling just wouldn't go away. It weighed on me for months. I knew I needed to come back home and make amends. Not so much for me, but for Isabel's sake. Because if anything should ever happen to me, I want you to take her, Alexa."

I don't want to consider the idea that Priscilla could die, even though I know that's a reality for all of us. But I know I would take Isabel in a heartbeat if anything happened to my sister.

"You know I would," I whisper.

"I want her to feel connected to all of you. Just in case. Besides, you're all her family. Dad is her grandfather. The only grandfather she will ever know. I want her to know him. But he and I had to take care of this unfinished business. We simply had to, Lex. And I'm sorry you had to hear it from me."

For the first time I think maybe in her mind running off to Europe was as much for my protection as it was for hers. If she had stayed, she likely would have blurted out the ugly truth at some point, and she very much didn't want that to happen. She wanted the truth to be exposed by the one who created the lie: Dad. And she knew that would probably never happen.

"It's okay, Priscilla," I say. "I understand why you did what you did. I really do."

We are silent for a few moments.

"Thanks, Lex. For bringing me to see him. For understanding. And for loving Isabel."

"You're welcome," I reply. After a moment I add, "Were you serious about coming home for Christmas?"

She smiles across the seat from me. "Isabel would love it," she says.

"So would I," I say.

"We'll see."

We're silent for a few minutes, and then I'm reminded of that conversation Priscilla and I had so many years ago when she told me she thought our names were preposterous.

"Remember that day you told me you thought our names were...were..." I can't think of a nice way of saying it.

Priscilla grins. "Outrageous?" she asks, supplying a word of her own.

I grin back. "Yeah. Outrageous. Do you really still think that?"

"No. And yes. I mean, I really do think Mom and Dad felt like fate had slapped them with a double whammy when we were born. They waited four years to have another child after Julian. It seems only fair they should have been granted a boy. But two girls instead? I used to think they gave us outlandish names to mock God and his mysterious ways, but Mom probably gave us those names to convince herself we really were worthy of being loved as girls and not a boy. Dad probably let her do whatever she wanted as far as the names went."

"You think so?"

Priscilla shrugs. "Actually, I don't think about it much at all anymore. What I do know is our parents never had a good marriage, Lex. It wasn't this precious, beautiful thing that cracked when Julian died and then split in two when Rebecca nearly died as well. I think their relationship had begun to crumble before Julian was born. We've just always kind of assumed it was those two tragedies that sunk their marriage. But my guess is if Julian had lived and Rebecca had never been in the accident, their marriage would still not have lasted."

"That's strange to think about. How different we would all be if Julian had lived and Rebecca had not been in the accident," I say, musing on the possibilities.

"Lexie," Priscilla says. "If Julian had lived, you and I wouldn't *be* at all."

I say nothing in response. Somehow I know she is right.

We are silent for a few minutes. Then I ask her what has been in the back of my mind all evening, even while I was being exposed to painful truths.

"Priscilla, what are we going to do about James Leahy?"

Priscilla sighs. "I don't know. I don't know if Mindy even knows what she's talking about. We don't know for sure that he died. I don't trust her."

"I don't either, but why would she lie about this? And why would Gavin have given into her demands for more money if it *wasn't* true?"

"I don't know, Alexa. I don't know anything for sure."

When we get back to the triplex it's nearly ten o'clock. Isabel awakens in a grumpy mood and Priscilla tells her a warm bath will help her relax and be able to fall back asleep. They head down the hall, and I take my cordless phone out onto my back patio. Stephen had told me to call when I got back from San Juan Capistrano if it wasn't too late.

Well, it's not too late.

He answers on the third ring by saying my name. One of the many advantages of Caller ID.

"How was your day?" he asks.

I hardly know where to begin, so much has happened today. "Can I hear about your day first? Mine is going to take a while. Did you see the oncologist?"

"Yeah," Stephen replies. "He's a nice guy. Honest. Didn't try to sugarcoat anything. He wants to get started right away."

"How soon?"

"Monday. I'll go in every day for five weeks. Then we'll do an MRI and see what we've got."

"Every day for five weeks? Wow."

"It could be longer, but Dr. Fridley told me there is every reason to think we can beat it."

"Really?"

"Yes, really."

"Although no guarantees."

Stephen kind of laughs. It's a nice laugh, void of all sarcasm. "You know there are no guarantees."

"But glimmers of hope here and there," I reply and I don't hide the tension in my voice.

"Oh, yes. Always those." His voice sounds soft in my ear. I have an immediate connection to the words "always those." Somehow they comfort me.

"If I can help you out, will you call me?"

"Of course," he says. "Thanks." We're silent for a moment, then he says, "Now tell me about your day."

"Where should I start?" I ask, sighing.

"At the beginning," Stephen says cheerfully.

It takes me fifteen minutes to describe my morning; how Priscilla and I learned the identity of Cosmo, about our conversation with Thelma Murdock and the fact that Rebecca is very likely now someone's wife. It takes another ten minutes to detail our meeting with Mindy and how it was that Rebecca came to be in possession of the check.

"Wow," Stephen says when I pause to catch my breath. "So what are you going to do? Do you really think Gavin killed him?"

"I don't know. I don't know, Stephen. But I can't just pretend I don't know that perhaps he did."

"Are you going to go to the police? I think maybe you should."

The same thought has been nagging at me for hours and I tell him this. I also tell him I'm not sure Mindy can be trusted.

"You don't have to ascertain if Mindy is telling the truth, Alexa. The police can do that. You're not responsible for knowing if it's true or not."

"I know, but this involves Rebecca too. She didn't think I would find out about any of this. She just wanted me to throw the check away. If the police are involved from my end, it will bring Rebecca into it."

"But she's already into it if it's true."

He's right, but I'm unwilling to be the one to go the police first if I don't have to. I would much rather Gavin turn himself in if, in fact, James is dead.

"I think I want to try and talk to Gavin first. I know it might sound crazy, but Stephen, he's not a murderer. He may have killed James, but I don't think he planned to. It may have just happened while they fought. And I'll tell him he should be the one to go to the police."

"And if he doesn't?"

I swallow back my apprehension that this could very well happen. "Then I will."

"I don't know, Alexa. This doesn't have to be your problem."

"I want to try it this way first. For Rebecca's sake."

"Please be careful, Alexa. I don't like the way this sounds."

"I will. I promise I will."

"And you will call the police the minute you think you're in over your head?"

"I promise."

"If you find him and then agree to meet with him, I'm coming with you."

I can't stop the spreading smile on my face. "I would like that."

"So you will call me if it comes to that?"

"I will call."

He sighs heavily into the phone. "So your visit with your dad went well?" he asks.

Oh. That.

By the time *that* part of my day is recounted, it's after eleven and Priscilla and Isabel have long since closed the bedroom door and turned out the light.

Stephen listens to most of my story in silence. Every now and then the silence is broken by a word or two of voiced compassion. When I'm done, he doesn't speak right away.

"Stephen?" I say, wondering if my phone has lost its connection to his.

"I'm here."

"The more I think about what Priscilla had to deal with, especially at such a young age, the angrier I get."

"I can understand that, but I don't recommend you let anger have its way."

His words sound strangely disciplinary. I'm a little surprised. If I have a right to any response to this, it's anger. "You don't expect me to pretend that I'm happy about all this, do you?"

"Not all, Alexa. It's just if your father really is sorry, and if he really has asked for forgiveness, then the only response that will bring you any comfort is the one where you give him what he asks for."

"Which is what?" I ask, a little confused, a little annoyed.

"Your forgiveness."

Those two words stun me into momentary wordlessness. To be truthful, I would very much like to be irritated with my dad for a little while. Maybe a long while. "But he doesn't really deserve my forgiveness," I finally say.

"No one who needs forgiveness usually does."

Again, he has said something that is altogether profound and yet madly frustrating. I feel as though I'm being poked with a sharp stick. I don't like it, yet I don't want to swat it away. The fact is, as soon as he says this, it rings true in my ears. I can be mad at my dad for as long as I want, but it won't make me feel any better about what happened. Not one bit.

"You're not mad at me, are you?" he asks all of a sudden.

I smile in spite of feeling severely poked. "No."

"Good," he says in response. I can sense the relief in his voice.

"It's late and I've talked your ear off," I venture.

"So you're taking Priscilla and Isabel over to your mom's tomorrow?" he says, ignoring my comment.

"Yes."

"And what are you doing afterward?"

I have no idea. "Nothing, I guess."

"Want to get together?"

It's been a long time since someone has said to me, "Want to get together?" and I've thought to myself, *This sounds like a date.*

"Okay."

"What time?"

This sounds very much like a date. "How about I call you when I get back from Coronado?"

"In the afternoon sometime?"

"I think so."

"Okay. It's a date."

There you go. I'm right.

Priscilla, Isabel, and I sleep in late the next morning. We walk down to a bagel place a little after ten and take our coffee—cranberry juice for Isabel—and bagels to the grassy area by Belmont Park. A white-railed, wooden roller coaster—the seaside park's historic landmark—is quiet and serene in the morning mist, but its many arches and plunges suggest it's not always this way.

I'm reluctant to let the day really begin. I'm anxious to see Stephen later, but I don't really want to relinquish Priscilla and Isabel. Priscilla doesn't seem to be in too much of a hurry, either. When we're finished eating, we walk slowly back to my place. Priscilla heads into the bedroom to finish packing her and Isabel's things, and I take our empty coffee cups to the kitchen to throw them away. As I do, I notice my answering machine is blinking. Two messages.

I press the button to hear them. The first is Mom. She has had my cell phone for five days, and this is perhaps only the second time she's used it. She wants to know when we're coming. I can't say as I blame her. She specifically says, though, *not* to call her back. She just wants us to know she is ready and that she wants to take us all to lunch. The second message is from Alicia, a co-worker. She just called to say she and the others in OT have missed me and that everyone is looking forward to seeing me on Monday.

I kind of forgot life would be returning to normal in a couple of days.

Normal.

Now there's a word that really doesn't mean anything, does it?

"So now we're going to Grandma's house?" Isabel is saying as she and Priscilla come into the living room from the back of the house.

"*Oui, mon coeur. N'oublie pas de prendre ton doudou,*" Priscilla answers. And while I have no idea what she's said, Isabel turns and runs back to my bedroom. She returns a moment later with her yellow blanket. Clement is safely tucked in her other arm.

"So you're ready?" I ask.

"I think so," Priscilla answers, winking at me.

We leave.

Priscilla and I decide to tell Mom about Rebecca's supposed marriage right when we arrive because Isabel will be distracted by Margot's and Humphrey's spirited antics—a dog duet that takes place whenever more than one person shows up at Mom's.

We're standing in her kitchen when we tell her. Isabel is in the living room with the pugs, laughing at their acrobatics and tossing rubber chew toys in the air to the dogs' utter delight.

"Why couldn't she tell me?" Mom asks quietly when we're done. I think she's a little hurt. "Did she really think I'd stand in her way? Did she really think I'd try and talk her out of it?"

I reach out and put my arm around her. "Mom, Rebecca's always been one to do spontaneous things. And I think we *would* have tried to talk her out of it. I'm pretty sure I would have. I think if you're honest with yourself, you'd have to admit you would have also. Remember what happened with Tim?"

"That was different. Tim was…Tim was incapable of being married to someone."

"But maybe Rebecca was convinced there was no difference between Tim and Cosmo."

Mom dabs at her eyes with a manicured hand. "But all I've ever wanted for her was for her to be happy," Mom continues. "That's all I've ever wished for."

"Then I think you've got your wish, Mum," Priscilla says. "I think Rebecca caught a glimmer of something grand and she went for it."

"But we don't know anything about this man. What kind of name is Cosmo?"

"Mom, it's probably a nickname. And from what we can gather, he seems like a decent guy. Rebecca said she'd write me, so I'm sure at some point we'll get to know him better."

"What do you mean Rebecca said she'd write you? You said she didn't leave a note," Mom says, looking up at me and frowning.

Oops. I didn't mean to bring up the note about the check. I think of a quick fix.

"She left a quick note about making sure her fish was fed. There was just a little postscript to me saying she would write."

Not exactly a lie. Just a blending of two truths.

Mom ponders the news for a few seconds. "So what are we supposed to do?"

"I guess wait to hear from her," I answer.

"And what about her room at the Falkman Center?"

"Well, she's paid up through the end of the month. If we haven't heard from her by then, I suppose she'll have to give her room up and we'll have to move her things out."

Mom sighs. "We'll never find another place like that."

"I don't think you're going to have to worry about that, Mum," Priscilla offers. "If she's married, she's not coming back to the Center."

"I guess."

Mom spends a few more minutes in quiet consternation. Then she seems to shake it off. I recognize this ability she has to shake off what she doesn't want to think about. She's been doing it for years.

"I'm ready for lunch," she says. "Let's go to the Hotel Del. My treat."

It's a little after two in the afternoon when I leave Priscilla and Isabel at Mom's. Mom has asked me over for dinner tomorrow night; Priscilla and Isabel's last night in San Diego. I hug them goodbye and tell them I will see them tomorrow at six.

As I drive back over the bridge, I'm aware of how intensely glad I am that I have plans with Stephen for this afternoon. I'd be in a sorry state if I had to return home to an empty house with nothing to do but start a load of laundry and pay bills.

I pull into my driveway and head inside my house, wondering if I should change into something more…more date-like. Maybe I had better see what Stephen has in mind first. I walk into my kitchen to pick up my phone and the answering machine is blinking. I press the button to listen to the message. The emotionless voice on the other end sends a shiver down my spine and I stand frozen as I listen to it.

"Hello. This is Kevin McNeil. It's a little after noon on Friday. My father is in town and would like to see you. He asks that you come to the house tonight. Seven o'clock. Please call me when you get this message."

Kevin ends the message by giving me his telephone number. It's different than the one in the phonebook, the one I already have. This one is probably his cell phone.

The message ends and I stand there in sheer amazement.

Gavin McNeil is in town.

And he wants to see me.

I have a funny feeling Gavin didn't just drive up from Palm Springs on a whim. I'm fairly certain he came to San Diego because of me. Because of what I found.

With shaking fingers I pick up my phone to make the call.

Not to Kevin, but to Stephen.

18

Stephen's first response to my news that Gavin wants to see me is concern mixed with doubt.

"I don't know if meeting him at the McNeil house is a good idea," he says. "Even if I come with you—and remember, I told you I would—I don't know if you should agree to meet anywhere other than a public place."

"But what if I insist Lisa be there? She doesn't seem like the type to just stand by and allow harm to come to me."

"I don't know," Stephen says. "Maybe."

"I just want to be somewhere we can all speak freely. Besides, despite what Gavin has done, I just don't think he's capable of premeditated murder. He made some pretty awful choices in the past, but I think, in his own skewed way, he was just trying to protect his family. He just chose a really bad way to do it. And he paid for it. We all did."

"If it's all true he did what he did to protect himself, who's to say he won't do it again?"

"Stephen, do you really think he's going to murder us both in his son's living room?"

Stephen is silent for a few seconds. "So I suppose you want to call him and tell him we're coming?"

"Yes, I want to tell him we're coming."

"You know, that isn't exactly what I had in mind for our first date," he teases.

"I'll take you out for coffee afterward."

"I don't like coffee."

His first flaw. I was beginning to think he was too good to be true.

"All right. I'll take you out for ice cream."

"Cherry Garcia?"

"Sounds good to me."

"So what do you want to do until then?"

I like the sound of that. "Can I come over and make you dinner?"

"*That* sounds good to me," he answers, and I can tell he really means it.

He gives me directions to his house and I ask to make sure his second flaw isn't that he doesn't like lasagna. He assures me he loves lasagna. We hang up.

I wait for several moments before pressing the numbers for Kevin's cell phone. I feel a strange sense of peace fall over me as I await the arrival of courage to make the call. I have a suspicion there is a man in Encinitas with his arm in a sling and his foot in a cast praying for me.

Kevin McNeil picks up on the second ring.

"McNeil," he says.

"Kevin, this is Alexa Poole. I got your message."

He says nothing for a second. "Can you come?" he finally asks.

"Will Lisa be there?"

"This has *nothing* to do with my family, understand? You keep them out of this!"

I feel a rush of Priscilla-like disdain welling up within me. "Look, Kevin, I have no plans to make threats to you, so I'd appreciate it if you would lay off making threats to me. I wanted Lisa to be there so that you would stop making them. And by the way, I'm bringing a friend with me, someone I trust. If you have a problem with that, then no, I will not come."

Kevin is silent.

"I apologize," he finally says. "I assumed you were…you were…"

"Well, you assumed wrong. All I want from you and your father is the truth. You can keep your money. I swear before God I don't want it."

"I really would rather Lisa wasn't involved with this," he says in a calmer tone. "She won't be there. Will you still come?"

I'm coming, but I pause for a moment before telling him.

"My friend and I will be there at seven."

I decide to change into white rayon capris and a pink-striped linen top. Serafina has told me I look good in this outfit. Even Patrick has said I look good in it. It's casual but in a dressy way. I want to look attractive to Stephen and in control to Gavin and Kevin. Before I leave, I put the check in my purse. I plan to tear it to bits in front of Gavin and Kevin, for Rebecca's sake, not theirs. They can put the tattered pieces anywhere they please.

I stop at a grocery store on the way to Encinitas to get the ingredients to make lasagna. I buy a fat bunch of sunflowers on my way out of the store.

Though I try to convince myself I'm not nervous as I follow Stephen's directions, my heart is beating way too fast when I finally park my car in front of his little apartment complex. He lives above the ocean in a forty-year-old building apparently inhabited by lots of other people who love to surf. Boards decorate every balcony.

I walk up the cement slab stairs with my bags and the sunflowers, wincing at the thought of Stephen negotiating these stairs with a broken ankle and elbow. I make it to the second floor and find his door. I can feel my pulse surging through my body, making my incision itch and my breathing rapid. I ring the bell.

It has been almost a week since I have seen him. The last time was Saturday. He was lying in a hospital bed watching ESPN. He had just found out he has a tumor in his brain. He answers the door on one crutch clutched under his good arm, smiling in an effortless way. I can't help but smile back.

"Alexa, are you a sight for sore eyes. Please come in." He limps aside and I walk past him into this apartment. His living area is furnished with nice things, but it's littered with magazines, empty water bottles, and bed pillows. I find my way to the kitchen, where I find a sink full of dishes that have been rinsed but need to be washed. When I open the fridge to put the lasagna-makings away, I notice that it's pretty much empty aside from a carton of orange juice, a jar of mayonnaise, and a package of string cheese.

"Stephen, what have you been surviving on?" I ask, putting my things inside the fridge.

He hobbles into the kitchen. "Yeah, I guess I am kind of low on stuff. People at church have been bringing me meals, so I haven't had to worry too much about that."

"Do you want to go get some groceries?"

"I'll go anywhere," he says with a smile.

We spend the rest of the afternoon getting groceries, talking about everything and nothing, and making lasagna. Stephen permits me to tidy up his apartment and wash his sheets and towels. The laundry room is two flights down; impossible on even one crutch with a loaded laundry basket. He tells me his mom will be by tomorrow to help him with the rest of his laundry. While the lasagna bakes, we sit on his balcony to watch the tide come in.

"I don't think I could ever live anywhere but by the ocean," he says to me as we sit on canvas chairs and look out over the water.

"Me, neither," I say. "I love that it's always constant, always dependable. The sound the waves make is as wonderful to me now as it was when I was little. I like that it will always be that way."

"For a long time I didn't appreciate that about the ocean— its persistence, I mean," Stephen says. "There were quite a few years where I didn't appreciate much about anything."

It sounds as though he wants to be honest with me about something. Something he thinks I should know before we go any further in our friendship.

"How come?" I ask, inviting him to tell me.

"Well, when my dad died, I kind of walked out on my mom and everything my parents had taught me about how to live. I caused my mother a lot of grief. And she didn't need it just then."

"How did your father die?"

"He got a flu of some kind, but it invaded his heart and never left. I was a senior in high school when he got sick, and he died a month after I graduated. I moved out, mad at the world, at God especially, and I started doing pretty much whatever I wanted. All those things that tend to ruin a young life."

Stephen looks over at me and smiles, though it's not a smile of mirth. "I became the guy your mother always warned you about."

I smile back. I don't tell him my mother really didn't warn me about anything.

"I got married too young to a gal I really didn't know very well, and we poisoned our marriage with fatal choices within the first few months." He looks away from me. "We were divorced two years later. That was eight years ago. I have no idea where Trish is now."

He doesn't sound as though he misses her nor that he still has feelings for her, but I can sense in his voice that he wishes there was a way he could fix what he broke. It's hard for me to imagine Stephen living the way he's describing. Something had to have happened to him to change him.

"But you don't seem like that kind of person anymore," I say gently.

He turns his head back around and the smile on his face is so very different from the one he wore only moments before. "That's because I'm not. Those years I was on a collision course I had a mother who was praying for me. She was praying that God would send someone my way, someone who could pull me out of the pit I was in. Someone I would have the wisdom to listen to. And I think that's just what God did.

"I was working for a guy who had a painting business. He was a Christian and I knew it when he hired me. He was always very open about his faith. When my so-called marriage fell apart, I got evicted because I couldn't pay my rent. I was living in my car. I kept showing up to work hung over, but this guy did the most amazing thing. Instead of firing me, he invited me home to his house. And not just for supper. He invited me to come live with him and his wife. They showed me compassion and unconditional love when I needed it more than anything else in the world. After a few months of living in their home, going to church with them, talking over the heavy stuff, like why God gave me a brain tumor when I was kid and why he allowed a good man like my father to get a virus that killed him, I gave what was left of my life to God. It was like being raised from the dead, Alexa. Nothing was the same for me after that.

"I went back to school, got my carpentry license, started my business, and I never looked back, except to see where I had come from."

I'm hearing all of this; registering it, but the words "it was like being raised from the dead," keep repeating themselves in my head. This is why I can't picture the Stephen I know living a twisted, marred life. That man is dead. It's startling to consider this.

"Wow," I say, unable really to come up with anything else. I feel tears at the corners of my eyes, and I'm completely taken aback by their presence.

"I wanted you to know where I've come from, Alexa," he says softly, fixing his eyes on mine. "And I wanted you to know where I'm headed. I want you to be very comfortable with both."

I think he sees what is lurking in my eyes. He doesn't ask me to respond. Then he does the most amazing thing. He reaches over and puts his hand over mine.

And we sit that way; just watching the waves hit the sand, until the timer on the oven goes off. Stephen somehow allows the heaviness of what he has told me settle around us in those quiet moments before we go in to eat. His hand on mine and his silence have a remarkably calming effect.

I'm not a whiz in the kitchen, but I do make pretty decent lasagna, and it's satisfying to watch Stephen eat three helpings. He doesn't want me to, but after we're finished eating, I clean up the dishes already in the sink as well as our own. At six thirty we make our way slowly down the stairs and to my car.

I don't say a whole lot about what we are about to do on the way over. Stephen lets me ramble on about my childhood growing up in the El Cajon valley, living in Mount Helix, and trying to learn how to ride a bike on winding neighborhood streets that challenged gravity. When I finally pull up in front of the McNeil house, I'm out of things to say. I turn off the ignition and simply stare at the house.

Stephen takes my hand, with his bad arm, actually, and holds it. "I'd like to pray with you before we go in," he says.

I am pleasantly stunned. I nod.

Stephen closes his eyes and, after a moment, I do too.

"Father God, go with us now into this house. Help us to set things to right. Give Alexa grace and wisdom to say and do the things that would please you. Guard our every step. Protect us from any harm, physical or mental. Enable us to bring peace and healing to this situation. Help Gavin McNeil to do the right thing. Give him courage and strength. We ask this in Jesus' name. Amen."

I whisper the word "amen." What a lovely word. As I say it, I feel the tension of the last few days ease on my head and heart. It is a strange and wonderful feeling.

Stephen squeezes my hand and lets go. "Ready?" he says.

"Yes."

I get out and come around to the passenger side to help him

out. We walk slowly up to the front door on a winding stone pathway that's lit by tiny solar-powered lights. When we get to the front door, I ring the bell.

Kevin answers it, as I expected he would. He hasn't changed much in the past seventeen years. His face is fuller, he has a bit of gray at his temples, and his gut is a little more pronounced. I imagine I would have recognized him anywhere. Kevin notices Stephen right off, standing there with his arm in a sling and his ankle in a cast, and I'm sure Kevin is wondering if Stephen is my quirky idea of a bodyguard.

"Hello, Kevin. This is my friend Stephen Moran."

Kevin nods to me and starts to offer to shake Stephen's hand, but with the sling and the crutch, he quickly withdraws his arm.

"Nice to meet you, Kevin. Don't worry about it," Stephen says pleasantly.

Kevin clears his throat. "Won't you come in?" he says.

We step inside the McNeil house. It feels strangely tomblike. There isn't a sound to indicate there's life within it. It's obvious Lisa and the kids aren't here. Even Gizmo the dog appears to have been banished.

"Please?" Kevin says, motioning us to the den, Gavin's former study. The very room where Gavin argued and fought with James Leahy, according to Mindy.

We step inside. Gavin is standing there with a tumbler of amber liquid in one hand. He looks the same, but very much older. Older than just by years.

"Hello, Mr. McNeil," I say.

His smile is tired and not very convincing. "Please call me Gavin," he says.

"This is my friend Stephen."

Gavin looks at my wounded friend, sizing him up. "Won't you sit down," Gavin says. He takes a chair by a large picture window. Stephen and I sit on the sofa where I sat with Lisa on Wednesday. Kevin folds his arms across his chest and leans against a built-in bookcase near his father.

"Can I get you anything?" Gavin says, holding up his drink.

"No, thanks," I answer.

An uncomfortable silence follows.

"Look, why don't we get right to the point," Gavin says. "I hear you found a check that I wrote and was never cashed. Kevin says you want to know why Rebecca had it. He told me you're going to call the police if I don't tell you why."

I clear my throat and feel Stephen move his arm closer to mine. "Actually, Gavin, since I last spoke to Kevin I found out why Rebecca has that check."

Gavin's eyes widen in surprise. So do Kevin's.

"Kevin mentioned Mindy's name in our telephone conversation," I continue. "He accused me of being in some kind of partnership with her to extort money from you. I assured him—and I assure you now—that is not the case. I just wanted to know the truth. Since Kevin wouldn't tell me, I looked Mindy up. My sister Priscilla and I met with her yesterday. She told me about the check. She told me everything."

I pause then to let my words sink in. I can see in Gavin's eyes that he's unsure what to do with someone who knows the truth and who's not interested in money.

"So you know about..."

"I know about James Leahy. I know what happened to him."

When I say James Leahy's name, Gavin visibly flinches in

his chair. He pauses for a moment before continuing our conversation.

"What do you know?" he whispers.

"I know that there was a fight. That when my sister and Mindy left this house on the day you asked them to bring James to you, James was lying in this study with blood all over his face. Mindy told me she was sure he was dead."

Kevin's face is now drained of color. He shifts his weight off the bookcase and takes a step toward me. "That's a lie! James wasn't dead! He just got knocked out. Dad broke his nose, that's all. And if he hadn't thrown the first swing…" but Gavin stops him before Kevin can finish his sentence.

"What do you want from me?" Gavin says every word slowly. "You don't want money. What is it you want?"

"There's nothing I want from you. If I could have Rebecca back the way she was before Leanne drove her car into a tree, I suppose I would ask for that. But you can't give my sister back her old life."

As I feel Stephen stir beside me, I sense that perhaps the conversation is not going where it should. I remind myself that Gavin never wanted anything bad to happen to Leanne or Rebecca. He probably never even really wanted anything bad to happen to James. But it did.

"I really don't want anything from you, Gavin. And I don't mean that in an accusatory way. I wanted the truth, but I got that from Mindy."

"You didn't get the truth from her!" Kevin snarls.

Gavin ignores him, puts down his drink, and studies me. "Then why did you come when Kevin asked you? You obviously haven't called the police."

I reach down into my purse and pull out the check. "I

wanted you to see that I'm destroying this check. Not because you wish it, but because it's what Rebecca wants. I also want you to know that I could use it to go to the police. I could take this check down to the police station and tell them I have information about a James Leahy, who I believe may have died in your house seventeen years ago after you fought with him. That you have a black belt in karate and dealt a blow that didn't just break his nose. That you paid my sister fifty thousand dollars to pretend she didn't know about any of this. But Rebecca asked that I destroy this check, so I will."

I tear the check in half, then in quarters, then in eighths. I place the pieces on the coffee table in front of us.

Gavin watches me, wide-eyed. When I'm finished, I sit back on the sofa.

"So you're not going to go to the police?" he finally asks.

"No, I'm not," I say. "But you should."

Gavin just stares at me.

"This is ridiculous!" Kevin shouts. "When that loser came to, my father paid him off and sent him on his way! There's nothing illegal in that!"

"Did you ever see James Leahy conscious again, Kevin?" I turn my head to him, wanting to believe that he is right, but I know he's not. "Did you see him walk out of here?"

Kevin's eyes widen, and he seems to turn to stone where he stands. He says nothing. I can see in his eyes that he suddenly realizes he had been deceived all these years, just like the rest of us. James did not regain consciousness. James wasn't paid off and then sent on his way. James Leahy died and Gavin McNeil never told a soul.

"Why should I go to the police after seventeen years?" Gavin says, closing his eyes when he says the word "seventeen."

"Dad?" Kevin's voice is crumbling into a sob.

"Because it's the right thing to do," I say. "His family, if any are still living, deserves to know what happened to him. You, of all people, know what it's like to lose someone you loved."

Gavin sits back in his chair and places his hand over his forehead. He rubs it gently, but his brow is furrowed nonetheless.

"Dad?" Kevin says again. It's barely a whisper.

"What will you do if I don't?" Gavin says.

I look at Stephen sitting next to me. I wonder what he would do if he were me. It doesn't take long to think of an answer.

"I will pray every day for as long as I have breath that you change your mind."

Several seconds of strained silence fill the room.

"I'm so tired of it," Gavin finally says, nearly whispering the words.

I lean forward, toward him. "Then be done with it."

I stand up then and Stephen clumsily stands next to me. "I'm leaving," I say, and I place my hand on Stephen's back as I help him maneuver his way out of the study. Gavin doesn't rise from his chair. He doesn't say a word. Kevin follows us to the front door, opens it wordlessly, and watches us leave. He also is unable to bid us farewell.

Stephen and I say nothing to each other as we make our way to my car. I help him in and then walk over to my side. I see that Kevin is still standing at the doorway, watching us. I get in and close my door, and Kevin finally closes the door where he stands.

Stephen reaches across the seat and takes my hand. "I'm so proud of you," he says, and his voice is laced with emotion such that I haven't heard coming from a man in I don't know how long.

"That felt good," I say in return.

He squeezes my hand.

"Do you still want some Cherry Garcia?"

He nods.

I drive away and my thoughts fly to Rebecca. I wish I could tell her, but I think she already knows.

She is free.

19

Stephen is quiet as I drive to the nearest Ben and Jerry's so that I can treat him to the promised Cherry Garcia ice cream. I pull into the parking lot and look over at him. He looks as though he is deep in thought.

Or perhaps in pain.

"Stephen, are you okay?"

He turns his head slowly toward me. "Would you mind too much if we just got it to go?" he asks, forcing a smile.

"The headache is back?"

He nods and looks away.

"Oh, Stephen. When did it start?"

He shifts in his seat. "A while ago."

"A while ago? How long?"

He turns to me again. "Don't worry about it, Alexa. It only started getting really bad just now."

"Do you want me to just take you home? We can do the Cherry Garcia thing another time."

"Maybe that would be best."

I get back on the road and head west on I-8. Stephen has his eyes closed. I feel so bad for him. There's nothing I can do except to get him home where I know he has pain medication.

"Hang on, Stephen, I'll get you there as soon as I can."

"No speeding," he mumbles.

"I promise. No speeding."

It doesn't seem like the time for small talk. Or big talk. I turn on the radio to a soft jazz station and keep the volume low.

Twenty-five minutes later, we pull into Stephen's apartment complex. As I help him out of the car, it startles me how much he's leaning on me. We take the stairs slowly.

I get him inside and help him to lie on his sofa.

"Where's your pain medication, Stephen?" I ask as I remove the one sandal he's wearing.

"Kitchen. By the toaster."

I go into the kitchen and find a butterscotch-colored bottle of white pain pills. I grab it and a clean glass from the dish drainer. I fill it with water and head back to the living room, reading the label on the medication. Stephen is allowed two pills every eight hours. I turn the lid and pour out two tablets into my hand.

"Here you go," I say when I reach him. I hold out the pills and the water and he takes them from me and swallows them. He lies back on the sofa pillows and closes his eyes. His brow is wrinkled in pain.

"Is there anything else I can do for you?" I ask. My voice sounds weak and young.

He shakes his head slightly and holds out his hand. I take it with mine. "I will be in lala land pretty soon. Don't you worry," he murmurs.

"Stephen, do want me to help you get to your bedroom?"

"Nah. I think I'll just sleep here tonight."

I let go of his hand to grab one of the bed pillows on the chair next to the couch. I place it under his head and then I take another one to elevate his ankle. Then I get up and tiptoe down the hallway and open a closet, assuming it's for linens. I am right. I find a light blanket inside and take it back to him.

As I'm covering him with the blanket he opens one eye to look at me. "Pretty pitiful first date, huh?"

I smile down on him. "Are you kidding? This is the best first date I've ever had."

He grins in spite of his pain. "Liar," he mumbles.

I kneel down beside him and tuck the blanket in around his shoulders. "The best first date I have ever been on," I repeat. I want him to know I mean every word.

He opens both eyes then and reaches with his good arm to gently touch my face. It's the softest touch I've ever felt, yet it nearly sends me reeling with its intensity. I just about topple over.

"Me too," he whispers.

He closes his eyes and drops his hand. I settle onto the floor, resting my head on the overstuffed arm of the couch. I'm about as close to him as I can be short of lying next to him.

"I'll stay until you're asleep," I whisper back.

He keeps his eyes closed and gives me a thumbs-up. Then he relaxes his fist and holds out his hand. I take it and caress it as the medication begins to work its way through his body.

After several minutes of just sitting there stroking his hand, I look up from our hands to see that Stephen is staring at me. He smiles—a sleepy smile—and then he gently pulls his hand out from under mine and places it under my chin, pulling me forward. He makes a concerted effort to lift his head off the pillow, a truly gallant gesture. Every instinct in me tells me he wants to kiss me and he doesn't think I should have to be the one to close the distance.

But I do.

I follow his lead, and bring my head close to his, my mouth to his mouth. It's *my* kiss that lands on his lips, not his kiss on mine, and the absolute beauty of it makes my eyes water. I have never known a sensation like this. It is something borne of the divine, I'm sure. Stephen's hand stays on my cheek, his thumb just below my right eye. He surely must feel the tears that are gathering there like bridled applause.

The kiss doesn't last long; Stephen hasn't the strength. Before he lowers his hand from my face, Stephen brushes his hand across my cheek, just below my closed eye. A tear falls onto his hand despite my feeble attempts to rein them all in, and I open my eyes to see Stephen fingering the wetness as though he were running his fingers through silk. I sit back on my knees and place my head next to his on his pillow.

Stephen reaches for my hand again and we say nothing as he drifts off.

I am speechless with awe.

When I'm sure Stephen is sound asleep, I rise quietly to run a little errand. I tiptoe out the front door, leaving it unlocked. I'm gone less than ten minutes. I return from the Vons grocery store nearby with a pint of Cherry Garcia, which I place in a prominent place in Stephen's freezer. Then I grab a tablet by his phone and write a short note that I hope he will find before his mother arrives in the morning.

Stephen:
Did you know fruit and cream make a good breakfast combo?

Check out the freezer. I'll call you Saturday night when I get back
from Coronado. Or you can call me.
Alexa

PS. I meant what I said last night.

I leave the note propped up by the water pitcher full of sunflowers on his kitchen table. I turn to leave, but I can't help but
watch Stephen for several minutes as he sleeps. On impulse I
walk over to the couch, lean down, and kiss him on the forehead.

Our second kiss.

It, too, is heavenly.

It's after one in the morning before I can relax enough to fall
asleep. My mind is full of a thousand thoughts, and the house
seems empty and lifeless without Priscilla and Isabel. When
I wake up the next morning, it's after nine and a whole day
stretches before me that seems bereft of purpose. I do the things
I've put off doing for two weeks, like laundry, vacuuming, and
tackling the pile of bills on my computer desk. I answer some
e-mail, scour my bathroom, sweep the porch, and clean out the
fridge. By one o'clock I'm restless and bored. I want to see Stephen. I want to be with Priscilla and Isabel. I feel wickedly out
of sorts. I could really go for a run on the beach.

I press my hand to my incision wondering how much it will
hurt. It feels tender, especially after cleaning, but not too bad.
Perhaps a light jog, nothing too strenuous. I can always slow to
a brisk walk if the jarring is too painful. It feels good to put my
running shoes on after what seems like a long time.

On my porch I attempt a few light stretches. My incision

protests somewhat, so I skip my normal routine and just start out with a slow jog down to the beach.

Usually when I jog I find a host of trivial, unrelated things to set my mind on. Sometimes I think of weightier things, like my family or my yearning to carve out an ordinary life for myself— one with a husband, kids, and a van with cup holders in the backseat. But today I find my mind is wholly set on Stephen and the things he told me last night; about his turning to God when his life was in tatters. It was an amazing story. Stephen is such a genuinely nice person; it would seem that he surely must have always been this way, but he is no liar. If he says he became the kind of person mothers warn their daughters about, I must believe him. I must also believe then that his transformation was real. I think this is why I have found his faith so appealing. I know it sounds silly. I have only known him two weeks, but he just seems so *real*. Especially the spiritual part of him. Religion has always seemed like a "put on" thing to me, as though it's something people wear, like a sweater or a mask, but it's not who they really are. But it's not that way with Stephen. His faith is like that tiny seahorse sparkling in the dirty Thames. It's something I never expected to find. And to think I could have missed it. If I hadn't been home recuperating from minor surgery, I wouldn't have met Stephen. The thought of this is disconcerting.

I can't tell what our future is, of course, but I can't help but feel that Stephen is part of my destiny. It's a scary, wonderful thought. Wonderful because loving Stephen is the nicest thing I can think of to do with my time here on earth. Scary because he may not live to see another summer. That's just the plain truth of it. But this fear is strangely not like the kind I would feel at being in open water where sharks are known to swim; it's more like the fear that grips me when a roller coaster I'm on is about to start and the sheer size of it assures me that I'm in for the ride of my life.

I slow down as my under-worked lungs and muscles whine and complain. I walk off the exertion, rubbing my incision gently as it starts to itch. I walk back to the triplex, taking in big breaths of air. Patrick is washing his car in his driveway.

"So, Alexa, is your sister still here?" he asks as he sponges the hood.

"She leaves tomorrow, Patrick."

"Going back to England."

"Yep."

He continues to rub the hood of his car. "Want to catch a movie later?"

"Sorry, Patrick. I have plans."

"Okay," he says, as though I'm missing out on real opportunity.

I inwardly cringe as I reach into my mailbox before going inside. Some opportunities are meant to be missed.

Once inside, I grab a bottle of water from my fridge and start to drink as I sift through the mail. Two credit card offers. The cable bill. A medical journal. A bank statement. And then a flash of color. A postcard. On the front is a picture of a wedding chapel with the words "With Love from Las Vegas" scrolled across the top.

I nearly spit out the swig of water in my mouth.

I slap the postcard over so that I can see what Rebecca has written.

Hi, Lexie!

I'm married! I wore a white dress that we found on sale at the mall. It's a prom dress but I didn't care and Cosmo said I looked like a queen! We are driving to some place where Cosmo has some cousins. Then we will wait for my passport to come. I will write you when we get to Italy. Maybe you can come visit me and I will make you spaghetti!

You can tell Mom. And Frances. Tell Priscilla too! Priscilla and I will be neighbors. Kind of.

Running out of room. Love you,
Rebecca DiMarco!

I read it three times before I'm fully able to process everything. Rebecca is moving to Italy. She got married. In a prom dress. She is waiting for her passport. She is going to learn how to make spaghetti. And thankfully not burn down her house.

Despite my mother's insistence that I not call her on my cell phone, I snatch up my kitchen phone and dial my number. I get the recording that tells me the cell phone customer I'm trying to reach is unavailable. Which means Mom has it turned off.

The stinker.

I will have to sit on this news for the next four hours.

Mom and Priscilla are sitting out on her patio when I arrive at Mom's front door at six. Mom hollers at me to come on in and join them. When I step onto the patio I see that Isabel has a little folding baby carriage and is giving Clement a ride around the backyard. Margot and Humphrey are following her like two Secret Service agents.

"Cute stroller," I say when I join them.

"Mum got it for her," Priscilla says. "I let her because it folds up and fits inside Isabel's suitcase. There would have been too many tears if we had had to leave it here."

"I would have gotten her a baby doll too, but she wanted

that seahorse to have the stroller," Mom interjects, laughing. "Can you believe it?"

I sit beside them.

I can believe it. I can believe a lot of things.

"I have some very interesting news for you both," I say.

They turn to look at me.

"I got a postcard from Rebecca in the mail today. She's okay. And she's married."

Mom's eyes widen in shock, and perhaps she feels a twinge of disappointment that I got the postcard and she didn't.

"Well, where is it?" Mom asks.

I have it in my purse, but I'm reluctant to show it to her. I think the line "You can tell Mom" is going to bother her. But if Rebecca were my daughter, I'd want to see it too. I reach down and pull it out of my purse.

"Let me see it," Mom commands.

"Okay, but remember she wrote it thinking only I would be reading it."

My mother takes it from my hand. Priscilla leans over to read it too. I watch their eyes move across the sentences. I can see when Mom reads "You can tell Mom." I can see when Priscilla reads her own name.

Mom shakes her head and then hands the postcard to Priscilla, as if oblivious that Priscilla has read it over her shoulder.

"She marries and moves to Italy, and she can't even tell me in person," Mom grumbles.

"Don't lose sleep over it, Mum," Priscilla says as she rereads the postcard. "It's done. If you want to stay on speaking terms with her, send her a wedding gift when you get her address and offer her your congratulations."

"She sounds happy, Mom," I add.

"I didn't know she was *unhappy* before. No one told me she was unhappy."

"I don't know that she was terribly unhappy, Mom. I think she just wanted a chance to lead a normal life. One came her way, and she went for it."

"I just can't believe she did this to me."

"Mum, please don't erect a wall of bitterness between you two," Priscilla says. "Believe me, it's not worth it. Let her go. Wish her well."

Mom just sits there, contemplating her options, I guess. Priscilla hands me the card and I place it back in my purse. We sit in silence for a few minutes, and then Mom does what she always does when life throws her a curve ball. She pretends she doesn't know how to catch. She changes the subject.

"I should have gotten Isabel the doll anyway," she says absently.

"Did you have a nice evening last night?" Priscilla asks me, pulling the conversation back to things that matter.

There is nothing I can tell her about what happened last night with Mom sitting right there. I can only hope I will have a few minutes alone with her before she and Isabel leave tomorrow.

"Yes. Yes, I did."

Priscilla looks at me and her eyes are questioning me. *Did something happen?* her eyes ask. *Oh, yes, something did,* my eyes say back. She nods slightly.

"What? Did you have a date or something?" Mom asks coolly, as though she's not in the mood for more surprises.

"Kind of," I answer.

"Did you see Stephen?" Priscilla asks.

"Who's Stephen?"

"The man who was fixing her house."

"The one who fell off her roof?"

I see Mom and Priscilla have discussed my current love interest. I wonder what else Priscilla has told her, but then I suddenly realize she can't have told Mom much of anything else. Because Mom would have said, "The one with the brain tumor?" instead of "The one who fell off her roof," if she had known more. There will come a time when I may tell her more, but not yet. If I told her I'm falling in love with a man with an inoperable brain tumor, it would have driven her right over the edge.

"So what did you two do?" Priscilla asks.

"Not a whole lot. We did some shopping and then sat and watched the ocean. I made lasagna for him. I used your recipe, Mom. He had three helpings. We went for a drive."

When I say, "We went for a drive," I cast a knowing look toward Priscilla, which I hope she picks up on. I need to tell her where we went. She nods her head toward me to suggest she understands.

"Well, we've had a wonderful time," Mom says, changing the subject again, which is fine by me. "We took Isabel to see a friend of mine who has a litter of Jack Russells. Oh, you should have seen her with those puppies, Alexa. It was the cutest thing."

"Go get your digital camera, Mum. You can show Alexa the pictures."

"Okay," Mom says, and she hurries into the house.

I know we haven't much time.

"Kevin called me," I say to Priscilla in a low voice. "I met with him and Gavin last night at their request. Stephen came with me."

"He did?"

"He insisted."

"What happened?"

"I tore up the check and gave it back to Gavin. Told him we knew everything. And Priscilla, he didn't deny *any* of it. I told him he should go to the police."

"Oh my goodness! Do you think he will?"

I shake my head. "I don't know. I can tell he wants to, but he's afraid. Maybe he will. In time."

I can say nothing more because Mom reappears with her camera, and she's clicking through the images. "Here we go," she says. "Now isn't that cutest thing you've ever seen?"

The check, Gavin, the past—Priscilla and I simply cease talking about it. I seriously wonder if we will ever discuss it again. We look at the pictures, which are indeed precious. Isabel comes running over to look at them.

"Now take a picture with me and Clement!" she says when we have seen them all.

"Okay, sweetie. Smile for Grandma!" Mom points the camera toward Isabel holding Clement in her arms and presses the shutter. "Now I want one of all three of you. Get closer, Alexa."

I move in toward Priscilla and Isabel so that our faces are close together. Clement's sequined head is tickling my chin. Mom snaps the photo and then shows the image to us. It's a lovely photo. Perfect. One I will want a copy of.

We have a nice dinner at the Hotel Del. Then we come back to Mom's place so that Priscilla has plenty of time to get her and Isabel's suitcases ready for the morning flight out. Mom, who has noted troubles with saying goodbye, doesn't want to take Priscilla and Isabel to the airport in the morning, and since I very much want to do it, we make plans for me to pick them up at nine.

My heart feels heavy as I drive home. The thought that I will call Stephen, unless he calls me first, cheers me, though. When I get home, I make a cup of tea and wait to see if he calls me. Fifteen minutes later, the phone rings and it is indeed Stephen.

"Hey, thanks for breakfast."

"Not a very healthy one. I'm sure your mother didn't approve."

"I ate it before she got here."

"So you had a good day? Feeling better?"

"It was all right. And yes, the headache's not bad at all today. But it's hard to be thirty-two and have your mother wash your underwear. I suppose it's probably good to be humbled every now and then, though. "

I laugh.

"So how was your day?" he says.

I tell him about Rebecca's postcard and my last evening with Priscilla and Isabel. I make no attempt to hide the sadness in my voice about them leaving.

"You just let too much time pass between this visit and your last one," he says. "I'm sure you and your sister won't let that happen again. Am I right?"

"You're definitely right. They might even come home again for Christmas."

"Well, there you go."

I pause for a moment as an idea comes to me.

"Stephen, would you like to come with me tomorrow to take them to the airport?"

"Really? I can't even carry a suitcase!"

"You know that's not why I want you to come," I say, smiling.

"I'd love to."

I think he's smiling too.

I'm at Stephen's by eight the next morning, and we are in Coronado by fifteen minutes to nine.

Mom is pleased to meet Stephen, I think. He's so personable and easy to like, but his broken elbow and ankle seem to puzzle her. As though she finds it very odd that I'm so deeply attracted to a wounded man. Oh, if only she knew.

Priscilla, on the other hand, has an immediate connection with Stephen that has less to do with us being twins and more to do with the fact that Priscilla has been right all along. There are worse things than falling in love with a sick man. I think it may be worse to not fall in love at all. In any case, they are fast friends. I'm glad Priscilla has had this chance to meet Stephen. I want her to know him, to see in him what I see—his very real faith in the midst of very real troubles. It's the part of him I'm willing to share with anyone and everyone I know and love. It's the part of him that I simply must know more about.

Mom is crying when we leave her house. She hands me back my cell phone as though it's a piece of spoiled meat. "Take this," she says.

"Bye, Grandma!" Isabel calls out as we walk down the cement path to my car.

Mom stands at her screen door and blows kisses with one hand and dabs at her eyes with the other.

At the airport, I'm not a whole lot different from her. So much has happened in the six days Priscilla and Isabel have been here. I feel as though I've aged far more than a mere week. My tears begin to flow as soon as their bags are checked.

Priscilla reaches for me and we embrace. She's crying too. "If we can't come at Christmas, maybe you can come see me," she says. "Maybe you can come by my place on your way to see Rebecca, eh?"

We laugh as our tears trickle down our cheeks.

We part and I reach down to hug my niece.

"Goodbye, honey," I say, wrapping her in my arms. "Aunt Lexie loves you so much."

"Clement wants to kiss you!" Isabel says as she unwraps herself from my embrace. She thrusts the mint green seahorse head toward me and places his smiling lips on mine. The crinkle of his fabric prickles my face. Isabel makes a loud kissing sound. "Now you kiss Clement!"

I kiss the seahorse head, unable not to grin at how this must look to anyone walking by.

"Nice to meet you, Stephen," Priscilla says, grabbing Isabel's hand. "*Au revoir*, Lex."

"Nice to meet you too," Stephen says. I rise from my goodbyes to Isabel and stand as close to Stephen as I can. He places his good arm around me, and I marvel at how nice it feels.

"Goodbye!" I say.

Priscilla and Isabel turn away and begin walking toward the security checkpoint line. My sister turns once and waves.

Then they disappear into a sea of people. I lean into Stephen and let the tears come. They're not sad tears. They're the tears that come from the ache of loving people. The most wonderful pain in the world.

20

A warm July sun is melting away the morning cloud cover over the beach at Encinitas. Sunlight is at last filtering its way through the miniblinds above the kitchen sink in Stephen's apartment as I mop his kitchen floor. The chore doesn't take very long. He tried to talk me out of it, but he's too fatigued these days to put up much of a fight. I've been winning all those battles lately. He's not far away from me though, just there on the sofa in the living room. He had been watching me, but I think he has drifted off to sleep. I know he hates being so tired all the time, but I love watching him sleep. I don't think he knows how much I love it. And I don't think I will tell him. He would probably find that very odd.

It's been three weeks since Stephen began his radiation treatments. I suppose you could say they're going well. He continues to tolerate them, although he has lost all his hair. He seems to be having fewer headaches, but it's too early to tell if the tumor is indeed shrinking. He's just past the halfway mark.

The first few treatments were pretty unremarkable, but by the third day, Stephen was starting to feel the effects. He was told the treatments would pretty much knock him flat. And they have. I had to go back to work the day he started them, and it bothered me that he had to have other friends take him to his appointments. But I did manage to take off one afternoon the second week so that I could take him to at least one of them.

Stephen's tumor is called a medulloblastoma. It's considered a fast-growing tumor and quite a troublemaker. It shows up mainly in children, so it's not particularly common for a thirty-two-year-old man to have one. It's what Stephen had when he was a child and, as I constantly remind myself, survived. Unlike the tumor he had as a boy though, this one is growing on the floor of the fourth ventricle of his brain, and it's this location that makes it inoperable. It's too close to the brain stem for any doctor to want to touch it. But the literature that Stephen has been given says that this kind of tumor is very responsive to radiation treatments. Every day that goes by, every time he comes home sick and fatigued from his treatment, is another day he's closer to being cured, if that is indeed in his future. There's nothing more we can do at this point except hope. If the radiation fails, chemotherapy will begin. If neither of these do the trick, Stephen's healing will only be found in heaven. But I can't let my mind wander there. There are too many reasons to hope for the best.

Stephen has had so many people from his church volunteer to help him, I sometimes feel I'm not needed. He insists that while he appreciates all the help from his church family, it's only my company that makes him want to brush his teeth and put on cologne. At first he resisted my seeing him bald and in such a weakened condition, but now that he knows that's the only way he can be seen, he has reluctantly given me a key to his apartment so that I can come in anytime, whether he's resting or not. He has also broken down and allowed me to wash his underwear. Better me than his mom, he says.

Since Priscilla and Isabel left, my dates with Stephen have consisted of doing his laundry, fixing him dinner, renting movies, reading to him from his Bible, and watching him sleep. I love our dates.

It was odd going back to work after my two weeks off. I felt like a completely different person. And I guess it's because I kind of am. I'm in love, for one thing, as wonderful a life-changing event there is. I also have the strangest sensation that I'm being stripped of my outer skin, as though I am shedding, becoming new. Stephen says it's the hand of God reaching down to pull away the shell of my old life, the one where I had no peace or purpose. It's all very complex and amazing to me. Stephen has been too weak to attend church, but I read to him from his Bible, and every time I come across something I don't understand, which seems to be often, we stop and talk about it. I have a lot to learn, but I'm getting the idea that when Jesus died— and I'm learning that he died for me personally—it was for this express purpose of making me new. I don't understand it, but I can feel it happening within me. I'm changing inside and out, it seems.

Coupled with this is no longer having Rebecca on which to foist my need for existing. I didn't realize how much I was dependent on her to give my life meaning until she left. When I told Frances that Rebecca had indeed gotten married and was moving to Italy, Frances could hardly think of anything to say. She was like all the rest of us. Shocked, surprised, but eventually glad that Rebecca had slipped away to follow love. I think

Frances may have switched gardening services, though. The day I went to move out Rebecca's things, the man I saw mowing the Falkman Center lawn was a complete stranger to me, as well as being overweight, balding, and sporting a wedding band on his left hand.

I told Marietta she could keep Rebecca's fish, and I also gave her Rebecca's books and magazines. I kept the baby book, of course. I gave away the clothes Rebecca didn't take except for a couple of sweaters and blouses I thought she might want to have with her in Italy. She hasn't written to me again yet. But I'm learning not to expect Rebecca to do what I would do. She never did. Not before the accident and not after. Everyday I check my mailbox hoping she has written to me. Someday I know I'll come home from work or from Stephen's and the letter will be there.

Mom asks if I have heard from Rebecca, although I can't believe she thinks I would actually keep that from her. Mom seems to be warming up to the idea of being vulnerable again; that is, feeling free enough with her love and devotion to risk being hurt again. She simply can't get enough of Isabel. In the three weeks Priscilla and Isabel have been gone, she has sent four packages to London, one of which was the baby doll she had talked about getting when Priscilla and Isabel were still here. Priscilla's last e-mail to me two days ago was nothing short of a desperate plea to tell Mom to stop. Or at least slow down. On the up side, Mom has purchased a pay-as-you go cell phone service. She never turns her new phone on except to call me once a week, but it's a start, I think, to living a life in the here and now.

The other amazing thing is Mom told me at lunch the other day that she thinks she and I should go to Europe in the spring.

Guess where? England and Italy. She even went to the federal building downtown and picked up passport applications. I have to confess, I really want to go. I miss Priscilla and Isabel like crazy. And I so much want to hug Rebecca, my married sister, and whisper in her ear, "It's done!"

And even if she asks, "What's done?" I won't care. It will be enough to know that it is and to see her married, happy, and making spaghetti in her own kitchen.

As for my dad, he and I met for a late breakfast last weekend. He drove down alone, and we met for lunch at a place in Del Mar that he likes. He wisely came without Lynne. It's going to take some time for me to be able to talk to her and be in her presence without thinking unkind thoughts about her. The weird thing is, she thinks—just like Dad did—that I have always known about their longtime affair. I think that's why she has always been aloof around me. She assumed I hated her. Why develop a friendship with someone who loathes you, she probably thought. But I don't hate her. I don't want to hate her. I just need time to adjust to the knowledge I now possess.

Dad asked me to forgive him, as tenderly as he asked it of Priscilla. I think when he told Priscilla a few weeks ago that people can change, he meant he's no longer the kind of person who would leave the woman he is married to and the children— or child—he shares with that woman. I told him I think forgiveness is a process. It's something Priscilla and I both want to be able to extend to him, but like any great work of art and sacrifice, it will not happen overnight. I don't know if he'll ever tell my mother that it wasn't her response to Rebecca's accident that drove him away, that it was something else entirely, but it's my prayer that someday he will. It won't change the past, but it might make it possible for my mother to live out the rest of her days without bitterness against God for the demise of her marriage. She and Dad let the marriage fail. It wasn't crushed by God's providential hand when Rebecca almost died. It's possible she might even allow herself the luxury of loving again if she knew the truth. As Priscilla said, sometimes knowing the truth makes living with it easier and sometimes it doesn't.

Of all the recent events that have happened, perhaps the most remarkable is a call from Kevin McNeil a few days ago. He wanted to let me know that his father had indeed gone to the police. He didn't tell Kevin ahead of time that he was doing it, he just called Kevin from the El Cajon police station and told him he had confessed to accidentally killing James Leahy and then disposing of the body. The police had asked to speak to Kevin too, to verify Gavin's story, but Gavin was adamant that his son was completely innocent. After the fight that day, and after Mindy and Rebecca had left, Gavin had sent Kevin to the bank to make a deposit to cover the checks he wrote—at least that was the ruse he gave Kevin. While he was gone, Gavin carried James' body out to his truck, drove an hour away to some undeveloped land he owns in neighboring Imperial County, and buried him. Gavin had explained his being gone so long by telling Kevin he drove James to Los Angeles and put him on a plane to New York. Apparently, charges against Gavin are pending as the authorities work to find James Leahy's next of kin, assuming there are any. And it could take months to find the remains, if they're found at all. What a mess.

I asked Kevin how Lenore, his mother, was taking all of this, and he said Lenore doesn't know. He paused for a moment and then told me that his mother suffers from dementia, that Lenore sometimes thinks Leanne is still alive and wonders why she never visits. I told him I was sorry. What else could I say?

Then Kevin did the oddest thing. He thanked me. He told me in spite of everything his father seems oddly at peace. And he said that his father hasn't been at peace since James Leahy set foot in his house, until now. Kevin had always attributed it to losing Leanne, but it was more than that.

It doesn't really surprise me that Gavin McNeil could find peace like that, in that way, in his confession. We're all of us looking for that glint of hope in an often-shadowy world. I think this is why Rebecca left as suddenly as she did. She saw the shimmer of what looked like fleeting loveliness and she grabbed it before it could slip away. Or before someone could snatch it away from her. And then I look at Priscilla and I see that she, too, has found her shining ray of beauty within the devotion she has for Isabel. I can see how she came to that place where she realized Isabel was a treasure not meant to be hidden away, but rather shared with the world—like the real Clement— a thing of beauty sprung from darkness and enjoyed by all who care to stop and look.

Even I have found my own glimmer of hope, my own sea-horse in a dark and mysterious river. And I can't help but feel that I'm on to something far grander than what Rebecca and Priscilla have found. I'm certain I've discovered something that truly lasts—something beyond the love of a woman for a man and even that of a mother for her child. The love I have for Stephen begins with the amazing love of God that I see shining out of him. This love calls to me, catches my eye; bids me to bend down and take hold of it, even though it's obvious the river's course is uncharted and perilous from time to time. I can't help but kneel down to embrace it. The alternative, which is walking away and pretending I've seen nothing sparkling in the dark water, holds no appeal for me.

As I watch Stephen sleep away his fatigue, knowing that tomorrow he will go to battle all over again—as well as the next day and the next—I'm reminded of what he said to me on the phone just a few weeks ago, when he came home from his first visit with the oncologist—when he told me that the outlook was favorable.

I had said, "But no guarantees?" And he had laughed, in that kind way of his, and had said, "You know there are no guarantees."

But glimmers of hope here and there, I had said, my heart aching with expectation. And he had answered me.

Oh, yes. Always those.

Epilogue

August 8
Naples, Italy

Dear Lexie:

We are finally here! It took such a long time and I was getting so tired of waiting, but no more waiting! We are staying with Cosmo's brother, Gianni, in Naples. Cosmo is going to write down the address on the envelope so I get it right. Then you can write to me. Gianni is very nice. He knows a lot of English. His wife's name is Marcella, and she knows a little bit of English. Cosmo's mother lives here too. And she speaks no English at all! She is very nice, though, and always says stuff to me in Italian. I have no idea what she is saying. Cosmo says that's okay 'cause sometimes she doesn't know what she is saying either. She coughs a lot. Cosmo told me his lovely mama is sick. I gave her my Halls cherry cough drops. She said, "Grazie." That means "thank you" in Italian.

When the whole family comes over there are like forty people in the house! Everyone talks very fast and they all hug Cosmo like he's been gone a million years. Marcella says everyone loves Cosmo, and I said of course they do! I am having a hard time remembering all their names, but Cosmo just said, "Join the club!"

Gianni has a restaurant, and he wants Cosmo to come work for him. Cosmo said he will, but he will miss being outside all day long. He told me soon we could get our own place and I will have a garden on the roof and he will help me take care of it. I hope you can come visit me soon. Cosmo says family is very important, and he wants you to come. He hopes you are not mad at him. Maybe you can come when we have our little house. And I will show you my garden. Cosmo says it won't matter that we will be in the heart of the city. He will make a little garden for me that will make you think you have come to the garden of Eden. He says it will be like a little spot of wonderful in a place where no one thought wonderful could be. I believe him. Cosmo is a good gardener. I have to go now. We are going to Cosmo's sister's house for supper.

I love you and miss you.

Love, Rebecca DiMarco

PS. I got a new headband. It's pink!

Author's Note
to Readers

When people ask me what *A Seahorse in the Thames* is about, I like to say it's about the wonder of finding beauty in an unexpected place. Sometimes we have to kneel down and wait to catch glimpses of loveliness in our often-troubled world. And if we are not taking the time to look for those snippets of splendor, we may miss them altogether. I love the idea that a fisherman found a beautiful seahorse in the weeds and shallows of the murky Thames when he least expected it. What a picture of hope.

I would love to hear what you have discovered as you read *A Seahorse in the Thames.* Please visit my web home at www.susan meissner.com to send me an e-mail or write me in care of Harvest House Publishers at 990 Owen Loop North, Eugene, OR 97402. Your comments mean the world to me. Discussion questions suitable for book clubs are available on my website, not only for this book, but for my other titles as well.

See you on the banks of discovery,

Susan Meissner

Susan Meissner is an award winning newspaper columnist, pastor's wife, high school journalism instructor, and novelist. She lives in rural Minnesota with her husband, Bob, and their four children. If you enjoyed *A Seahorse in the Thames,* you'll want to read Susan's other novels…

Why the Sky Is Blue….What options does a Christian woman have after she's been brutally assaulted by a stranger…and becomes pregnant? Happily married and the mother of two, Claire Holland must learn to trust God "in all things."

A Window to the World….Here is the story of two girls—inseparable until one is abducted as the other watches helplessly. Years later the mystery is solved—and the truth confirmed that God works all things together for good.

The Remedy for Regret…Tess Longren is 28, single, and at a crossroads in her life. She finally has a job she enjoys as well as a proposal of marriage from a man she loves, but Tess can't seem to grasp a future filled with promise and hope. Her mother's long ago death remains a constant, though subtle, ache that Tess can't seem to move past. Here is a masterful novel about finding the courage to change a painful situation and bearing what cannot be changed…about understanding the limitations of an imperfect world and the vast resources of a perfect God.

In All Deep Places…Acclaimed mystery writer Luke Foxbourne lives a happy life in a century-old manor house in Connecticut. But when his father, Jack, has a stroke, Luke returns to his hometown of Halcyon, Iowa, where he reluctantly takes the reins of his father's newspaper for an undetermined amount of time. Memories of Norah—the neighbor girl with whom he shared his first kiss—cause Luke to reflect as he spends night after night alone in his childhood home. Soon he feels an uncontrollable urge to start writing a different story altogether. Norah's story. And his own.